Amanda Sington-Williams

The Eloquence of Desire

Sparkling Books

A CIP catalogue record for this title is available from the British Library.

First published in hardback in June 2010. This edition August 2010.

2.1

BIC code: FRD

ISBN: 978-1-907230-16-5

Edited by Anna Alessi.

For more information visit our website *www.sparklingbooks.com*

Printed in England by JF Print.

The Eloquence of Desire by Amanda Sington-Williams, reviewed by Dr. Stephen Wyatt

The Eloquence of Desire is an engrossing and atmospheric novel. This story of a married couple in the 1950s banished to Malaya after the husband's affair with the boss's daughter has the sharp edge, clarity and narrative drive of a Somerset Maugham novel.

But Amanda Sington-Williams brings her own distinctive voice to the material. The descriptions of Malaya evoke the people, landscape and climate vividly and sensuously. The sounds and smells are almost tangible and there is a palpable background of unease and tension as the political situation constantly threatens to explode into violence.

At the same time the writer has a wonderfully compassionate and insightful view of her all too human and believable characters. This is particularly true with George, the husband. On one level, this man is a selfish serial adulterer but we are lead to understand his motives and he emerges as a complex, if fallible, human being. The same understanding is offered to all characters, major and minor.

Thoroughly recommended!

Stephen Wyatt

Award-winning writer of *Memorials to the Missing*

To Christian and Emily

The Eloquence of Desire

Love from Amanda

Amanda Sington-Williams grew up in Cambridge and Liverpool. She has lived in Japan, Spain and Australia and has travelled extensively. She now lives in Brighton. Many of her short stories have been published in magazines and anthologies. She has an MA in Creative Writing and Authorship from Sussex University. For this novel she won an award from the Royal Literary Fund.

This book is dedicated to the memory of my mother, Priscilla Kent, whose recollections of colonial Malaya were central to the formation of the narrative.

Chapter 1

The tube rattled and shook. A punishing series of jerks swung George round into awkward, precarious positions as he clung onto a strap. The light bulb above his head flickered and swayed; the crossword clues jumped. Newspaper clutched in one hand, he took to watching his fellow commuters, observing their untroubled, ritualised state. At Chalk Farm, several seats were vacated; he squeezed past a man just about to deposit his mackintosh on the seat beside him. Their knees collided. They grunted apologies, acknowledgements; the other man resumed reading his paper. George lit a cigarette. Would he really miss this journey to and from work? Inconceivable to believe that this was the last time he would travel from a respectable job in the City. But he enjoyed this irksome form of travel: the daily struggle to find a seat, the jostling, the intimacy of strangers' bodies - a constant source of jocular comments with the secretaries when he finally arrived at work. Besides, the journey gave him a feeling of belonging, of fitting into place. Now, he would be left to flail, aimless, purposeless, without status or recognition. Exactly in fact what Moorcroft had in mind when he made his decision, when he chose the penalty for his employee; one that would mean there was no risk of them meeting again. George thought of Moorcroft's flattened tone, the anger held in, zipped up behind the doughy features. The plans for George's future in the firm useless, discarded, his place taken by a nodding, cheerful young man.

He watched the newly arrived commuters as they stepped into the carriage, pushed their way down the tube, the odours from their damp clothes mingling, giving off varying degrees of mustiness: London grime, or smoke from airless offices. A woman wearing a blue swing coat glanced along the carriage, casting around for an empty seat. Her pale skin, the searching green eyes, reminded him of Emma. Briefly, he felt his breath catch; he stood, clambered back over his neighbour and indicated for her to take his seat. And so his mind stayed with Emma when he knew he should be working out a strategy for telling Dorothy his news. But Emma was never far away; like the glitter balls in dance halls, she would slowly rotate in his memory, different facets reappearing, as the hues changed in her auburn hair.

The tube had come above ground; it continued to roar along the track, as if desperate for this newly found fresh air. Finally, it stopped at Golders Green. George stepped out on the icy platform, buttoned his coat and started the walk home. But he took his time, ignoring the freezing temperature that was numbing the blood in his veins.

When he stood with his hand on the gate latch, he could not stop his hands shaking. Studying the house, he tried to calculate Dorothy's mood. There was a time when she would instinctively know when he was outside the house, the front door would open, a smile would welcome him in. He made his way up the path and stamping his feet on the doorstep, remained, fighting the impulse to turn and run. His fingers gripped and turned the key. No point in delaying further. He pushed the door open and stood on the mat, puddles forming at his feet. Not that he could be blamed for that, or the snow which he would soon be treading into the carpet.

"Darling," he said, when Dorothy appeared. "Sorry I'm a bit late."

"I was beginning to wonder…," she began.

She hung his coat and umbrella under the stairs, put his briefcase in the corner; everything as normal, routines maintained. Had she forgotten about his meeting with Moorcroft this afternoon? Or was this simply her way of coping?

Bending forward he went to kiss her on the cheek. The pleasure he felt when she turned her face towards him gave him renewed strength; a hurdle had been cleared. He followed her into the sitting room, watching her skirt ripple round her legs as she walked quickly across the carpet. Standing with his back to her, he poured out two sherries. Suitable ways of telling her ran through his mind; he wondered whether the letter in his pocket had become sodden and illegible, the message completely destroyed. He should have planned this moment more efficiently, now he did not know how to tell her, had not considered how to soften the impact of his news.

"What did Moorcroft say?" She was sitting on the leatherette sofa, her legs crossed neatly at the ankles, the toe of her black pump tapping the carpet.

Absurd of him to think she had forgotten, even momentarily. She extracted a cigarette from a packet and stared at him expectantly.

"You know that my firm has contacts all over the Far East?"

She nodded, placed her lit cigarette in a glass ashtray, where it balanced uncertainly. She rolled the beads of her necklace between finger and thumb. The smoke rose in twirls from her cigarette; she watched it deliberately, studying the patterns with wide eyes, waiting. It appeared to George she had not made the connection, did not think this fact relevant to their future.

He slid along the sofa towards her. "Moorcroft has found a new position for me in Malaya. A town called Ipoh. Export business." Done, he had told her. His shoulders slackened. A hand was placed on her knee. "Sorry," he said. "I'm truly sorry for…" She removed his hand and stood.

"Malaya!"

He could almost follow the trace of blood departing from her face.

"Malaya," she repeated. "Abroad. I've never been abroad before. No." She retrieved her smouldering cigarette from the ashtray, inhaled deeply, started to cough, moved unsteadily to the bay window. "No," she said again.

Swallowing hard, George kept his eyes on the bars of the electric fire, glowing like the devil he felt was in him. All he could think of saying now was the repeated apology.

"When? What about Susan?" She was standing over him now. "Can't he get you something different? Here?"

He shook his head, tried to touch her hand before it was snatched away. "I've got a letter."

The contents were memorised, but he extracted the letter from his pocket, unfolded the crumpled paper. "We have to leave quite soon. The boat departs on the tenth of January."

She stretched her hand out. He should have bought that box of Milk Tray, for once bypass his dislike for queues with dilly-dallying females, loitering, chatting to the shop-keepers. An attempt to sweeten the poison would have been worth the wait.

He watched her face as she scrutinized the contents. Her hair was neatly tied in a blue chiffon scarf, the same colour as her eye shadow. A wisp of brown hair had escaped from the scarf and tumbled down a cheek. She started to shake as she discarded the letter beside her. But if he tried to comfort her, she was bound to push him away. Suddenly he realised how cold the house was. There was no fire in the grate, a wind was whining down the vacant chimney; it blew the letter back onto the floor again where it lay, the spidery handwriting uppermost, the imparted news laid bare. Moorcroft's face returned to George, stubbornly remaining in his vision.

4

"And do you have any choice in the matter?" Her voice was toneless, measured.

"I could always turn it down. Try my luck back in Manchester."

"Start from the bottom again? Impossible. I won't let you." Her clenched fist landed on the arm of the sofa.

Relief passed through him. What would he have done if she had agreed to that? Manchester. Rain, grey, descending in icy torrents; colourless offices in gaunt, humourless buildings. No, he could not have returned to Manchester.

"Moorcroft is punishing us, George. Susan and me, for your actions. For your thoughtlessness, your selfishness... what you did. Does he realise that? It's us he's punishing. Not you."

Everything she said was true. His actions had disgusted, appalled everyone that now knew. Moorcroft had said as much a few hours earlier. He picked up the letter from the floor, folded it, replaced it in his pocket. He noticed how cold Dorothy looked; saw the tips of her fingers were pink. He asked her if he should light a fire. She stared at him.

"What about Susan?" she asked again. "Her school, her friends? What plans do you have for her? Where will we live? What about all this, our furniture? My new settee?"

Hands steady now, she poured herself another sherry. George waited expectantly, fiddling with the empty glass on his knee. No top-up was offered. A bauble on the Christmas tree caught the light as it turned. Fleetingly, his eyes strayed to it.

"What will I tell my parents? Can you imagine Grace's reaction?" She tugged at a strand of hair.

So many questions. What else did he expect? But if there was a way of being transported back two years, of reliving the meeting

5

with Emma, he would not be able to resist breaking the same rules. Only given a second chance, he would take more precautions, adhering to the principles of care, of secrecy. How many times had he relived the moment of discovery, reinvented the passing of events? And still he did not know how much Dorothy had told her family, her friends, the neighbours. It would not be like her to admit to her shame; for that is how she saw it, he knew that. Lifting the electric fire to one side, he poked at the ashes in the fire place.

"When is Susan due back?" Uncertain whether to build a fire, he traced a circle in the fallen ashes. Though he longed to feel some warmth seep into him, bring some cheer into their home, he replaced the poker against the surround.

"I'll tell her." Dorothy stood, moved away. "I'll do all the explaining. She's staying at a friend's for tea after Guides. Not a word from you when she comes back. Not until I've spoken to her." She was staring at a photo of Susan, taken the year before on Brighton Pier. George looked too, remembered the day he took it, the wind catching Susan's dress, blowing it out like an inflated beach ball.

She turned, so her back was to him and he wondered whether she was about to cry. Would she respond to a show of gentleness, the care he still felt for her?

"All day I've been thinking about this meeting. I even caught myself praying this afternoon." There were no tears in her voice; instead she gave a forced laugh. "I thought they'd give you a second chance, simply not promote you for a couple of years. Perhaps even a transfer to another office. But this? I never imagined this. I don't want to go to Malaya. I like it here. Why can't he give you another job here?" Her voice was rising. "Can you ask him for an alternative?"

Best that she did not know how close he had got to joining the queues at the Labour Exchange, for that is how it might have been. He stared down at the rug and told her no, there was no point in that.

"Moorcroft knew my father," he said. "Said he was being lenient because of it."

She said nothing to this, but stared blankly at the Christmas tree. "I'll get supper." A waft of her perfume caught him unawares as she reached towards the table for her glass. He looked up at her; their eyes met for a second, before she straightened and left the room, her petticoat rustling beneath her woollen dress.

The fireplace looked forlorn, abandoned, ash with dust forming a thin skin on the hearth. He shifted his eyes to *The Times* lying on the footstool, the crossword still empty, beckoning. Folding the newspaper carefully into four, he tucked it into his pocket and went through to the dining room.

The hatch was closed and for a minute he hesitated, listening to Dorothy bustling in the kitchen, filling a saucepan with water, lighting the gas. He opened the hatch, peered through into the kitchen, watched her stir gravy on the stove, one hand resting on her hip. "We'll have servants to do all that. An amah, a cook. You won't have to lift a finger." Surely, Dorothy would like that, at least.

There was no reply. He sat down at the table. The smell of steak and kidney pie grew more intense with her footsteps as they neared the dining room. Ignoring his eyes which followed her every move, she settled the pie on the table, retrieved the plates from the hatch. "And boarding school's not so bad. It can be quite enjoyable." Perhaps the regime was not so cruel for girls. Involuntarily, his left eye started to twitch.

"You told me it was awful, that you'll never forget it. I remember you saying how the experience had affected you. Forever, you'd said." She was staring at the pie. Steam curled gracefully towards the ceiling. "Do you think she'll manage any better than you?"

He recalled the terror of watching his own parents disappearing into a cloud of steam, the friendly chug altered to a mean hiss, as the train moved away, taking them to India. But that was before the war, such a long time ago.

"It's different now. Susan will be fine. She'll like staying with Grace and Tom in the holidays," George said.

"Grace will think her prayers have been answered. At last an opportunity to have a child." Dorothy's tone was bitter, full of sarcasm. "A prime opportunity for her to mould her niece in her ways." A deep sigh followed. "Couldn't she come with us?"

He did not answer. He was remembering standing in the corridor outside the dorm: mid-winter, no shirt, bare feet. He jolted as she repeated her question.

"We'll have to see." Now was not the time to tell her of the drink with Jenkins, the information he had gleaned about Malaya, the reason he was late.

The potatoes and peas on his plate were growing cold. He picked at the pastry for a while, then gave up. Rubbing his eye he looked across the table; Dorothy was staring at her untouched food, her hand turning the fork over and over. Desperately, he wanted to confide in her, tell her what he knew about Malaya. It would be cruel not to give her some inkling, at least impart a proportion of what he had learnt. But he had to allow her time, give her that at least. The initial outburst was only natural, but he knew that tomorrow she would want to know more details. The newspapers carried so little news of British outposts, preferring only to relay the good, the ceremonial events; or, when they chose to report on disturbances in the Empire, embellishing the stories with tales of British heroes. And why would she bother scouring the papers for news of a country in the South China Seas? Of the Emergency in Malaya, even he had known very little, before his chat with Jenkins. A disagreement between the natives, he remembered reading in *The Times* that was dealt with effectively by the British Army. Too many wars, Jenkins had said. The public are sick of them, scared of the Communists, terrified of an invasion. Best to keep them unaware of the reality of the Emergency.

Dorothy collected the dinner plates. He touched her lightly on her arm, a token of their old bond. Her eyes closed briefly, before she returned to the kitchen. But she had not pushed his hand away, or lashed out at him, as she had a couple of weeks before.

A gust of wind rattled the window; he got up and drew the curtain back, listened to cats howling, scrapping in the dark. His face stared back at him, from a blackness he could not penetrate. Adjusting his focus, he caught sight of the frozen lawn. The snow had stopped, the branches of the apple tree were motionless. Shadows, elongated, wandering in the wind, gave an unfamiliar, peculiar look to the garden. And the door to his shed creaked and moaned; the place where he used to sit on sunny Sunday afternoons, thinking of Emma, dreaming of touching her silky skin.

Dorothy returned with the coffee. No pudding tonight; he was tired of the after-taste of tinned peaches anyway, cloying, like paper glue.

"I hear there's a magnificent array of tropical fruits in Malaya. You might like them." He leaned across the table towards her. "You can learn to play bridge." There was a time, he remembered, when Dorothy's mouth would turn up, and dimples would form when he brought the cards out to play his tricks for Susan. A sigh dispelled the vision. "It could have been worse," he said. Immediately, he regretted his futile remark.

Picking her knife up, she played with it, running her finger along the cutting edge. "Have you forgotten why you've been sent there?" She dropped two sugar lumps into her coffee, her features rigid.

In a curious way, her question was equivocal. The reason for his exile would never be far from his thoughts. He could not forget Emma, despite all his attempts to rid her from his conscience. Lately, he would attempt to remove the image of her face, he would try and replace her memory with a picture of Dorothy, her angular features, with brown eyes, deep and questioning.

The front door burst open and Susan's voice filled the emptiness between them.

"Not a word to her," Dorothy said, her voice low. "Understand?" She stood, gripped his wrist. Her face was devoid of colour. "Let me deal with this."

Turning to face the opening door, George watched his daughter as she entered the dining room, saw her smile slowly dim, as she looked first at Dorothy then at him.

Chapter 2

Dorothy stared at the gas jets burning in the open oven; at the blues and yellows merging, turning into a shimmering haze. Malaya: pink on the map like so much else; apart from that, she barely knew where it was. For a brief moment she felt sorry for George as she imagined him in Moorcroft's wood-panelled office, shuffling his feet, his head hung in shame. But why Malaya? Why so far away? Weeks after the telling, her mind still turned like the flypaper that hung in her parents' grocer's shop. Why had George not tried harder? Why not somewhere nearer? And would George have asked the same question of his boss? But he had sounded as if Moorcroft were doing them a favour; the mention of George's father, the old school loyalty.

A pile of newspapers, rescued from under the stairs, lay discarded on the table. Picking up the top one, she searched through the foreign news again, for the third time that morning. She glanced over an article about Yugoslavia and the UN vote, turned the page over. But there was nothing about Malaya. Before, she had always glossed over news posted from Reuters about countries so far away; now they all seemed to evade her.

Exhaled smoke filled the kitchen; a fog clinging to the ceiling. How many cigarettes had she smoked, sitting there since before dawn? She went to open the window a fraction. The snow was still thick on the ground, with footprints of birds running across the lawn. A robin briefly settled on the honeysuckle then flew off to better pickings. The postman was whistling *Jingle Bells* as he made his way up their path.

She heard Susan call out as she clattered down the stairs. Turning her wedding ring round on her finger, Dorothy wondered how Susan would react to the news. Quickly, she raked her fingers through her hair, threw the contents of the ashtray into the bin.

Susan stopped in the doorway and stared at the cooker. "Why have you got all the burners on?"

"I'm going out in a minute. I was just cold. It's so cold, don't you think, darling?"

"Are you all right? Is everything…" Her eyes came to rest on the newspapers.

"Everything's fine. You'll miss your bus." A quick kiss. "Got your homework?"

Susan nodded and studied the cold toast, butter congealing on the surface. Her eyes rested on the empty cigarette packet, nothing escaping her observation. Muttering goodbye, she left for school, dragging her satchel behind her.

The delay of telling Susan could not last another day. Dorothy decided she would sit her down that night, but first there would have to be some careful thinking, some planning, a way of getting it all in order. And Susan did not need to know everything. It would be better for her that details were scanty.

The windows had steamed up and the kitchen had an unhealthy warmth to it: a sweatiness, permeated by the fumes of coal gas. This is how Malaya would be; steamy jungles, unbelievable heat. What would their house be like over there? She remembered seeing pictures of houses on stilts with the staircase on the outside, the front door at the top of the stairs. Would she, too, live in an upside-down house with its innards showing for all to see? How would she sleep with mosquitoes whining round her, insects scratching at the walls? And would she have to tolerate one prolonged season? No winter in Malaya, no need to wear her fox fur and matching hat. No more snowmen, ducking snowballs, or sitting in front of a blazing fire, supping brandy egg flips. She tipped the toast into the bin, washed her cup and saucer. Servants to do all that, George had said, as if this would make all the difference.

"I'm going to the hairdresser's," she called up the stairs.

There was no answer. Again, she called out, her tone louder, more insistent. George appeared at the top of the stairs, naked from the waist up, a towel draped over his torso like a robe. His muscles appeared more developed, his shoulders broader, better toned than the last time she had looked at him properly and she wondered why she had not noticed before. As he came down the stairs towards her, she found herself gazing at his chest, at the curve of muscle, the hollow above his collar bone; the place she used to brush with her lips. Had Emma done the same? Turning her back to him, she put her hand to her eyes; she would not cry anymore. Her profile in the hall mirror looked no different from the usual one, as if the grief and anger of the past two weeks had forgotten to leave a mark, to change the shape of her features. She applied some more lipstick, dabbed her nose with powder and tied a scarf round her head.

"I'll be back a little late tonight. Things to tie up, then I'm meeting up with Jenkins. And that's the truth." He stayed on a step halfway down the stairs and put his hands out, imploring. "You must believe me. I'll get some introductions for Malaya," he said. "Make life easier for both of us out there if we have introductions." He reached the bottom step and the towel slipped off his shoulders. "Did you manage to sleep last night?" he asked, his voice concerned, innocent.

"No," she said and wondered how long it was possible to exist without sleep. Already, she felt the onset of unreality, an edginess that made her fidget and jump at sudden sounds.

13

He went to touch her face, then withdrew his hand suddenly. "If Susan's already in bed when I get back, say goodnight to her. Have you told her yet?"

Dorothy knew he was staring at her, felt his eyes fastened to her profile. "No," she said again.

"Maybe tomorrow. The two of us. Not fair to keep it from her for so long." He picked up the letter from the hall table. "This is from the new school, isn't it?"

She nodded, took it from him, dropped it into her bag. She would read it first, she told him, then she would decide.

"Decide what?"

But she chose not to answer and he did not press her. As she left the house, a pile of snow slid down gracefully from the roof with the closing of the front door. The air was thick with a greyish smog and the wind felt Siberian. She turned her coat collar up and headed towards the local shops. Tears, brought on by the cutting wind, fell down her face as she walked, head down, past the bread shop, crammed full of shoppers, yeasty aromas, spreading out into the street. She opened the door to the shop next door, her hairdresser's. The sudden warmth, a nebulous perfumed mist of shampoo, of setting lotion and fragrant bodies was reassuring for Dorothy; a feminine space, a delightful haven. It was like visiting an old friend.

Adelina sat her down in front of the mirror. Dorothy patted her hair and put her head on one side. "I think I'd like something different today." She turned round and looked at Adelina "I want a complete change. A perm maybe?"

"A curl will suit you." Adelina lifted the hair up from her nape. "Something like this?"

Their eyes met in the reflection. "For Christmas? A present for your husband, yes?"

Dorothy smiled, moved her focus to her own face, noticed a darkness under her eyes.

"Yes, a perm is very fashionable," Adelina continued. "Would you like to put this on?" She held out a cape, the same pink as the marzipan wrapped round a Battenberg cake. Slipping it on, Dorothy continued to stare at herself, at her cheeks changing to a rosy colour, warmed by the artificial heat. Watching Adelina as she sorted through her hairdressing implements, picking out a fine-toothed comb for Dorothy, she wondered if she knew much about Malaya, had picked up information from a client, perhaps heard a reference to the colony on the television she was so proud to own.

A blast of cold air from the opening door made Dorothy wrap her arms round herself. Another customer walked in. Adelina greeted the newcomer and escorted her to the back of the salon. Dorothy half-listened to their chatter about the weather and preparations for Christmas. The rhythmic hum of hairdryers bobbed in the background as she closed her eyes. Did she have to go to Malaya? Were there choices for her? There was always the possibility of divorcing George. Harriet, her school friend, had managed without her husband, had two children to take care of, though of course, her open-minded parents helped out. But could Dorothy do the same? There would be her sister to deal with: she imagined Grace's reaction if she were to divorce George. There would be references to the holy sanctity of marriage and implicit pointers to the physical comforts George had brought.

Adelina returned with a catalogue of photos of women in soft focus; their hair curled, faces glowing. Turning the pages, Dorothy stopped at a picture of a woman with pouting lips and pencilled eyebrows, happy, relaxed, carefree. Hair swept off her face, framing her delicate features.

"I want to look like that."

"That'd suit you really well," Adelina said. Fingers flew through Dorothy's hair. Shaking her wrists like a magician about to perform a conjuring trick, Adelina flicked the hair, fluffed it out, drew it back from her temples, then led Dorothy over to a basin. A stream of warm water cascaded onto her head. The tears started, this time real tears. Impossible to stop them, unaided. She grabbed a towel, pressed it to her eyes, tried to concentrate on the sensation of gentle hands massaging soap into her hair, lifting the strands with well-practised manoeuvres.

If she divorced George, what would she do for income? Perhaps he might agree to only provide for the bare essentials. She could stay in the house in Golders Green, keep Susan at the local school, ask her parents to help her out, work in their grocer's shop. But she would not be allowed to forget all she had thrown away. Her father thought George a nice young man, still referred to him as such, even after their fourteen years of marriage. Her mother said he looked after her, gave the best to Susan. "At least you won't have to slice ham every day of your married life," she said on Dorothy's visits, as they sat amongst the familiar odours: cheese, biscuits, pork pie.

No, Dorothy could not bear the idea of going begging to her family, dealing with their disappointment, the cover up. For they were bound to tell their friends she was a widow; that is how they would cope, by eliciting sympathy and understanding. And if she were to try it alone, to leave George to deal with the tropical outpost without her, would she be strong enough to put up with the dis-tasteful looks, the shuns by other women that Harriet had endured? More to the point would Susan be able to defend herself? How would she handle being the only child in her class with a divorced mother, the wrongdoer? For that's how it would seem to them. Breaking up the family home; Dorothy would be blamed for that.

Adelina was dribbling cold fluid over the curlers. It smelt like drain-cleaner, made Dorothy shiver unexpectedly, but still she carried on smiling at their two reflections. A net was pulled over her head, cotton wool secured, covering her ears.

"Are you looking forward to Christmas?" Adelina asked as she shepherded Dorothy to a row of dryers.

"Indeed I am." The gracious lie, well-practised of late. A magazine was placed on her knee. Her eyes fell on an advert for gravy powder, the happy family set round the table, all present and correct.

The alternative to divorce, thought Dorothy, was to grit her teeth and depart for Malaya. She pretended to doze under the hooded hairdryer.

It was eleven by the time she left the hairdresser's. A man was sweeping the streets, making piles of snow blackened by the sooty fog, filthy puddles forming where it was turning to slush. The sky was murky, ashen, the pebble-dashed houses colourless, their grey windows like closed eyes. No one she knew passed her by. More than anything she wanted to be invited in for a cup of tea, another ear, an alternative view point, but no opportunity arose. She leaned into the wind, and struggled home, keeping a tight hold of the scarf round her hair.

At home, she examined herself in the hall mirror. The curls were pretty, framing her face, accentuating the roundness of her eyes. But still she was disappointed; she looked nothing like the model in the magazine.

It was time to write to Grace. Sitting at the dining room table she doodled on the blotter, drawing spirals that expanded across the page. She wrote about the bitterness of the wind, the snowball fights in their neighbours' gardens, the Christmas tree glittering in their bay window, the pudding in the larder and how much she was looking

17

forward to seeing both of them and having a family Christmas once again. She fiddled with her ring and sat staring out at the garden, at the bare trees, their branches bent towards the ground, the snow weighing them down. *I bet he's in St John's Wood now* she thought, *not at work, not making final arrangements, or meeting Jenkins.* All nicely clean shaven and smelling of Old Spice, his hair styled like Dennis Compton's.

She sighed, rested her head in her hands. The pen dropped to the floor. Pushing her chair back quickly, she stood, made her way into the sitting room and poured herself a glass of sherry. As she took the first sip, then the second, a warm glow spread from the pit of her stomach, a reassurance that her inclination, her decision on the matter was right. The middle road was a sensible option.

Back at the table her pen hovered over her letter. *I have some news to impart to you* she wrote. *George has been very fortunate at work. You know how much he is appreciated there.* She chewed at the end of the pen. Words about apt punishment, the evil of telling lies, came back to her, drilled in by her mother. The sherry glass stood empty by her side. She fetched the decanter, refilled her glass *He has been offered a promotion to Malaya. The opportunity is such that he has decided to take it. We will be sailing out there on 10ᵗʰ January, and we would like you to be Susan's guardians while she remains at school here.* She paused and drew a jagged Christmas tree on the blotter with a large-winged fairy to top it. She thought of George with Emma, all the trouble, the anguish he had caused. Now both she and Susan were paying for his selfishness, his narcissism, his sheer stupidity.

An hour later, Dorothy was in the sitting room, perched on the edge of the sofa, her feet warming in front of the newly-lit fire. A tray was laid on a footstool, one cup and saucer, a glass, two plates, butter, raspberry jam and a dish of crumpets, steaming, fresh from the oven. The front gate clicked open and she heard Susan's footsteps running along the path.

Susan said nothing at first when Dorothy told her. Stunned, she slumped in her seat, as if all her energy had been forcibly removed, and Dorothy was not surprised when she started to wheeze. The ghastly medicine, the vile spray, had been prepared, brought downstairs ready, just in case. With her arm round Susan; she helped her recover, stroking, patting her back as the sound in her chest quietened.

"Not much time, is there?" Susan said eventually when her breathing eased. "Jane's parents were given six months before they went to Rhodesia." She refused the freshly buttered crumpet. "Why can't I go with you? I don't want to go to boarding school. Why can't Daddy turn it down? You've never said anything about him wanting to go abroad. Why now? At Christmas?" She stopped for a minute, drew a breath, her freckles pale, the colour of oatmeal. "Do you think there's a chance he might turn it down?" Fixing her gaze on her untouched milk, she said, "I knew there was something wrong, something going on. I wish you'd told me before." She took in another breath. A wheeze was still squeezing her lungs.

Dorothy reached out for Susan's hand, and began rubbing it, caressing the fingers. "There's absolutely nothing wrong. You mustn't think that. It's for the best. You'll see in time." The words sounded so convincing to Dorothy, she almost believed them herself. "And your school is so near to Auntie Grace and Uncle Tom, you'll be able to visit them at weekends. Then you can visit us. Come out to Malaya. It'll be fun, you'll see."

Susan's eyes fell to the ashtray, to the letter from the school secured underneath, its school crest visible. "Can I read it?" she asked.

"Yes, of course." A shard of coal spat from the fire as Dorothy waited for Susan to finish reading. Her hand shook as she lifted a cup of tea to her lips.

"I'm going to Carol's house for tea," Susan said suddenly.

"What do you think of it? Your new school?" Dorothy nodded towards the letter. "Looks jolly nice to me."

"I'll be back in an hour," Susan said.

Shaking off Dorothy's restraining hand, she stood and screwed the letter into a ball, threw it onto the floor. "It's not fair." Tears were bubbling in her eyes. "I don't want you to go."

She rushed out of the room, slammed the door. The following silence was interminable. The only break in the quiet was the slow drip-drip of water as snow melted in the gutters, and the carefully constructed snowman shifted, its axis collapsing as the thermometer slipped above freezing. A throb started over Dorothy's eye. *No stopping now,* she thought. The lie has been told. She rested her head in her hands, leant over towards the fireside, waiting for Susan, then George, to return home.

Chapter 3

George picked up the paper chain from where it had fallen to the floor and draped it back round the mirror over the fireplace. A quick check at all the other decorations reassured him that everything was in order. To prevent any irritation on Dorothy's behalf, every little action helped, exasperated though he was with the compliance she sought to aid her with her plans. Of her need to obtain approval he understood, but it was the deluge of story lines that he found irksome. And he really had no choice but to agree, to keep up the layers of tales, though they were becoming troublesome, impossible to recall with the exactitude needed to maintain the façade. It was not so much that he blamed her; he could understand how she felt, her anger, her disappointment. But he would have preferred the true reason for their exodus to Malaya to be out; he had prepared himself for the rebuffs, the disbelief and horror at his actions. And now there was no going back. The Christmas visitors had arrived two days early with their congratulations and good cheer. On that day of all days when he had to get away, could not, would not change his appointment, the only chance he would have before leaving for Malaya.

Tom was rocking on his heels, warming his bottom in front of the fire.

"I couldn't be more surprised," he said. "Never thought you were the type to want to go abroad." A smile of understanding passed across his face. "Was it for Dorothy? Is she behind the promotion? Looking for a better life? The grass is always greener?" He chuckled. "They're very alike, aren't they, in some ways, Dorothy and her sister. Though Grace of course is always seeking to better herself through

Him up above." And he raised his eyes to the ceiling. "But we are delighted to be Susan's guardians while you are away. A gap in our lives it has been. Not to have been blessed as you have." Putting his hand to his mouth, he coughed and George saw two red circles forming a deep flush on his cheeks.

But the reference to the desertion of Susan made his stomach rage in turmoil of terrible guilt. If there is a God, he thought, it is His duty to watch over Susan, and not to allow her to pay for her father's indiscretion. But he knew no God existed, had seen the burning cities of Germany from three thousand feet above, his finger on the button to annihilate it all. Every Christmas he thought of this, as though the date was set as a reminder. Turning towards him, he noticed Tom looking at him curiously, as if he was trying to read his mind.

"We are very grateful to you," George said as he glanced at the wall clock. He would have to leave soon, he wanted to be early for his appointment; a suitable excuse for Dorothy had not yet formed in his mind. Then there was Susan with her quiet fury, he would have to make amends for the absence he would soon generate. Tom was going on about Susan, telling Dorothy that there was no need to worry, that she would soon get used to being apart from them. And George was concerned too, but for now he had more pressing demands on his mind. Would he have time to change into more suitable attire? Calculating fast, he dispelled this idea, he would have to leave as he was.

Grace was singing Noel, the descant part, as she carried a tray of steaming mince pies into the sitting room. Strange that she and Dorothy were sisters, so unlike, despite Tom's belief that they shared the same ethos, had so much in common. He watched Grace as she dished out the mince pies into the best china, her pale blue twin set buttoned to the neck, a pearl necklace laid over the wool, her hair grey at such an early age. But her complexion was as fresh as

22

Dorothy's, the same bloom on her cheeks. On hearing Dorothy call up the stairs to Susan, he began to fidget with his tie, sliding his fingers under his collar; he still could not think what to say to explain his departure from the family gathering.

Then Dorothy entered the room, her Blue Grass perfume following close behind. She had made a special effort, had swept her hair back to show off her neck, was wearing a blue dress with a matching stole, not an outfit he had seen before. Her smile was demure, another reminder of how easily she had fallen into the role of a willing partner to their removal. She nodded in the direction of the sherry. There was no alternative but to tell her now. Easier to tackle with his back to her, he made his way to the decanter, held it up to the light, then poured some into a glass, hesitated before turning to hand it to Grace.

"I'm afraid I have to go out in a bit. Well now, actually. I'm terribly sorry. Bad timing. Business, of course. Nothing I can do. Very sorry as I say. But I won't be long." Handing Dorothy her glass of sherry, he caught the hurt in her eyes. She knew he was lying, but what could she say if she was to keep up the front?

"What a shame," said Tom. "But I expect you have a lot to sort out. We understand, don't we dear?" Briefly, he touched his wife's arm.

"Can't you wait until Susan comes down?" asked Dorothy, her voice high, strained.

"Sorry, no. I had better be off. The sooner I go..." He kissed Dorothy on her cheek. Innocent, pretending not to know about the remonstrations, the questioning and tears he would suffer tonight while the rest of the household slumbered.

It was sunny at first when he left the house, this day of his last meeting with Emma; a low winter sun dazzled unexpectedly. The ground remained sodden, soaked from the melted snow, and the torrential rain of the night before. Later, as the tube crawled along, he stared up at the silhouettes of chimneys and roof tops against the clear sky, and noticed a cloud, black enough to hold a downpour, spreading slowly across, until eventually the sun was obliterated.

Then the rain came. Puddles formed on the straggly grass which passed as lawns in the back gardens, water flowed from leaking gutters, and spread from drains blocked with leaves. The tube shuddered to a stop; a sodden solitary sheet hung, forgotten on a line in a yard directly in his vision. Until it was replaced by the blur of a tube train travelling at top speed going in the opposite direction, before his tube picked up momentum and shot underground.

At Euston, he got out and pushed his way through the crowds. He queued at the bottom of the escalator, his nose nearly touching the gabardine mackintosh of the man in front of him. Outside, people were bad-tempered in the rain; they hurried without looking where they were going, holding umbrellas as if they were weapons with which they might strike. He decided to walk the mile to the Café Royal, he was in fact half an hour early, he had left extra time in case of an emergency: the tube breaking down, a body on the line, as happened sometimes, on grey days similar to this.

When he reached the place where he knew the Café Royal stood, he at first thought he had come to the wrong building. He had not expected the scaffolding. In his mind's eye, he had pictured the grand pillared steps up to the double door, painted red with the ushers waiting to take his coat, show him to his table. But, of course, his memory of the coffee house belonged to two years earlier, his first secret meeting with Emma. He had not considered it might have changed, had forgotten about the headlines in September of the fire which nearly gutted the building and destroyed the art deco facades. Would Emma pass the building by as he had nearly done? He toyed with the idea of waiting outside in the rain for her. But then she would see him bedraggled, desperate, his face tinged with blue from the cold.

He was shown to a table in the bow window. The cafe was nearly empty, as he had expected at this time in the morning. The coffee machines hissed and spluttered like a consumptive, but the smell was glorious, thick and heady.

"Would you like to order?" A waitress offered him a menu. "We've got a large assortment of cakes too," she said and indicated to a trolley where cakes sat, uncut, untouched. He could see walnuts, cherries on sponges and crystallized oranges on white icing. Or mince pies piled on a red and gold plate.

"I'll wait thanks, I'm expecting a friend," he said. Maybe she could not get away. Had this been a foolish idea of his? He stared out of the window for a minute, to avoid the waitress' gaze. It was still raining, a thick fog had descended, headlights swirled in the gloom.

At that moment Emma came through the door. She saw him immediately, smiled at him as the waitress took her coat and led the way to his table. She was breathing hard, and her face was flushed. She quickly looked over her shoulder before she sat down next to George.

"I can't stay long," she said and leant over towards him, her scent fragrant, light.

He saw she was wearing an ivory blouse. It emphasised the green of her eyes, her pale skin. The fineness of the fabric made him want to undo the top two buttons, to feel the warmth of her breast.

Reaching for her hand across the table, he thought how supple it was. "We'll make the most of it, what little time we have." Disappointment made him swallow hard. Somehow he had imagined them spending most of the day together.

The waitress arrived, trolley in tow with her chat about Christmas festivities, her questions about their plans, what parties they would be attending. Eventually, after too long, she backed away, perhaps, at last, conscious of their desire to be left alone.

"I can't believe you're leaving so soon. It's all happened so quickly." She shook her head slowly, closed her eyes for a second.

He caressed her hand, lifted it to his lips. "I'll come back," he said. "I'll come back."

"Sometimes I hate my father."

"No, no don't hate him."

She turned and looked out of the window, and he noticed her brooch catching the light. "I never dreamt he'd do such a thing."

"But will you wait for me? Or will you marry your Lieutenant, the man your father approves of? You might forget me. That's what your father would like."

"No, no. Don't speak like this. How could I forget you?"

"I'll write. Every day if I can…" George said.

"The letters will take such a long time from Malaya. But when I get them, I'll read them over and over, then I'll tie them all in a silk ribbon. I'll write long passionate letters by return of post." Her voice was a near whisper.

"If only you were coming with me." He sighed; a deep sigh. "Ludicrous, even to think of such an event. Sometimes, though, it does no harm to dream."

She removed her hand from under his and took a sip of her coffee. "He couldn't have sent you much further away. To such a dangerous place too."

"I hear the Emergency is just about all over now. No need to worry about me on that account. I'll be fine. Though it will be intolerable without you. Without our meetings to look forward to. Sometimes I wonder how this can happen. How can we part now? I never believed in fate before. Didn't believe in anything. But it is as though…" He did not know how to put his feelings into words and it was clear that she was close to tears. Leaning forward he touched her cheek, and she held his hand there until she was able to maintain a posture of calmness, her hair smoothed back into place. They resumed talking, tears always a possibility, kept at bay in a public place.

"I have to go now," she finally said. "I'm already late."

They were the words he had been dreading. Reaching for his hand she returned it to her face and closed her eyes.

***

George's return journey, the damp clothes smelling of city smog, the mounting of stairs, the clamour of the underground passed over him, as if he were a spectator, a visitor to a strange world. Soon he was at his front door, his key in his hand, the strains of *Come all Ye Faithful* sifting through the cold night air...

"That's over with," he said as he entered the room. Straight for the sherry, he downed a glass in a single gulp.

Looking round he saw Grace and Dorothy squashed together on the couch, a conspiratorial look on their faces. And he wondered whether Dorothy had decided to reveal all, that the calmness with which Tom was playing Scrabble with Susan was a silent front for the row which would follow. If that were the case, he really did not care at the moment. Anything would be sufferable, bearable compared to that final goodbye to Emma.

Susan turned her body towards him, knocking over her Scrabble set. Her eyes looked rounder than usual as she stared at him. "Where've you been Daddy?"

Dorothy stood, adjusted a bauble on the tree.

"Business. Boring business. At work. What have you been doing?"

The record scratched to a stop, but the needle spun on. Susan sucked her cheeks in. "Nothing," she said.

"Another carol I think, don't you?" Grace's voice.

"You've never been to work at Christmas time before."

"Susan," Dorothy said. "You shouldn't talk to your father like that."

"Sorry." She got up and stood by the door. She stared at the Christmas tree for a minute then returned to Tom and the game of Scrabble.

Chapter 4

Dorothy pointed to an empty table by a porthole and allowed George to lead the way. He opened his newspaper while she picked up her book and surreptitiously looked around the café and the other occupants. The ship owners had done their best to make it look comfortable and welcoming, and although the table and chairs were functional, more in the style of a canteen, they were spotless, looked brand new. On the ceiling, huge domed lights surrounded by mirrors gave the room a feeling of depth, of immensity with their upside-down images of people strolling across the room, making her long for the homeliness of their house in Golders Green. And there was a continuous low hum of the engines, vibrating slightly as the ship rocked gently through the waves. It was hard to comprehend that they would be floating on water for so many weeks. But she continued to take in their new surroundings. For there was no escaping it now. She found herself envying the laughter, the air of companionship that everyone else seemed to share. She wondered why they too were sailing out to the Far East.

But reading was impossible; no matter how many times she studied a page, she could find no sense in Agatha Christie's world just then. Instead, she wrote her first letter to Susan, though she had planned to do that later, when George was in the bar. In her letter, she described their cabin with the brown and blue striped bed covers on each bunk which reminded her of a rug that used to lie by Susan's bed, the chest of drawers, and how it was polished that morning by a man who smelt of the spices she had put in the Christmas pudding. And she told her how she had placed the matching mirror brush and comb set that Susan treasured, on the top of the chest, along with her favourite photograph of her taken on Brighton Pier, one hand holding onto a hat, a mischievous grin on Susan's face. She told Susan how much she missed her and reminded her to keep her finger nails clean and to work hard at her new school. She hoped, Dorothy wrote finally, that the other girls were nice and that Susan was making new friends.

Looking up, she saw that George was engrossed in yesterday's newspaper, his thumb flicking at a pen held between two fingers. He signed Susan's letter after a quick scan of the contents, smiled at Dorothy.

"Settling in?" he asked. "Everything all right?" He put the pen on the table and started to massage his nose with his thumb and forefinger.

"You don't seem to miss your daughter," she said quietly.

"Of course, I do. But it's only been a couple of days since we saw her."

Biting her tongue, Dorothy resisted the urge to lay more accusations on him. Too many people around, and she was tiring of the arguments, the rows that circled them every day. She needed to stretch her legs, leave his company for a while. So she told him she was going to powder her nose.

"Fine, fine," he said. "I'll get you another coffee, shall I?"

Both lavatories were engaged. Dorothy waited behind a woman with grey hair, cut very short, brisk with no attempt at style. Another woman, dressed in white, matching white gloves folded on the sink edge, leaned towards the mirror. She was painting on a fresh layer of lipstick, stretching her lips like an elastic band. And her hair was curled and bouncy, like the picture in Adeline's, as Dorothy's hair was supposed to look. Tears irritated Dorothy's eyes. Sniffing, she turned her face away from the two women. But the room was so tiny, it was difficult to pretend she was not crying.

"Oh my dear, what's the matter?" the woman in the white dress asked.

Perhaps it was being referred to in such caring tones that made Dorothy cry even more. Suddenly she felt helpless, vulnerable, as Susan must have done when they left her at the red brick school. The woman handed her a white handkerchief. It was folded into four with a faint lipstick mark in the corner. A whiff of perfume caught Dorothy as she wiped her eyes.

"I just miss my daughter so much." She felt like crouching in the corner, sobbing. Letting it all out, bawling and screaming.

The other woman took her arm. "Come on, let's go somewhere else," she said. "I'm Hannah, by the way."

Dorothy pictured Susan's face again, distorted with tears and fear.

"There's a lounge upstairs." Brushing a stray hair from her face, Hannah added "It's quiet up there."

The lounge had a few men sitting at tables reading papers, and a family in the corner playing a card game. There were four children, three boys and a girl. The girl's hair was long like Susan's, though a dull brown, and curly. A row of mottled green chairs with upright backs were facing away from the portholes. Hannah pulled two out so they were at an angle and sat in one, patted the seat of the other.

"What's your daughter like? What's her name?" she asked.

So Dorothy told her about Susan, about her hair, how she had inherited the colour from her grandmother, and about her asthma, the way her lungs would wheeze, the concoctions the doctors prescribed, how Susan hated them and the fear Dorothy had, that now it would worsen with her being so far away.

Hannah listened attentively, patted Dorothy's hand and made soft clucking noises. A sense of ease made Dorothy relax. She liked being with this sweet-smelling woman. Would the journey be made more tolerable if she had this woman as a friend, a confidante who seemed to understand her loss?

"Have you got any children?" Dorothy asked.

Hannah tucked some hair behind her ear and it bounced out again immediately. She took out a packet of cigarettes and offered Dorothy one. Stretching across the space between the chairs, Dorothy allowed Hannah to light it.

"No, we haven't any children," Hannah said. "Have you got a photo of Susan?" she asked, leaning back against the chair as she exhaled smoke. She turned to look towards the entrance of the lounge. Following the direction of her gaze, Dorothy saw two nuns moving silently, almost gliding across the floor before they sat at a table at the far end of the room.

Hannah put the back of her hand up to her mouth. "I think they're following me," she said. "They share a cabin with me. Can you imagine?"

And as Hannah giggled like a girl, Dorothy couldn't help smiling. Hannah described in a low voice how the night before she had taken a look at their faces as they slept in their bunks, and that there appeared to be no visible aging signs she said, and, they made snuffling noises as they snoozed, but that even these were discreet and anonymous. She laughed again. Touching Dorothy's arm, Hannah continued in a whisper, "This morning one of them told me they're going to Borneo to be missionaries." She raised her eyebrows. "They hunt heads there, put them round their doors as trophies so I heard, and they live in trees." Her eyelids fluttered. "You're not going there, are you?" she asked.

Dorothy shook her head and wondered whether the ship's crew had put the three women together as some kind of a joke. She glanced back towards the nuns, at their faces, pink and scrubbed, with lips pale and bloodless. One met her stare, and Dorothy pretended she was examining a painting of Big Ben, behind.

Taking a snapshot from her purse, she remembered the day it was taken; in a booth, both she and Susan pulling faces at the hidden camera.

"It's not very recent," she said. "But I do like it. Susan has such an impish grin. Her hair's longer now; she wanted to grow it, to be like her friend."

Hannah studied the photo. "She's got a pretty face, hasn't she? And I love the hat you're wearing."

Dorothy laughed. "I remember Susan put it on for one of the photos. Pulled the veil down over her face and pouted at her reflection." She replaced the photo, fastened the catch on her bag. They chatted for half an hour about the latest fashions, until Dorothy saw the lounge was emptying and she realised she had been there longer than she had planned.

"I must get back to George now. Thank you for…"

"Don't mention it. Glad you feel better now. We're bound to bump into each other again soon. You're lucky to have her." She crushed her half-smoked cigarette in the ashtray.

George was watching the entrance when she walked back into the café. He waved and walked towards her, his hands smoothing back his hair. "I was going to send out a search party. You've been nearly an hour. Never mind. You're here now," and he took her arm, steered her back to the table.

Had she been away that long? She watched his face; a twitch that he had lately acquired in his left eye started its spasmodic movements. Wiping the condensation from the porthole, she stared out at the grey sea, looked out beyond to where the horizon merged with the ocean.

Chapter 5

Dorothy sat back in her deckchair and smoothed out a wrinkle in her new summer frock. Resting in the open air somehow made the reason for them being on ship easier to bear. The days drifted into each other, lazy, as she had become herself. But she was finding the heat difficult, discovering the fierceness of the flat ocean sun gave her frequent headaches, caused her skin to itch. But at least today she was pain-free, though she was as ever sleepy, too drowsy even to open her book. A man in a turban bent and filled her tea cup. Perhaps George was right. Getting used to servants would not be so hard.

Hannah was sitting next to her, the chair pulled back into the shade. She was wearing her white dress again, and Dorothy remembered George at breakfast that morning as he skimmed the outline of Hannah's body. Of course he thought Dorothy did not notice. Luckily for her, Hannah appeared oblivious; her attentions purely concentrated on a man who worked in the Colonial Service, a younger man who played tennis everyday.

"You'll love it over there," Hannah said. "It's really the perfect life." She sipped her tea and looked about her at the other passengers. "Obedient servants, who adore us, none of the drudgery of housework for us, enough gin and ice to cool the brow. Bridge in the afternoons. What else could a girl want?"

"It does sound attractive," Dorothy said.

Hannah described her house, the large veranda with the swing seats made of rattan, the flowering plants in elaborate pots, the bell she would use to call the servants. The afternoons spent there reading, writing, sipping gin and tonic, or just resting, dozing in the heat of the afternoon. And the cook who knew English recipes like

Hannah knew her times tables, the gardener who bowed when Hannah picked flowers to decorate the house.

"I used to have help in the house in London," said Dorothy. "For a short while." She held her cup and saucer out to the waiter. "Tell me, why didn't your husband go with you to England?" The hand of the man pouring her tea was dark and smelt of scented soap.

"Seasickness," Hannah said. "Don't suppose we'll ever leave Malaya. He refuses to travel anywhere on a boat. Not since last time."

"How awful for you." Dorothy hesitated. "But how will you, I mean both of you, ever get back?"

"That's exactly what I say to him." She ordered another tea, no milk, just lemon, she said to the man, and Dorothy watched as Hannah looked at him, unblinking, bold, and smiling. "I might have to come back with somebody else." Her laugh was breathy, hoarse from the strong brand of tobacco she preferred. Leaning over towards Dorothy, she described in a low voice how one or two of her servants would, besides serving meals, or pummelling cushions, provide comfort of a more sensual nature. "A little ding-dong," she said, "can make a girl feel wonderfully young." Her eyes closed and she pulled the brim of her hat further down her face.

Dorothy read her detective book for a while: a naked woman had been found in a ditch, a look of agony in her eyes. The second murder of this type, with blue stains round the mouth. Dorothy shifted herself so she was sitting further back in her chair and put her book face-down on her lap.

"I hope our servants are as accommodating as yours," she said to Hannah. "Though they don't appeal to me in *that* way." She thought of last night, the look of disappointment on George's face as she pushed him away again. But what did he expect? It astonished her that he appeared surprised at her rebuffs, that he thought some form of normality could be attained already. The raw stage had not passed, and she could not foresee when she would allow him to touch her again.

"We'll be arriving at port soon," Hannah said. "You take a look at the natives; they're so romantic, with their soulful eyes, and dark skins. You'll see what I mean."

The sound of wood scraping against the deck made Dorothy look behind her. The two nuns were settling into some deckchairs in a patch of shade. They started to whisper to the crosses that hung around their necks; their Bibles were open on their laps. They turned the pages, their movements quick, furtive. But they did not stay long, nor did they acknowledge Hannah and Dorothy's presence. Maybe they just wanted a bit of sunlight, a respite from the dark corners they inhabited. Dorothy suddenly felt sorry for them. Always trying to convert, never thinking of themselves. And she wondered about the head hunters of Borneo, whether the nuns would ever show fear. Then she saw the port taking shape as the ship neared the land, and a rush of excitement pushed the nuns' destiny out of her mind. At that moment, more than anything, Dorothy wanted to disembark at Port Said, to stroll around in the crowds of foreign faces and take in the admiring glances she felt she would receive from the robed men she could just make out on the quay. But most of all she wanted to link arms with Hannah, to wander around the bazaars and choose a souvenir for Susan.

But an epidemic of typhoid had overtaken the port; no one was permitted to disembark. She listened to the call to prayer coming from the mosque she could see quite clearly, up on a hill away from the shuttered houses with their flat roofs. The call made her melancholy, the sound was so pure. She thought of Susan, wished she were beside her hanging over the rails.

And a familiar sense of disappointment, of unfulfilled dreams occupied her mind, as she watched the other passengers throw coins into the water. Young Arab boys dived to retrieve the money, their bodies smooth and glistening as they rose from the depths, shaking the water from their hair.

"They can stay down for hours," Hannah said as she pulled herself back from the rails. "Well, a long time at least."

They watched a boy as he raised his right fist to his friends and swam back to the harbour.

"Poor mites," said Hannah. "As I said, we're lucky. Got it all."

The sun rose higher; Dorothy's skin was starting to prickle and burn despite her efforts to keep to the shade. She wanted to take a bath and told Hannah she was going to have a lie down for an hour or two.

The darkness of the inside of the ship momentarily blinded Dorothy as she made her way down the steps and, as she reached the cabin area the quietness mollified her, the dim light soothing her eyes. There was the sound of running water; she could hear a baritone singing: *Never do a tango with an Eskimo.*

She turned the key to their cabin and opened the door. George's aftershave hung in the air; she could almost taste his presence. She sat down on her bunk and picked up the photo of Susan. What was she doing now? Perhaps she was using her sketchbook and pencils. Dorothy put the photograph back. George's fountain pen fell onto the floor, dislodged by the frame's support. It was still warm from his grip. Slowly, she rotated it between her finger and thumb. Who was he writing to? Not Susan, he had just scrawled a note at the bottom of a letter written by her. She tugged at her wedding ring, drew it backwards and forwards over her knuckle. A worry, always present, hovering in the back of her mind, slipped to the forefront, made her light-headed and perspiration form on her brow. Was he still in touch with that girl?

She pulled open the top drawer and searched through his socks and underwear, his rolled up ties, his folded handkerchiefs. There were footsteps along the corridor. Closing the drawer she remained still, controlling her breath. The footsteps passed the cabin. She rifled through the second drawer, pulled out a writing pad. Here it is, she thought, and her hands shook as she leafed through the thin pages. All empty, not even a mark on the blotter. She tried the bottom drawer. Nothing.

His bunk - if he had written to her, he would put it there; keep it next to him while he slept. One final look, then she would give up. Maybe he really had no more contact with her. That was always a possibility. There was nothing under the pillow, or inside the pillow case, she made sure of that. She pulled the covers off the bed, threw them onto the floor, yanked the sheet off the bed. A folded piece of paper fluttered to the carpet.

My darling Emma,

The distance is increasing between us, but I do not feel I am further apart from you. I think of you every day. Sometimes I find it difficult to express my feelings to you when we are together, and now when I want to put them on paper, I find I do not possess the words that would give justice to this love I have for you. But it is greater than anything I have ever known. We will be together again, one day I am sure of it, it has to be. I simply cannot tolerate any other possibility. We are approaching Port Said and everyone on the ship is happy, rejoicing that they will be on land again...

The door opened. "What on earth are you doing?" George asked. His face was grey.

As she sat on the edge of his bunk, the half finished letter shaking in her hand, she found that she was speechless.

"Give it back to me," he said.

Screwing the letter up into a tight ball, she threw it across the room. "How dare you?" She stood, kicked at a pillow on the floor. "How dare you?"

"I'm sorry," George said. He looked wizened under the fluorescent light.

"No contact you said. You promised. I should have left you while I had the chance."

"I'm sorry."

"Why did I believe you? I should have taken Harriet's advice. She told me to divorce you. How many times have you written?"

He remained silent.

"How many letters?" Her voice raised a pitch. "You told me she didn't matter anymore. So how many times have you written to her?"

"Please don't shout. Everyone will hear."

"I'm not shouting. Do you think I want everyone to know what a scheming husband I have?"

George sat on her bunk. Put his head in his hands.

"Don't try that little boy lost with me." She stood in front of him. "It won't wash anymore George."

He stood, fetched the letter; tore it into small pieces, put it in the waste paper basket.

"I don't deserve this," Dorothy said. "Why are you writing to her?"

" I was just… I don't know. Sorry."

There was a knock on the door. "Hello Dorothy, it's me."

"You've lied to me again," Dorothy said. Nausea was making her dizzy. "Just a minute, she called out towards the door. Steadying herself, she turned to the mirror, powdered some colour onto her face, poked at her hair, retouched her lipstick.

"Where are you going?" He lowered his head and sat on his bunk. A trembling hand smoothed back his hair.

"You'd better make your bed," she said.

Outside their cabin it was as still and quiet as before.

"You all right?" said Hannah. "You look as if you've seen a ghost."

She walked up the staircases, holding onto the rail.

"What's wrong?" Hannah asked as they reached the second deck.

Dorothy did not reply.

They reached the top deck. The crowd was still at the rails.

"Come on," said Hannah and she led her to the Veranda Café where a man was swabbing the floor with a wet mop. They sat at a table at the far end of the room, away from the smell of bleach.

"You're in a bit of a state, Dorothy." Hannah's face was close, close enough for Dorothy to notice a crease in her green eye shadow.

"Nothing. It's just the journey, you know."

Hannah brought out her cigarettes. "I think it's more than that."

Dorothy inhaled deeply. She coughed. "I should never have come. I could have stayed in England. I'd have been fine there, on my own, just Susan and me."

41

Hannah patted her hand.

Dorothy looked towards the man with the mop. He was cleaning the floor in wide circular movements, working his way up towards their table.

"I thought you were looking forward to life in Malaya," Hannah said. She drew deeply on her cigarette. "My dear, what's happened?"

Dorothy was silent, she fiddled with her wedding ring, thought of going out on deck, chucking it into the ocean, watching it sink.

"I've just found a letter," she said eventually. She had to tell someone. No longer could she keep it to herself. "He'd written a letter to another woman."

"Another woman? Who?"

The man with the mop had reached their table. He drew a ring of suds round them; his movements were slow, exact, as if he were painting on a canvas. She waited until he had moved along, out of earshot, then sighed, and let her shoulders go loose.

"He was having an affair."

"Oh you poor thing. I'm so sorry."

"He first started seeing her in June, year before last. I got that much out of him."

Hannah pursed her lips. "I bet that took some doing."

"I always thought he was happy with just looking, you know. He thinks I don't see, but I do." She turned towards Hannah. "You know I never thought he was the type to have an affair."

Two men entered the café. "Jolly hot up there, isn't it?" one said.

Dorothy squashed her cigarette into the ashtray.

"And now we're going to a Colony. I've got to pay for his stupidity."

"The brute."

"I don't know how many letters he's written to her." She glanced over at the two men. One of them laughed and looked towards Hannah and Dorothy.

There was a loose thread in her dress, she picked at it, wound it around her finger Hannah put her hand over Dorothy's. "You'll tear your dress apart."

"I've got a terrible headache now." Dorothy put her hand to a spot above her right eye. It throbbed; a rhythmic beat, like her pulse.

"Let me get you a cup of tea," said Hannah. She was standing, looking towards the two men. "I've got some aspirin. I'll fetch you one."

Dorothy sat up. "You mustn't tell anyone else."

"My lips are sealed." Hannah picked up her bag and left the room.

Dorothy wondered whether she had told Hannah too much, she might spread it around the ship, like Chinese whispers, despite her promise. She would not be able to tolerate the glances, the gossip. And of course they would blame her. Better not to say anymore.

Ten minutes passed.

She heard the door open and turned her head. The two men watched Hannah in silence as she crossed the room.

"No tea or coffee. Only Bovril. Do you a power of good."

The hot liquid scalded her lips; she blew on it, cupped her hands around the warmth.

43

"Do you know what I would do in your shoes?" said Hannah. She crossed her legs, put her arm across the back of her chair.

And Dorothy was reminded of Harriet.

"I'd leave him."

Dorothy drank some more Bovril, swallowed the aspirin.

"Do you really think he won't write to her again? Do you think he won't see her again? Or do it again? With another girl? Out for a good time."

"He told me he wouldn't contact her again. He promised. Not that the letter would ever get to her. The fool."

Hannah raised her eyebrows.

"How can I possibly leave him now?"

"Best thing you could do. Start a new life."

"I've got nowhere to go."

"You know what I would do?" Hannah said again lowering her voice. "I'd leave him now, before he does it again. Get off at the next port. It's now or never." She sat back. "Ceylon is beautiful, you'd be fine there on your own."

"I can't do that." Dorothy thought of Harriet, her recounts of divorced motherhood, her regrets when she was snubbed by another mother. And now, here was Hannah making it sound very easy. But the idea of packing a small bag and giving George the slip as they walked together through the port suited her mood well. Disappearing, making him worry himself sick. Could there be anything better? She pictured George as he waited for her in the scorching sun, looking at his watch every minute, clearing his throat, pacing. Maybe she could pick up work, a private tutor or a secretary, and live in a beautiful house where hibiscus hung over the porch, and a man in a turban served her tea all day. Susan would go to a local school and they would weave flowers into each other's hair as they sat in the coolness of the summer house.

One of the men in the café called out goodbye to them both.

"It'll be all right," she said. "I'm just a little upset. Of course I'm not going to leave him." She stood up and looked at Hannah, and wondered what sort of man her husband was. "There's simply no way I can leave him."

Through the porthole, she could see the waves were higher, the sunlight shone through the swell. Two sea birds rode on the water. Looking back at Hannah she watched her as she sipped her drink.

Chapter 6

It was the first landing since leaving the Essex Marshes; the first time they were to be allowed on shore. A desperate need consumed Dorothy; to have her feet placed on a surface which remained static, which was not surrounded by water. She felt George's hand resting on the small of her back, guiding her as the other passengers surged forward.

Stepping onto the quay in Colombo, the motionless air, stiff and dank, hit Dorothy full on. No ocean breeze to cool, only the solid heat; it was suffocating, like an invisible veil that had become tangled and damp. Thick sweat of sailors and vendors filled the air, mixing with the putridity of bird lime, gutted fish. Exotic perfumes broke through the stench. Local women drifted past, their saris floating, midriffs bare, jewelled ears, belly buttons glinting in the sun. She watched the fishermen, their backs glistening in the morning sun. Birds circled their nets. They fought, their beaks stabbing at the catch, and as Dorothy waited for the passengers to disperse, she saw a boy, feet bare, sitting cross-legged. He turned and stared at the passengers, at her. Was he puzzled by her pale face, her neat attire?

A man carrying a box yelled at her and George, gesticulated for them to move aside. Gasping, she allowed George to pull her out of the way. Porters poured from the ship, balancing suitcases and trunks on their heads, chattering in a clipped, guttural language. Bizarre-looking vegetables with spikes and hairy matting were piled onto stalls, wheelbarrows, bicycles. A rapid pulse was beating in Dorothy's eye. Was this how Malaya would be?

At last she, with George close beside her, reached the end of the quay. "Soon be at the shop," said George as calmly as if he were taking a stroll through Regent's Park. He pointed to a street beyond the quay, down some steps. "We won't stay long," he said. "If you don't want. If you find it too noisy, too hot." A smile, shy, as if he were wooing Dorothy, passed quickly across his face. He brushed some hair back from her eyes, lightly touched her cheek.

She was pleased to have George take her arm, to guide her down the steps. His sorrow, the disgrace bore through her, burrowed under her skin. She looked around her at the other couples laughing, heads together, comfortable, as they sauntered down the street. Buildings, nearly toppling, crammed with shops on their lower floors, open, no doors, the shop's innards strewn across the cobbled stones: pots, saucepans, bulging sacks, grains scattered across the road. Dorothy told George that she would be fine, that she would get used to it, and needed to be on land as long as possible. Despite the chaos of the scene, she was curious to explore it with him.

A ring of laughter, bold and careless, rode above the noise of the dock. Dorothy swung her head round, back in the direction of the ship. Hannah was strolling towards them, calling out, her skirt rotating round her hips as she waved. A sense of uneasiness made Dorothy turn quickly back, but George shaded his eyes with his hand and watched her progress towards them.

"Mind if I join you?" Hannah asked. She wore a different hat, wide brimmed, one that flattered her face, brought out the blue of her eyes, the careful tan of her face.

"Of course you must," George said to Hannah, his eyes wide open, with gentle smile. "Can't have you wandering round alone."

Always she and Hannah had shared their time alone, a pleasant way to spend the days on board, drifting, wandering the decks. But this was supposed to be Dorothy's day. It was George's promise, his effort to make amends: a small step towards her forgiveness. She felt herself shrinking into herself. Her hair had become frizzy from hours spent sitting in the open, her skin was peeling, unused to the ferocity of the Indian Ocean sun. Would George now make comparisons, be reminded of the girl in London?

The other passengers had spread across the uneven road, taking their individual, their separate routes, but still there was little space to walk. Hawkers hassled, mules headed across the way, laden down and heaving, cows ambled down the cobbled stones. The three of them kept close together, bumping together in the narrow streets. Hannah dawdled, stopping in shop doorways, touching the silver jewellery on display. Men were squatting nearby, staring straight ahead, spitting into the dirt. And George waited patiently for Hannah, his gaze fixed on her bronzed, silky neck.

They reached a shop with swaths of material hanging in the doorway like sails to a mast. It was full of passengers, skins pallid with lobster-like patches at the neck of shirts and summer frocks. They looked dowdy, compared to the Singhalese women with gems in their noses glittering, and tinkling bangles on their slender wrists. Rolls of fabric leaned against walls, piled up to the ceiling, propped against rickety chairs. Tea was offered, hot and sweet. Dorothy watched as Hannah fingered a yellow sari wrapped round a dummy. Threads hung from its stitched eyes. Lipstick, bright red, was newly painted on its mouth.

Dorothy chose a blue sari, the colour of an English summer's day.

"Complements your eyes," George said as he sipped his tea.

She held the sari up against herself; the material draped from her shoulder.

"What about this? Do you like this colour? Don't you think it's rather splendid?" Hannah was standing in front of George, turning. She fluffed her hair, smoothed the fine fabric over herself. The sari was a translucent green.

George nodded, slipped his eyes downwards. Studiously, he drew a line with his foot. Then looking back up at her he cleared his throat. "Very nice," he said. A spot of pink was forming on each cheek.

Dorothy watched as Hannah, aware of George's gaze, examined her profile in the mirror, lifting her face a little, eyes downcast, revealing a soft spread of eye shadow.

Was Hannah's performance a deliberate act? Or an innate response to George's obvious admiration? And why was it that he played along with her? After all his promises about the girl in London, the letter, his fear, despair at the discovery. Dorothy had chosen to try again, to ignore Hannah's warning. But her day was ruined now, thoughts of reconciliation rapidly diminishing, as though bleached out from excess use. She felt weak, empty, as she sank into a chair. Of course Hannah was right. Correct in her assumption that George would no longer be satisfied with her alone.

Her throat tightened; she swallowed hard, mouth dry. A woman in a brown and yellow dress was listening to the exchange, watching the turn of Hannah's hips. Dorothy remembered her at dinner the night before; she had laughed and guffawed with increased gusto the more she drank. As she watched the woman turn to her husband, Dorothy recalled her mother forcing her to drink bicarbonate of soda when she had returned from a dance excited, exuberant, so talkative, full of laughter and music, her mother assumed she was drunk.

"I thought I might buy a bangle too," Hannah was saying. "You should as well," she said to Dorothy and picked one out of a box lying on the counter.

"Of course you should." George stood, rattled the change in his pocket. "You must have whatever you want."

So Dorothy looked for a bracelet, helped by a young woman in a cerise sari. The one she chose was silver with intricate carvings of serpents and flowers. The blue stones matched her new sari. The Singhalese woman pushed it onto Dorothy's arm, showed it to George and smiled. Fragrances, myrrh and musk of warm sensuality, oozed from her oily skin.

***

After a downfall of rain in the afternoon, Dorothy returned to the upper deck of the ship. Alone, she watched the expanding sea, the landless horizon ahead. Small waves rippled on the ocean, the surface disturbed from a past unruliness. She tried to imagine what her life would be like in Ipoh. It was difficult not to picture the house as being identical to the photo Hannah had shown her. A high veranda with an Indian man standing behind Hannah, a tray of tit-bits, of drinks and glasses balanced in one hand.

Leaning over the rail, Dorothy watched the wake churn, throwing froth from the retreating ship. She wondered at the depth of the ocean, felt light-headed, unreal. Trying to penetrate the surface of the water with her vision, she imagined tiny fish and sea-horses swimming along with the current like the picture hanging in the dining room, of fish that looked like humbugs or were coloured as brightly as parrots.

She heard Hannah talking. A low conversation, soft words spoken with the man who worked in the Colonial service. She was starting to question Hannah's motivations. Perhaps she should not have told her about the letter to the girl in London. Why had she allowed her secrets to spill out to a woman she barely knew?

Some dolphins were leaping, playing in the water. A small crowd gathered round, exclaiming, pointing. Aware that Hannah had passed behind them, was leaving the deck, Dorothy stretched forward to peer at the dolphins, conscious of a man pressing close behind her.

"Aren't they lovely? God's creatures." The nuns appeared beside her. The sun glinted on the smaller one's glasses. "They are a pleasure to watch. Don't you think?" she continued in her Irish lilt.

"I've never seen dolphins before," Dorothy said with a smile.

"And will this be your first time in Malaya?" the same nun asked in her next breath.

"Yes, yes. My husband's been promoted there." Too late, the words were out; the lie so easy to tell. But to tell an untruth to a Holy Order... was this blasphemy? Would retribution now come her way? "And you?" Dorothy asked pleasantly. "Have you been out there before?"

"Oh, indeed we have," the tall nun said. "Not long to go now before the end of our journey. Two weeks and we'll be there. With the Almighty's blessing." She covered her cross with one hand, closed her eyes. Her face was pale, like stretched parchment. Then they both moved away, gliding across the deck.

The dolphins had vanished beneath the water and the crowd of onlookers dispersed. A few stragglers stayed on, hoping for another sighting. Perhaps they were desperate for more entertainment to provide relief from the hum-drum of the journey.

Dorothy's new bracelet glittered and shone in the sun. Putting her arm out in front of her, she admired the engravings; delicate, with a life-like quality. The man who had been close behind her stepped to her side. Startled, she realised he was the man from the Colonial Service. His eyes were screwed up as he looked out to sea. Taking out a pack of cigarettes from his pocket, he offered one to Dorothy.

French writing covered the packet. She refused his offer, aware of his beefy breath.

"Couldn't help overhearing," he said. "First time out there for you?"

Dorothy looked about her; searched the deck for Hannah.

"Didn't Hannah tell you?" she asked.

He carried on looking out to sea. "She did mention it, come to think of it. Are you looking forward to it? You and your husband?"

"I expect it will be very different." Had Hannah mentioned anything else about her?

"Of course it will get better soon. The situation out there. It is Ipoh you're going to, isn't it? That's where it all started. Did you know that? Not that that will make any difference to you. Long time ago all that caper."

"I'm afraid I don't know much about Malaya. I was told The Emergency was nothing to worry about." She paused. "How did it start in Ipoh?"

"Three rubber planters murdered by the Chinese." He stopped looking out to sea, turned to face her. "The British are getting the upper hand now. It'll be fine for you. For you and your husband. You'll have a super time." There was no smile in his eyes, but the corner of his mouth lifted a fraction.

"Is it dangerous?" Desperately, she tried to hide her concern.

"Oh no. Not for non-army personnel."

"Not at all? "

He resumed searching the horizon. Maybe he had not heard her.

She repeated her question. Sweat trickled down her back.

"As long as you don't take unnecessary risks. But you wouldn't do that, I'm sure."

"I hope you're not trying to frighten the life out of the poor girl? Of course it's not dangerous." Hannah's voice was clear, determined, and made Dorothy swing round. How long had she been standing there listening?

"Just making conversation," the man said. He slipped his arm round Hannah's waist.

"Well, don't." Hannah poked the man in the ribs. "There's nothing for you to worry about, my dear," she told Dorothy. "Used to be much worse." She rolled her eyes towards the man, then extracted a cigarette from the pack in his hand. "I've been out there for years."

"But you have a gun, don't you? For when your husband's not there?"

Dorothy knew the man was watching her, observing her reaction. She gripped the rails, picturing Hannah by the light of the moon, a pistol in her hand, snatched from under her pillow. Was that how it was going to be for her? Would she have to barricade herself in, ready for an assault? Her hand went to the beads round her neck. She twiddled them, tugging at the string, slipping them between her fingers. The necklace snapped suddenly and the pearls scattered on to the deck. She saw one roll under the rail, overboard.

"Oh dear!" Hannah crouched, started to collect them. "Duncan. Go to the bar. I'll see you down there in half an hour."

Some of the pearls travelled across the deck, vanishing under chairs, slipping into cracks. A waiter appeared, helped to retrieve them, then handed them to Dorothy in a paper bag.

53

Hannah put a hand on Dorothy's shoulder. "Let's go and sit down," she said. "In the shade."

Dorothy hesitated.

"I want to apologise," Hannah said. "I know you thought I was flirting with George. I know you're cross with me."

Dorothy followed her to a row of deckchairs out of the sun. She waited, twisting her bracelet round her wrist as Hannah ordered the drinks. After the steward had gone, Hannah pulled a parcel out of her bag.

"I brought you a present," she said. "To say how sorry I am. I was only having a bit of fun in Colombo. Can't help it sometimes. But I mean no harm." She handed the parcel to Dorothy; green paper, with matching string. "I thought you might like it."

Hiding her surprise, Dorothy unwrapped the parcel. A silk shawl unfurled from the wrappings. It shimmered and slithered over her arm: turquoise bordered with silver.

"Thank you," she said. "It's beautiful."

"Promise me you'll come and visit me. It gets lonesome on that rubber plantation." Hannah patted Dorothy's knee. "I am truly sorry if I upset you. And ignore old Duncan. Malaya's not nearly as bad as he makes out. Do you think I would stay there if there was any risk? I would be the first one to be off. Believe you me."

But Dorothy did not believe her. In her mind she turned the ship round and steered them back through the steaming waters of the Indian Ocean, slicing the waves of the Mediterranean until they arrived back home.

Chapter 7

Their boat was beginning to feel like home. But it suited George, this state of temporary existence. Though occasionally he thought the cabin, with the iron framed bunk bed, the washbasin with its leaky tap, the scratched mirror, and the ever present smell of damp that pervaded every corner, was a place in which he was destined to endure as part of his punishment. At least in the confines of the cabin, he could dream of Emma's soft perfumed skin beneath his fingers in much the same way he used to relive their secret meetings in his potting shed at the bottom of the garden. Replacing the cap onto his fountain pen, he went to the porthole and looked out. Not long and they would be landing. Then to Ipoh and on to the export business. Doing his bit for the remnants of the British Empire is what Moorcroft had said, as if George's love for Emma had affronted all that England stood for. The Empire needed rubber to mould the tyres of motorcars, for the backs of carpets that everyone wanted fitted in their houses. Its uses were immeasurable, a vital material to the success of the post-war boom. But rubber was a smelly, dirty business. Not clean and ordered like the insurance company that Moorcroft headed.

He extracted the letter to Emma from his pocket. Just written, with an ear open for Dorothy's footsteps, the swish of her skirt, he knew only too well. So many years together. Too many without this new passion, these unbearable emotions discovered with Emma. The love he felt for Dorothy was mild, brotherly, a genuine fondness. Now, she barely spoke to him, only sat next to him at meal times. It was Hannah's company she sought out. An unlikely friend. Bit flighty. But then who was he to know about such things?

He had attempted humour in his letter to Emma, as he described the other travellers, the man who every morning marched along the deck swinging his cane, the woman with a different feathered hat for every day of the week. He told her he was finishing crosswords at record speed. Then he wrote how much he missed her. For two pages, his looped handwriting formed the crux of the letter as he detailed his love for her using language that had never before flowed from his pen.

He folded the pages and slipped them into the envelope, sealed it, uncapped his pen again and wrote the address, Emma's girlfriend's address in St John's Wood. It was as well they had one ally. How else would they have kept in touch? The alternative: years ahead, blank, without contact, none of her letters to break up the tedium of his days, was not worth contemplating.

He peered out to sea. He knew every mark on the glass, every scratch in the paint on the metal surround. The view was limited by the swell of the ocean. And as much as he squinted, he could see no sight of land. Letter in pocket, he opened the cabin door. Apart from the ever present throb of the engine, all was quiet. He guessed everyone was on deck scouring the ocean for land. Like a thief with the family silver, he sneaked down the stairs and made his way along the lower deck. His knock was answered immediately.

The steward dipped his head in a slight bow and George found himself wondering again at the intricacies of a turban.

"Can you post this for me when we land at Port Dickson?"

He felt the man's eyes burrowing into him, asking him why he could not post it himself. Now, George felt he had to explain, or was it that pang of guilt, the little voice at the shoulder telling him he should know better.

"Family business. The wife is upset, you see," he said.

"Of course, sahib. We will land very soon." He took the letter, bowed and retreated back into his cabin.

George strode up the stairs and out onto the deck. It didn't take him long to spot Dorothy. As he approached and called her name, she turned and waved to him. A wide-brimmed sun hat threw a shadow across her eyes, but her lips were painted a fashionable red and they formed a smile that said everything was fine, as if there was nothing more she wanted than this new life as an expat in a far flung British colony.

After a while, a cheer rose from the crowds leaning over the rails and there boomed across the deck, the boat's hooter signalling the imminent arrival at Port Dickson. The sun was strong up there on the deck, with the boat nearing port, as the breeze from the ocean grew still and there was nothing to blow away the stench of rotting fish, or the garbage strewn along the quayside. Men with cloth wrapped round them, stood, or sat, or squatted in a patch of shade watching as the boat was pulled into dock. There were shouts as two men wound the rope round a capstan and the stink of fish grew stronger every minute. George touched Dorothy's hand. More men yelled instructions as the gangplank was pulled down.

"We'll get transport to the station," George said as they waited to disembark. He was aware of Dorothy standing silently beside him, looking on, her hands fiddling with her freshwater pearl necklace, a recent Christmas present from him.

***

George walked with Dorothy hanging onto his arm, down the station platform to where their train was waiting. The shade of the station provided no respite from the sweltering heat of Port Dickson. There was a mass of travellers; breaths of bourbon, cigars, the strange sugary smell that some women breathed, leather suitcases with their musty odours, trunks that emitted aromas of camphor that mixed with the sweat of the men who carried them. George repeatedly cleared his throat. How he longed for the order and brisk wind of a station platform in England.

"Shall we get on?" George asked. His voice was deliberately soft, gentle.

He took her hand, helping her up onto the train, noticing that her yellow dress had a smudge of dirt on the flounce. Her face was pale, with a half-drugged look about her eyes. The smile of a few hours ago had vanished along with Hannah.

He found an empty compartment, slammed the door and refrained from slumping into the padded seat.

"I didn't get a chance to say goodbye to your new friend," he said trying to make his voice sound jolly.

"They live up country. Her husband met her in his car."

Was that a reprimand, a reminder of their wandering status? Never sure, he was beginning to read disapproval into most of her utterances. He took to staring out of the open window, listening to the slamming doors, watching the passengers climb on. Many from the boat, women in colourful summer dresses, men wearing pale suits and panamas. Young men in army uniform watched from the sides, guns slung over their shoulders. Should their presence ensure safety? Or indicate the dangers of the Emergency? He thought back to his meeting with Jenkins. An uprising encouraged by the Chinese Communists, he had said just before he bought another drink and patted George's shoulder in commiseration with his growing concern.

George leaned closer towards Dorothy. "We'll be all right. You might never want to go back." He found these, his own words oddly comforting, as if the idea was a real possibility.

She sighed, removed her hand from under George's and fiddled with her hair. "That's unlikely, I think. Under the circumstances." Turning her face towards him, she said: "I'll never get used to being without Susan. I'll never get used to being here. I hate it already, this heat, the flies, the strangeness of the place. I'll put on an act. Not for you, George. Because I have to. Don't ever forget that."

Before George could think of a suitable response, the compartment door slid open. It was the man with the cane.

"Anyone sitting here?" The seat opposite George was tapped with his cane.

George told him no and nodded to the man. He was still reeling from the unexpected outburst from Dorothy. He wondered whether Hannah had encouraged Dorothy to take this position of continuing outrage. But they had to share some kind of existence together. Why would she not make an effort?

"On the boat, weren't you?" The man put his hand out. "Jolly good sailing, I thought. Wouldn't you agree? Been on a few rough rides. Everyone going green. Sick bay full. That kind of thing." His hat was removed and placed beside him. "Hot one today."

"Does it get cooler then?" asked Dorothy.

"'Fraid not. Beastly weather out here. And with this rotten war, Malaya isn't what it used to be. Be back in Blighty this time next year. Retiring from my Colonial Service. Can't wait to put my feet up. How about you?"

"First time out here. Promotion," George said, conscious of Dorothy's body next to his, tightening. Had the conspiracy taken its toll? Was she regretting the transformation of his exile into this ludicrous pretence? But she was in this case, quite right. For what else could they have said?

"Promotion? Well done," the man said raising his eyebrows. "Well I never." Reaching into his inside pocket, he took out a flask. "Partake?" he said. Without waiting for an answer he lifted the flask to his lips, took a drink and screwed the lid back on. "Time enough for a snooze before we get to KL."

A whistle blew. More doors slammed. The train heaved as if just roused from a deep sleep, chucking steam out across the platform. George watched a couple of porters fold themselves into a squatting position and the men in army uniform standing to attention. The train creaked, then began to move. The figures grew smaller, eventually vanishing from George's view. An ache in his stomach grew in intensity as his body rocked with the momentum of the train. He looked up at the sky. It was streaked with rain clouds; the threat of a storm rumbled in the distance. He dabbed at his face with his handkerchief, turned to look at Dorothy who appeared to be absorbed in her book, at the man sitting opposite him whistling and blowing in his sleep. Would George change into a man such as this if he stayed here long enough? He closed his eyes resting his head on the antimacassar allowing himself to sway with the rhythm of the train. He dreamt of sailing on the ocean and the words of his last letter to Emma spun through his mind.

A jolt woke him. The train had stopped at a tiny station. Outside the window, women held up hands of bananas, mangoes in baskets, water melon cut ready for eating and plates of orange and red balls of rice. Boys standing on crates waved a bottle of tonic water in each hand. A couple of dogs lay sprawled out in a patch of shade. Chickens scratched in between the flagstones, their soft clucking noises just audible above the hiss of the train. Standing in the shadow, just in view of the train, a young soldier looked on.

"You buy, sahib," the women called out to him. "I give you good price." They smiled their big smiles, showing their missing teeth. Their heads were draped in scarves and green, blue, red clothing hung from their tiny forms. The women reached up and offered their wares.

"Would you like anything, darling?" George asked.

In the presence of someone else she played the charming wife and George could not help admire her acting abilities. "Doesn't this heat make one thirsty?" she said in a voice that did not belong to the Dorothy George knew. She settled for a tonic water, he the same, although he would have liked a banana, or a slice of melon. But if the juice had dribbled, he would have looked the fool. The man with the cane took another swig from his flask.

"Be plenty more of those. The drivers stop even where they shouldn't to give the vendors a chance of selling."

"How very thoughtful of them. And they are not reprimanded?"

"Things are different here," he said and resumed sleeping.

A whistle blew and the train moved off. George stared out of the window. Barefooted children lined the platform edge, waving and grinning as the train crawled past. And George thought about Susan, her polished shoes, the way she sucked the end of her plait when she played Scrabble. Closing his eyes, he allowed his dreams to be carried by the momentum of the train, to recreate the rooms of his house in Golders Green, to remember Moorcroft's panelled office with the portrait of his father; he dreamt he was sailing high on the ocean, that it was to the rock of the boat that he swayed. And always Emma was there.

The train stopped again and again. Each time he looked out of the window at the women in the scorching sun, smiling offering snacks and fruit, at children in rags with their bottles of tonic water, and the endless goats and chickens chewing the straggly vegetation, at the soldiers loitering in the shadows looking on. Despite the thunder and flashes of lightning, there was no rain and the air remained heavy, full of moisture.

Hours later, the train arrived in Kuala Lumpa. 'I'll be off then." The man tapped his cane on the floor. "Good luck with your promotion."

And it appeared to George that everyone was disembarking, that he and Dorothy had been deserted, left alone in this train. The ache in his stomach returned.

"Soon be there."

"Yes," she said. "I know." She closed her book, straightened her dress, crossed one leg over the other.

The train started off again taking them out of the city, gathering speed as it travelled north to Ipoh. In the distance, a snake of ocean light sneaked in between the trees and settlements, winking in the late afternoon light. George looked on as the sun began to set, as red streaks shot across the sky turning the sky to purple. Then it was dark. He heard Dorothy kick off her shoes. He pulled the blind down and slept.

Someone was tapping his shoulder and for a minute or two, George thought he was still on the boat, that the jolt he had felt was the vessel hitting the quayside.

"We arrive at Ipoh, sahib."

George looked up at the ticket inspector, at the peaked hat resting on oiled hair. "Aha," he said. "So we're here at last." Allowing

Dorothy to disembark first, he glanced round the station, as if seeking clues, as to the workings of this town, at the domed structure that rose above him, at the tiny birds pecking at crumbs, at sweepers and cleaners, backs bent as they worked. And he marvelled how much it resembled a railway station at home. Apart from the men in army uniform positioned at the barriers. He walked, his hand cupping Dorothy's elbow, out onto the concourse. He attempted a stride, to look purposeful, as if arriving in Ipoh was a customary event, but a dread overshadowed him, like an approaching sickness that he was powerless to prevent.

"Shouldn't be long," he said. He searched amongst the other male expatriates for the man he had been told would meet them. He rubbed his eyes and watched the minute hand of the station clock. It was fifteen minutes now.

"What if he doesn't come? He might have forgotten…"

"The firm have arranged it darling. Maybe he got held up." It was then that he saw a man with a moustache hurrying towards them, holding his hand up as if in a salute. Stopping a short distance away, he looked at some papers, then walked in their direction.

"Mr and Mrs Johnson?" he said as he approached. "Henry Golding." He extended his hand. "There's been a spot of trouble. That's why I'm late. So sorry"

"Trouble?"

Henry beckoned to a porter. "I'll explain in the car. Good trip?"

"Do you mean trouble with the firm?"

Henry ran his fingers through his hair and smiled at Dorothy. "Not the firm. No. We must get on. Bit late."

At the exit to the station, two small boys were kicking a coconut shell around. Dorothy was looking at them, frowning. George knew that she was thinking of Susan, wondering if she had found new friends in the red brick school that was now her home.

"What do you think has happened?" she asked in a low voice. "This trouble, he's talking about?'

For a moment, George felt warmed. She was confiding in him, seeking his reassurance. Perhaps she did not hate him. "I'll find out," he said.

A warm night-time breeze cooled the air a fraction and George saw rising to the sky a palm directly opposite the station entrance, silhouetted against a moonlit sky. A lawn stretched out beneath it, the grass visible in patches of pale light. The chatter of vendors approached them and George smelt spices, fried chicken. He remembered the Christmas turkey of a few weeks ago. His mind slipped to Emma and their last meeting…

"Here we are," Henry was saying. He opened a car door. "Would you like to go in the front, Dorothy?"

It was agreed that he should sit in the front so that the two men could become acquainted. Once inside with the doors closed, any freshness from the night air vanished immediately. Henry glanced over his shoulder at Dorothy, pushed back his hair and started the engine.

"Best not to open the windows," he said. "The mosquitoes are very bad this time of day."

"My wife is very worried about what you said before."

"Yes. Quite understandably. Not the best situation." He offered George a cigarette. "It happened this afternoon. Not that long ago, actually. The Palfreys were a well established family. Been here longer than us..."

"*Were?*" Dorothy said. She was leaning forward. "They *were* a family?"

"Still are. Sorry. My mistake. But I understand... no never mind about that." He swerved to avoid a group of women crossing the road. They walked in a leisurely fashion, the colours on their sarongs lit up in the headlights. "Thing is, they were attacked. It seems by their own servants. Apparently they've all fled at any rate. The army are searching for them of course. Road blocks. All that kind of thing... they weren't actually hurt, the Palfreys, I mean. Badly frightened. I understand Mrs Palfrey... well you don't need to know everything that happened."

George wondered whether Henry was gaining some kind of satisfaction in holding back on details. Was it possible he was exaggerating for effect? A street market caught his eye, the stalls lit up with red lanterns; the flames under the cooking pots making the vendor's faces look macabre.

"This is the Old Town," Henry said. "We live across the bridge."

"Where are the family now?" So close to him now, Dorothy's hair was brushing George's cheek.

He saw they were driving over a bridge. Beneath it a train was crawling along, belching out steam. Perhaps it was the train on which they had just arrived.

"Safe enough now. But, I heard they're already making plans." Again, that hand through his hair. "Rare for these events to happen. But bad luck on your first day."

"Yes. Indeed," George said. "Perhaps it would have been better if you hadn't told us."

"No point in that, old chap. You'd have found out sooner or later anyway."

Aware that his right eye was starting to twitch, George put his hand to his cheek while he gazed at the wide road they were driving along. Peeping above the tall gates he could just make out mansions built in the style of Grecian villas. The street was deserted. A strange silence hung like an impenetrable mist. A dog fled across the road. Overhead a night bird cackled. They drove for ten minutes longer. Here the road was narrower, the houses less grand, not enclosed by walls as the mansions of the previous enclave were. But still quietness pervaded.

"Your house is just up here," Henry said as he slowed down. "I'll just see you in, then I must be off."

Climbing out of the car, George looked up at the house, at the flight of steps that led up to the front door, back at Dorothy's face, ghostly pale in the moonlight.

Chapter 8

George looked closely at his reflection, pulled his forehead flat, stretching out the creases with his fingers. A cock crowed in the distance. He moved to the window, looked down at their garden. Apart from the lack of apple trees, it could be England. Even the lawn was kept a vibrant green, a constant with all the colours in Malaya. He resumed soaping his face, and as he shaved slowly, thoughtfully, manoeuvring his razor over his chin, his face took on different expressions. Two hollows had appeared beneath his cheekbones where there was flesh before. He wondered whether Emma would prefer this new lean look. The time and distance between them had done nothing to stop his yearning. It was her figure lying naked, head supported by her hand that continually hovered in his thoughts.

A beetle crawled onto the soap; it crouched, nibbling the block. It was huge with long mandibles that waved around as it feasted. Picking up the soap between finger and thumb, George lifted the blind with his other hand and tipped the insect out. Best to rid the bathroom of all tropical creatures before Dorothy rose to have her bath. He hoped that today she would be less nervous, that her imagination would be reduced in its activity. But she seemed to be in a constant state of fear, believing there were gangs of Communists waiting to attack her the minute she stepped out of the door. And it was difficult trying to calm her down, when she knew that is what had happened to the Palfreys. While he dried his hands, he wondered how the Palfreys must have felt at discovering a servant, a trusted member of the household had betrayed them. But they were in a different position. Working for the British administration carried these dangers, as he tried to convince Dorothy. To no effect it seemed.

The few times she had ventured out, her head was wrapped in a scarf, not dissimilar to a native woman. If her terror was not so alarming he would have laughed; she looked like an insurgent herself and her insistence that it was the heat of the sun she was escaping, her denial of her own trembling fear, made the entire act more farcical.

It was true, however, that the climate did not suit her. And even he had not been prepared for the power of the equatorial sun. The humidity was relentless and, as the hottest months drew nearer, he felt he would implode if the temperature rose anymore. Then there were Dorothy's headaches, another popular topic of conversation and another reason for her to turn from him. Not that he blamed her; it was not her fault. Nevertheless, he had tried to entice her, to flatter her as if he were courting her again, repeatedly telling her how lovely she looked, encouraging her to go out, to mix with the other expatriate wives, allow herself to relax, have a good time. To no avail, although she declined his advances in a fashion that bordered on politeness, as if she were refusing a second helping of ice cream, he felt like an outcast and sometimes he despaired at her enforced isolation; not to mention the physical frustration which made him almost weep for Emma's touch. The ultimate rejection was last night when Dorothy had finally locked her bedroom door. In his dreams, he had forced the lock, thrown off the thin sheet to see Emma lying in her usual position, the other arm resting on her hip. The solitary pleasure, after he had woken damp, agitated, was unsatisfactory, a worthless resolution.

As he knocked on Dorothy's door now, he called her name out four times. There was no answer at first and he felt bile rise in his throat, and shock waves passed through his gut. Had he misinterpreted the signs? Maybe she was really ill; sickening for some dreadful tropical disease. Then he heard her voice telling him to come in.

The room smelt of sleep and face cream. A stream of sunlight shone onto the dressing table, making one of her perfume bottles glint and wink in the powerful beam.

"Darling," he said. "Why don't you join me today?" He neared the bed, saw her chest rise and fall. He longed to touch her, for her to respond to his needs, but he dare not move his hand from where it remained rigid at his side.

"I've got to an exciting bit in my book. Nearly finished it now. It's too hot to go out today, anyway," she said. "You know how the bright sunlight gives me a headache."

"Yes," he said. "I wish I could do something about that for you." He pulled the curtain tight, closed where the chink of light shone through a gap. Her suffering made his guilt worse. "But I wish you would." He stared at her flattened form under the sheet, at the nightdress strap, loose on her shoulder.

Closing her eyes, she put her hand to her head. "I'll come with you next Saturday," she said.

It was a stifling day; he had to agree with her there, one of the worst yet. Putting one foot in front of the other was an effort. It was constant, no relief; whichever room he stepped into. Even the flies had stopped hovering, their buzz silenced as they dozed, lulled into a trance. The door to the kitchen was open and he could hear the loud chatter of the servants as he made his way down the steps of the house. He came out onto the veranda.

"You back for lunch, sahib?" Liam asked.

George paused on the bottom step and watched a tiny lizard scurry under the house. This one was green with pink markings. He liked seeing these pretty reptiles with their dainty claws. Sharing his territory without invitation, catching mosquitoes with their tiny tongues.

69

"A late lunch for me," he told Liam.

He got into his car, and sat for a while flapping the door to and fro until the sweat on his face had dried. As he started the engine and set the wipers going, he watched the blades smear minute insects across his windscreen. Death must have come quickly to them, destroyed as they would have been, by the impact of the glass windscreen. The tyres crunched against the stony path and he drove out onto the street. It was unusually quiet and still, perhaps there would be a storm later with some rain. A welcome relief; he longed to feel drops of cool water on his face.

On an impulse he took a longer route, through the area where the more established expatriates lived. The avenues were grander, the houses wider, with neo-classical pillars supporting the verandas. Gardeners raked lawns, pruning the fruit trees; an English suburb transformed into the tropics. Seeing Henry and Matilda's house first, he took a peek through the wrought iron gates at the neat lawn beyond as he slowly drove past.

He pulled up outside where the Palfreys used to live, but the overgrown foliage obliterated his view of the house. No need to trim it now the occupants had flown. A bird cackled in a tree and a cat sped down the street. There was no one else around. He got out of his car and walked to the start of the driveway, then craned his neck so that he could see the house. He gazed at the veranda, at the urns and swing seats and spotted a large padlock hanging against the door. The house was obviously vacant, closed to the outside world. He felt strangely satisfied. So there was a way out. But to go through this, the violence, the fright. Best to keep a low profile where politics were concerned.

He took one step nearer, treading on weeds and fungi that had sprouted between the paving stones. To the side of the house a solitary swing hung in the garden, the chain already starting to rust.

A picture of Susan flashed through his mind. Putting his hand to his head, he felt the weight of guilt again. He missed Susan's call down the stairs, the funny faces she used to pull, the lightness she brought into the house. Deciding not to loiter, he returned to his car.

He arrived at the Club. As he entered the lounge, he heard the rumble of male laughter. The haze of tobacco smoke and the collective sound of English vowels made him acutely aware of what he had left behind. He took out his handkerchief and blew his nose, then straightened his shoulders and searched the room for a familiar face.

Henry was at the bar stroking his moustache. He looked up from his paper and beckoned George over. "How's your wife?"

"She's fine. Reading in the shade of the veranda." Why did he feel he had to lie about Dorothy? But there was shame, embarrassment at having a wife who refused to socialise.

While Henry ordered drinks, George saw Sarah come in through the Club door and join her husband at a table. Catching his eye she lifted her hand, held his gaze as she removed her jacket. He turned and leaned over towards Henry. "Let's sit over there old chap, under the fan with Dick and Sarah."

Henry nodded, tucked his newspaper under his arm and led the way to the table. Sarah crossed her legs, allowing her skirt to ride up a little. Also crossing his legs, George sat back so he had a good view of her legs. Their shape was perfect, very pleasing to the eye; curved and muscular with delicate ankles. She was rotating one round and round just in time to the ceiling fan. Shifting his eyes across to Dick, he found himself wondering at the strangeness of her choice of spouse. Beneath his thin shirt, Dick's stomach could be seen straining against the white fabric.

"This time next year, maybe? Independence. So many changes," Henry was saying.

"Independence is a huge mistake," said Dick. "The Communists will undo everything; bring the country to its knees."

George thought of the Palfrey's house, the air of desolation or was it defeat? He tried to picture the attack again, but it was too ghastly to imagine, too close to his own fears.

"This chap Tunku Abdul seems to be on the right track, doesn't he?" Sarah said. "And he's got us, the British on his side."

"Can't see how they'll manage it, though," Dick said. "When we go, it'll be up to them. They'll be on their own."

"They seem more interested in sitting around contemplating than getting down to real work," said George.

"But Tunku Abdul was educated in England, wasn't he?" Sarah said. "That must be good." She cupped her face in one hand. "You have to give them an opportunity to try and self-govern."

Dick looked across the table at her, then at George. "This country's in a strategic position. Mao's bully boys still have their eye on it, and it'll take more than a few handshakes and a couple of signed charters to keep them out."

George cleared his throat. "By the way. Have you got any news of the Palfreys? What are they going to do?"

"Run scared, didn't they?" Dick said. Something was flicked from his trouser leg. "No stamina. Though in a way I quite understand them going. Terrible business. But it's not what I would have done. Best to stick it out. Show the blighters what you're made of."

"They've got a posting to Australia, I believe. In a couple of months time. That's what Jean told me anyhow," said Sarah. "But they're not the only ones to be leaving, are they? And he would have been killed, wouldn't he, if that officer hadn't called round. Jean too." She swilled her drink while staring at it.

"They were offered another posting in Kuala Lumpur, so I heard," Henry said, wiping the whisky from his moustache. "Anyway, it was their choice. It'll all be over soon, all this fighting; the ambushes are fewer these days. Army's doing a grand job at ridding the country of the troublemakers. Cutting off their food supply is an excellent move."

George nodded and picked up his drink, watching the ice as he turned the glass round in his hand.

"Chaps been arrested now, haven't they?" said Henry. "The ones who attacked the Palfreys. Be in detention by now." Picking up his paper he straightened it noisily, punching it with his hand.

Sarah looked quickly at George. "I've got their keys. Jean asked me to look in on their house now and again. They still have furniture there."

Had she seen him there this morning? Maybe she'd been watching him watching the house. Was the padlock fastened? He could not remember now. "Aren't you frightened?" he asked.

"She's not frightened of anything," Dick said. "Made of stronger stuff than that." He put his hand on her arm. "But you never go there alone do you, my dear?" A pat on her knee, as if she were his favourite dog. "Best to be on the safe side."

"Indeed. One never knows, though of course it is unlikely other sympathisers would return to an empty house. They've done what they set out to do. No need to return," Henry said.

"No, I never go alone." Slowly, Sarah uncrossed her legs, patted her lips with a tissue.

He thought of her inspecting the rooms of the Palfreys' house, coming across the escaped terrorist. Another picture came into his mind of her bound to a chair with George untying her slowly, deliberately, her sultry breath on his face and neck, the warm touch of her finger tips opening his shirt.

Dick was reading the financial sector of Henry's paper. It provided an opportunity for George to scrutinize his face, to take a look at his sagging jowls, at the small wart-like protrusion at the end of his nose.

"They're not interested in us anyway," Henry said. "The CT, I mean. We're not involved really, are we? Not like Harry Palfrey. He was an obvious target for the Communists."

"Rather the Palfreys than us," George said and laughed. "They must have misplayed their cards somewhere along the line."

They all looked at him.

"Not very sporting of you, old chap," said Dick. "Terrible thing to have happened. We have to stick together, us Brits."

George suddenly felt uncomfortable in Dick's presence. It was time to leave.

"Must get back to Dorothy," he said.

"Of course," said Henry. "We'll have that game of tennis sometime, shall we?"

Dick held his hand up. "Be seeing you."

George got up and walked to the door, aware that Sarah was behind him. What was she doing? What was she thinking of?

"I need someone to come with me next Saturday," she said when they were outside the bar.

"Sorry?"

"To the Palfreys. I've agreed to oversee the men who'll move their furniture out."

"Can't Dick go with you?"

"No, he'll be in Kuala Lumpur for the next few Saturdays." She stood with her back pressed against the wall. "It'll only take half an hour. Everything's all packed and ready."

"Why me?"

When he saw her colour, he wished he had not asked. The attraction was obviously mutual. But if he went, it would be on the basis of helping out. Nothing more.

"I am very busy. So much to do in the office, then there's Dorothy, my wife, she's been ill, you see..."

"Oh, I'm sorry. It doesn't matter. I'll ask Henry."

He hesitated. "What time?"

She told him. Without thinking it out, he agreed and stood in the passageway after she had gone, leaving her perfume lingering in the air.

He mused over his rash agreement to help. Dorothy would not approve. What would he say to her? Another lie? He should have refused, not given in to his curiosity. But he could cancel, make an excuse, say it was impossible, that Dorothy needed him to be at home. Putting these thoughts to one side, he walked down the Club steps.

The pounding heat hit him as soon as he walked out of the building. Fortunately, he had remembered to park the car under the shade of a palm tree. There were two Malays round the other side of the tree also in the shade, just squatting on the ground. They could sit like that for hours without sign of discomfort or cramp. His haunches ached just to look at them. They watched him, and he returned their stare for a minute, but could not tell what lay behind their eyes.

He should return home. Dorothy would be expecting him soon; he thought of her fretting, fiddling with the amber beads she had bought for herself in Colombo. But for now, he wanted to snatch a bit of time alone, even though he spent most of his time in solitude at home, he needed to be away from Dorothy's pressing anxiety, her unspoken misery. He pushed the window open and started the engine.

In five minutes he was outside his office block. There were, as he expected, a couple of employees inside and he greeted one as he passed his room. The fans were off; the absence of the familiar whirring left a silence that was death-like. And he could not stay there long without puddles of sweat forming at his feet; there was already an odour of male sweat, permeating the fabric of the building, drifting through the empty rooms. He went straight up the stairs to his office. The letter was where he had put it in the bottom drawer to his desk. No prying eyes here. He took it out from its envelope and reread it:

The blossom is out in the parks. But it means nothing when you are not here to see it with me.

Footsteps halted at his door. Not now, he thought.

I think of you all the time, I'll never forget you. The months that pass do not make it any easier to bear.

There was a knock, and his door opened.

"How's things?"

"Fine. Absolutely fine."

76

"Unusual to see you here on a Saturday."

"No peace for the wicked." George said, laughing.

"Indeed not. Just thought I'd say hello."

"Nice of you."

"Bye then. As you say, no peace."

George's door was closed quietly.

I had thought of you returning, of us running away together as you suggested once, but the cold reality of you not returning for years is slowly dawning.

This last line, he read several times, as he had done yesterday, as he knew he would repeatedly until the next letter arrived. And again he posed the same questions to himself: What was Emma saying? Was she hinting that she was giving up on him? Holding the letter to his face, he tried to smell her perfume he so sorely missed; exotic, musky, sweet and warm. But the journey had stolen it; all that remained was a faint odour of engine oil and the tropical dampness that invaded everything. Stumbling against the chair behind him, he conjured up her face, heard her laughter, her gentle voice.

He could not bear to think of being out here for years. He would write and explain that to Emma, tell her he would turn over every stone to ensure his speedy return, that as long as they remained in communication, then their love would survive. Standing, he put the letter back in the drawer and straightened the papers on his desk.

He decided to take a scenic route home. Apart from anything else, it would delay having to return back home. Besides, he had really seen so little of the country surrounding Ipoh. He had a desire to see waterfalls cascading, to see the sun shine through the canopy, to find some beauty in what little remained of the day. How far would he have to travel to see vistas such as those he had seen in the National Geographic magazines?

It did not take him that long to reach the outskirts and, after half an hour driving, the road narrowed and there were no other cars. He came to a fork in the road, dithered for a minute or two, then decided to follow the road in the direction of Butterworth. The name gave him a comfortable feeling, and made him think of cows grazing in meadows, of rotund women with aprons tied round their waists.

He drove for half an hour, leaving the settlements behind; nothing on the road except a few absent-minded goats wandering into the path of his car. He turned up a road. Perhaps this would lead him to those views. But there was no vista of jungle-clad mountains. He could not see anything through the high trees. Ferns, with fronds sprouting like enormous wings blocked any view he might have had between the trees. The whine of insects got louder; the smell of tropical vegetation became more intense. There was no breeze coming in through the open window and he was being feasted on by dozens of mosquitoes. Ahead of him, the road narrowed to a rough track and he decided to turn round; there really was not any point in going further. He had started to turn the wheel when he heard a gun go off. He jammed on the breaks and listened, feeling suddenly very alone. Another shot. Sweat trickled into his eye. Putting the car into gear, he reversed too fast and hit a boulder. There were two more shots followed by rapid gunfire. He could barely grip the steering wheel, his hands were as slippery as butter. Out of the corner of his eye he saw some foliage move apart. Slamming his foot on the accelerator, he bounced over potholes back onto the tarmac road. Perspiration was seeping from every pore. His heart was pounding. He concentrated on the road ahead. The tyres squealed at every bend.

He drew up outside his house. Back to normality, a return to the everyday. As he opened the front door, the smell of roast pork and custard drifted out from the hallway. In the hall mirror, his face stared back at him, eyes wild, cheeks blotchy, red. He straightened his tie, smoothed back his hair with a shaking hand.

"I'm back," he called out to Dorothy.

He noticed Liam in the shadow of the kitchen doorway. How long had he been standing there?

"She is in dining room, sahib." Liam indicated with a jabbing hand.

Dorothy was sitting in her usual place. She was wearing a green and red flowery dress with bows on the shoulders straps

"Did you eat at the Club?" she asked.

"No, I'll join you." It would seem that she had noticed nothing. With her fork, she cut a slice of mashed potato.

"Dorothy." He waited for her attention, blinked, looked across the room through the window, back to her. Desperately, he wanted to tell her, to share his fear, to hear comforting words. But what would be the use of recounting the incident? He would have to deal with her hysteria, her terror.

Liam placed a plate of roast pork in front of him. He sat down, picked up his knife and fork and began to eat.

Chapter 9

The rain had started during the previous evening. It was the noise of the torrent, like fists beating on the roof, which had kept George awake most of the night. And now, as he sipped his morning coffee, he looked out at the descending water as it fell into an expanding puddle at the edge of the veranda. The rain soaked the ground, flower heads drooped, leaves bowed under the weight. But it was different from the rain of England: muggier, clammier, indistinct from the moisture of humidity. But it was pleasant to be in a temperature that did not consume, draining the energy, like sap dripping from a tree. Quite easy to spend the remainder of the morning watching the mud form, listening to the splatters on the roof. But it was ten o'clock, nearly time to go and besides, the rain would clear soon. Clouds were already parting to show blue patches, and the plops of water from the cheese plant to the right of him were subsiding. Then there was bird song from the trees at the bottom of the garden. He searched the greenery for the source of the sound. A couple of bright streaks flew out of the jacaranda.

Dorothy's book was splayed open, the spine stretched apart; she was playing solitaire, placing each card in its place with a meticulous snap. George watched, transfixed, while she completed the game, then she glanced up at the sky and returned to her book. He remembered a time when he could almost read her thoughts, when conversation was not always necessary. Her hand moved swiftly, flipping the page over; it was curious how her reading taste had changed so dramatically.

"How are you spending your day?" he asked Dorothy as he studied a crossword clue. *Weigh down, six letters.*

"I've got a lot to do." She looked out towards the garden. "I'll come with you to the Club next Saturday."

She said this every Saturday, it was a well-practised performance, an unspoken agreement; and for once he was thankful she had not changed her mind. It would be typical if she had decided to go with him that day.

He slipped his hand under his shirt, scratched his stomach, then started to fill in the space that had been bothering him. *Anchor* he wrote.

"I'll be back for afternoon tea," he said and bent to kiss her on the cheek. She lifted her face a fraction then resumed dealing her pack of cards again.

Squinting at the sky, he got into his car and steered through a muddy puddle outside the house. Uncertainties about the day ahead troubled him. He had expected this arrangement to be cancelled again, had thought the hurried note handed to him the week before would be the last he would hear of it. But now the second arrangement had been made. A refusal at this late stage would be rude, unforgivable. But first he wanted to go to the Old Town and buy a present for Dorothy.

Soon he was nearing the Old Town and saw there was some kind of commotion up ahead; clashes of cymbals followed by a male Chinese voice through a loud speaker, angry, though they often appeared such to George. Maybe it was just the way they communicated. No subtlety in their strange tonal sounds, a spitting brusqueness, never soft. There was an explosion in the distance. Gun shot or firecracker? How was he supposed to differentiate? Sweat soaked his shirt; it trickled down his face, blurring his vision. He turned the car round, but his way was hindered. A crowd of rebelling Chinese: women, tiny, bent with children bundled on backs, squatters in dirty singlets and men dressed for the town, all heading in the direction he had just come from. Keeping his eyes to the road, refusing to meet those who stared in at him through his window, he steered, his jaw locked, inducing pain. Open palms were banging on the boot, the bonnet. Faces glared in at him. Heart racing, he kept his hand on the horn. He remembered the back doors were open; someone could climb in, bash him over the head. A policeman came towards him and the crowd started to retreat.

"You go on," he said, after George had slowed down, opened the window a fraction. The policeman was a youth, could not have been more than eighteen. The beret gave his Polynesian features a childish, almost cheeky look.

George nodded, kept his foot steady on the accelerator, until eventually only a dog, with protruding ribs, was barking at him. Dorothy's present would have to wait for another day.

Ten minutes later he arrived at the calmness of the wealthier expatriate enclave. The Palfreys' house looked much the same as it had done three weeks before; though this time he strode up to the steps and stared out in the direction he had just come. He looked at his watch, then walked around the veranda to the French doors at the back and peered in. He imagined the room as it must have been before. Now the glamour of chaise longues, the brocade settees, the Persian rugs, and the clinking of champagne glasses had been replaced by dust sheets and a family of beetles which had made their home in the corner of the doorway. Strange that he should be invited here in these somewhat unusual circumstances.

Five men walked up the path towards the house. As they neared him, he caught sight of their faces; dark and clean shaven, smaller than the Malays'.

"You'll have to wait. I haven't a key," he said to the tallest man who stood in front of the others.

The man nodded and spoke rapidly to the other men. Sitting on their haunches, they spat into the grasses and chattered, their hands moving with the rhythm of their language. They appeared unperturbed at the long wait, as if they had nothing else planned for the rest of the day, and kept pointing to something towards the horizon. But their strange, earthy smell was somehow an assurance, a comfort to George's jittery nerves. He was becoming impatient; she was half an hour late now.

He looked about him, at the large garden, at the mango trees with their dropped fruit rotting in the earth and at the still neatly-mown lawn. He could see the ha-ha if he looked hard enough; he had spotted it before on that first visit and had been reminded of himself as a boy chasing imaginary friends up to his parents, pretending he was the only one that did not tumble, that he won the race every time. He turned back to the men and saw Sarah coming up the path. She was wearing a blue and green dress, caught in at the waist, and a lighter blue hat with a large brim. As she strode towards him, he saw her white high heeled shoes flashing through the grass. The Indian men watched her in silence, stood, started their chattering again.

"I had an accident." She put her fingers to her brow, rubbed the flesh, let her hand drop. "I thought you might have given up on me."

"Are you all right?" Of course now he felt guilty for cursing her timekeeping and noticed the paleness of her face with traces of tears in her eyes.

"I knocked a child down, a Malay child." Her hand reached her cheek and she bowed her head. "It was terrible, terrible. At first I thought I'd killed him. I was a bit hysterical. But then he got up and ran off."

83

"Christ. Is he injured?" Rapid thoughts of hospitals, doctors, questions ran through his mind; Dorothy finding out where he had been.

"He's fine, but it was a terrible shock. I thought I'd killed him at first," she said again.

"Come and sit down. This can all wait for the time being." He touched her shoulder, lightly; an innocent gesture.

"No, I'm fine." She lit a cigarette. "He couldn't have been injured badly. He disappeared down a track into the jungle fast enough. He couldn't have been seriously hurt, could he?"

"Doesn't sound like it. But it must have been a shock for you both."

Dropping her cigarette to the ground, she crushed it with her foot, took a compact out of her bag. "I don't want to keep them waiting any longer." She looked towards the men. They were quiet, waiting instructions. Or were they trying to catch the drift of their conversation? Maybe they planned to pass it on, discuss it as they sat crossed-legged in their homes that night.

"Let's get this stuff moved, then I'll tell you more of what happened. Can you tell them we're ready now?" she said.

Stepping across to where the group were still standing, now murmuring to each other, he rubbed his palms together. They all looked at him.

"Right then, chaps. Time to start moving that furniture."

They removed and carried the items down the steps, working in solitude, each article to a man. As they lifted the items high to their shoulders and walked, George thought of his father's funeral and the way his coffin had been carried to the graveside.

He caught a whiff of something burning; the men stopped and looked to the horizon. Now he could see what they had been pointing at. A thin trail of smoke rose from the hills beyond, dissolving into the clouds hanging over the forests. Hardly noticeable, but definitely there.

Sarah had her eyes closed and was rubbing her face with her hands. "A rubber plantation. Destroyed. Like so many others. That's all they seem to be interested in. Destruction and killing."

He stared at her, but said nothing. Just, he could distinguish the smell of the burning rubber. An odd, acrid smell that was carried intermittently on the slight breeze. It reminded him of the distant factories he would pass on the train up to Manchester. Poisonous odours that could damage the lungs. His heart was thudding, but it would not be good to show his fear. Besides, the plantation was probably far away.

"They had the right idea, the Palfreys. Get out while you can. That's what Jean said. It's too dangerous to stay," Sarah said. She took a deep breath.

The wind was carrying the smoke cloud in another direction. The grey haze was dissipating further into the clouds. And the men mumbled to each other, their hands cutting through the air in horizontal slashes. Were they mimicking the destruction of the plantation, or worse? He remembered the gun fire echoing across the valleys. He thought of the faces at his car window, yelling, accusing.

The house was empty now, stripped, erased of memories. An old newspaper page covered in dirt, used matches strewn across the floor, a crooked nail protruding from the wall. He locked the padlock and waited for Sarah to check through a mound of paperwork before the men were sent away.

"Let's have a cigarette," Sarah said and beckoned him to follow her to a bench under an orchid tree. "Thank goodness that's done."

George sat beside her, lit her cigarette, watched her inhale, her head thrown back.

"I wonder how long it's been burning. Do you think anyone was hurt?" He took a hurried look towards where the plantation must lie. A couple of miles away, maybe more, difficult to calculate. Although he squinted and searched, now he really could not tell the difference between cloud and smoke. He took a deep drag on his cigarette. The wind picked up, blew some leaves across the lawn.

"Feeling better?" he asked.

"I don't want to stay here. I thought it might have been quite refreshing - sitting here in the calm, but I feel uncomfortable, as if we're being watched."

It was true. Although the house was devoid of occupants, there was an eerie sensation sitting here in a garden, looking around the grounds so peaceful, birds cackling in trees, flowers blooming. He tried to picture what it must have been like knowing what the terrorists could do, familiar with their cruelty, and feeling so helpless, out of control. Then expecting the knife, the bludgeon, a shot in the head, or worse. Any minute, then suddenly saved. So had the fear become part of the house, locked in the fabric, trapped in the rooms? He had heard of such things.

"I could do with a drink. I don't live far. Let's go there," she said.

Her voice was unsteady, wavering. A smudge of dust lay along her cheek bone. Would it appear too intimate to offer her a handkerchief? He glanced down at her legs, took a sidelong look at her neck, her throat. Hard to abandon her here, she was in a bit of a state, obviously needed someone to talk to. And besides, she still had to tell him about the accident. He looked in the direction of the smoke cloud, at the abandoned house, at a loose shutter swinging in the wind. A shudder, uncontrollable, ran through him.

"Thanks," he said. "Sounds good, I have to agree with you. A drink would be most welcome."

They took her car; she said she wanted to show him where the accident had happened. Watching her drive, he found his eyes drawn to her hand as it rested on the gear stick. It was small, like Emma's with long fingers; a ring with a cluster of blue stones lay over her wedding band. He wondered whether they were sapphires from Rhodesia, where Dick and she had lived before.

They were heading back through the Old Town. The crowd had dispersed. Maybe they had gone to rest in the midday sun, too hot to cause trouble, or mingle at close proximity to each other's moist bodies. George stared up at the gold on a temple that winked in the sunlight.

Soon they were driving out of the town. Either side of them long grasses bordered the narrowing road with huge fronds beyond leading to jungle, disappearing into mist. Just as he was about to protest, she pulled up.

"It was here." She pointed. "He ran out into the road. Didn't look. Just appeared in front of me, as if from nowhere. Come on, I'll show you." She got out of the car. "He ran back through there."

There was no one else around. A scan of the road where they had come from and the direction the car was parked. Nothing. So quiet.

"It may not be safe," he said.

But she was already heading along the road. He followed her to where she was standing, looked about him, fancied he saw some

87

palms being spread apart, an opening being made, but it was nothing, a breeze, a tiny animal perhaps.

Look," he said. "I'm not sure this is a terribly good idea." He touched her lightly on the top of her arm. It was warm and damp. "Some of these villagers may be sympathisers."

"Not this close to Ipoh." She turned and pointed. "They live through there,"

"How far?" It looked dense through the trees. Dark, forbidden, noiseless.

But she did not reply, was balancing on a rock looking down the track.

"What about that drink?" he said.

"I want to go and check he's not been hurt too badly. I know he must have been hurt, but he ran off like a scared animal. Down there." She pointed down a track. "I followed him for a bit…"

"A bit dangerous, don't mind me saying."

"It was these shoes." She looked at them. "Not ideal for that kind of terrain."

A noise started him; turning quickly he searched behind. Something rustled in the undergrowth; it retreated and left them alone.

"And, I have to admit I thought it might be unwise, on my own."

So she wasn't entirely foolhardy.

"Would you come with me, to check he's not injured too badly?"

She was putting him on the spot again. How could he admit to her he was not the brave kind?

"It's been a bit of a day," he said. "I'd rather have that drink right now." There was always the chance she would forget about this escapade, with a little persuasion. "And you'll need to change your shoes."

Taking his hand, she allowed him to help her step down onto the path. "We'll go back to my house then," she said. "We'll have a drink. I'll change, then we'll feel a little refreshed. Won't we?" She smiled as she opened the passenger door for him.

His stomach was grumbling. He hoped Sarah would offer him some lunch. They had been driving for at least twenty minutes when she told him her house was just in the next road. He was surprised at the size of her house, even larger than the Palfrey's. It looked a bit like the Club with its mock timbered exterior and, if it was not for the palms towering above the roof, they could have arrived at a residence in a Surrey suburb. There was even a tall hedge to the side. He wondered whether it was privet, or whether such hedging, accustomed to the climate of England, would shrivel and die out there.

A woman came to the door and greeted Sarah. She was smaller than Liam, and her face was more lined, with the yellow tinge the Chinese seemed to acquire with age. She gave a small bow, something Liam never did, not that he wanted total servility. He followed Sarah into the sitting room.

She pointed to a rattan sofa. "Have a seat. Chuen will bring you a drink, while I change."

"Righto," he said but he did not sit down.

It was he noticed, much cooler than his house, with an ambience of leisure, of comfort. It was furnished with rattan chairs and loungers, a nest of side tables and the ubiquitous Persian rug on the wooden floor on which a mahogany gate-leg table stood. He scratched his stomach and went over to study a picture on the wall.

His hunger pangs grew and he heard his stomach rumble again. The picture was an oil of a lake and mountain, and, from the purple heather, the sheep on the slopes and the ash-coloured cloud in the distance, he guessed somewhere in the Lake District. George remembered his honeymoon, walks along the fells, trips across Lake Windermere. He remained in front of the painting for some time, then moved over to the window. It was divided up into Georgian panes through which he could see a large garden, and another smaller house at the far end. On the wall to the right of the window was a photograph. It was of Sarah, a younger Sarah with a laughing boy in shorts on her knee. Footsteps descended the stairs. They were Sarah's, now dressed in a greyish skirt which dropped to below her knees, and simple white blouse. She had changed her shoes too.

"That's Peter, my son," she said in a flat voice. "He's a lively little boy."

"I see the resemblance. The same colouring."

"Yes," she said briskly and turned away from the picture. "I've asked Chuen to make a light lunch," she said. "You must be hungry, I know I'm famished." She sat on a chair to the left of the Lake District picture.

"Will Dick mind me being here, having lunch with you and all that?" he asked.

"I think he'd consider me very impolite if I hadn't offered you my hospitality in return for your help this morning." She crossed her legs, wound one ankle around the other. He raised his eyebrows, sat down in a chair opposite her.

"Well, it's very kind of you, but I must be getting back. After lunch, you know."

"That's a shame." She was rotating her ankle again. "I am so disappointed. I really must go and check he's not harmed too badly." She paused. "It won't take long. I promise."

He walked to the window. Her insistence was relentless; her mood not unlike Emma's when she was determined to get what she wanted. A rush of memory: Emma leading him by the hand into the summerhouse at St John's Wood. Swallowing hard, he tried to dispel the image of Emma's laughing face as she pulled him through the door. He watched a gardener rake leaves off the lawn, his arms sinewy, long. The man looked towards George, leaned on his rake a minute, then went back to his work.

"I can't today, I'm afraid," he said. "I really must get back soon."

"I'll have to go on my own. I must find out if the boy needs anything."

The clinking of crockery and cutlery made him turn from the window. An aroma of chicken stew, carrots and potatoes, flooded into the room.

"I think lunch is ready," Sarah said and started to walk to the door.

"All right," he said. "I'll come with you to find your injured boy, but it'll have to be a quick visit. I must get back."

Turning, she kissed him on the cheek; a feathery touch and fragrance of spring flowers. "I'll owe you," she said. "Thank you, I am a bit nervous about going on my own."

The gardener pushing the wheelbarrow across the lawn, glanced up at them both.

Chapter 10

The journey back to the palm forest seemed to take less time than before lunch. George followed the route closely, taking more notice of where they were going. A shallow river ran alongside the road; on the other side, a palm grove. Through the trunks he could see curved roofing. Gold flashed in the sun.

"It's a Chinese temple," Sarah said. "Hewn out of rocks."

Sarah's knowledge about her surroundings, her interest in politics, her lack of a timid attitude was refreshing, like an iced cocktail on a hot afternoon. He looked up at the mountains beyond, at the mist hanging over the highest peak. From here the jungle looked beguiling, mysterious. He remembered the gun shots he had heard the other day.

"Tell me?" he said. "Is it true that all the Palfreys' servants were in it together? Ganged up on them, I heard."

"The amah had a brother who was a sympathiser." The car slowed down. Sarah was searching the forest that lined the road. "None of the others were involved as far as I know." Pulling up, she parked under the shade of a tree. She was looking at his hands, as they tapped out a rhythm on his knee. "Poor Jean. I believe the amah had been with them for years. Ted Palfrey was on a review committee. It was common knowledge that he was against the releasing of detainees. I knew Jean very well. She called the attack a blessing in disguise. Couldn't wait to leave."

George stopped tapping. He wondered whether Jean Palfrey had come here under pressure, forcibly removed from her home, forfeiting the sweetness of the English garden, gentle spring rain.

There was almost complete silence once Sarah turned the engine off. Sweat glistened on her face, dampening her hair. He heard a rustle from a gap in the palms. His mouth dried, heart pumping fast. A bird hopped out from the undergrowth. Closing his eyes briefly, he swept his hand over his head. He was no good at this, should not have agreed to come. How was he going to manage in the palm forest if every movement was going to startle him?

"And you don't think there'll be sympathisers down here?" He pointed in the direction of the path through the forest. Just one final check, then no more on the subject.

"No. They'll be small-holders." A faint smile. "Native Malays living off the land."

Was she patronising him? Hands on hips, she was waiting for him. "Probably better if you go first. Better that they see you before me."

Now to get on with it. He smacked his thighs and climbed out of the car. Dorothy would be fretting. He thought of her sitting on the veranda, her book open, feet resting on a stool. Or had she returned to bed, the heat too much, a headache to contend with? He hoped she was not suffering too much.

The path was slippery in amongst the thick of the palms and the air smelt of decay, of rotting vegetation. The sunlight was almost entirely blocked by the towering trees. A feeling of insignificance struck him, here in the shade of the giant fronds, of primordial growth. It was as if nothing survived, nothing grew other than the palms high above his head. He raised his eyes to the canopy, searched through the trees, heard the creak of wood shifting in the slumbering breeze. Mosquitoes fought for his blood. Leering vines planted suckers on his bare skin, tore at his shirt. Feeling a tickling sensation down his leg, he lifted it. A trickle, bright red, ran down his calf. He thought back to Henry's tales of tropical jungles, the remedies for defeating the creepy crawlies that habituated foreign parts. Lighting a cigarette, he pressed it to the leech, watched it drop to the forest floor.

He turned, waited for Sarah to catch up. "You all right?" he said to her when she arrived at his side. He was aware that his voice had a whiny edge to it. They had been in the forest for more than thirty minutes.

She gave him her handkerchief, neatly folded, laundered white. "Use this," she said. "To wipe the blood off your leg."

It was hard to see the houses at first, being made, he supposed of the material from the forest. All that was visible were the roofs, thatched and pitched. As he climbed over tree roots, holding back branches for Sarah, the smell of wood smoke and fresh dung grew stronger. A large clearing opened up to them and several houses on stilts became visible, each surrounded by dense foliage bearing pods. He peered at the settlement. It looked cool, restful, a peaceful village at repose. Standing still, he observed his surroundings. The land surrounding the houses was cultivated and shaded by banana trees that bordered the plots. A cat was stretched out in the shade, its tail twitching, jerking to and fro. George watched a man in a clay coloured sarong as he turned and raked the soil. He looked up at them, flicking his eyes to George, to Sarah, back to George. The man called up to someone in one of the houses, carried on with his task.

Sarah put her hand on George's shoulder. "I'll be all right on my own now. You wait here."

George watched Sarah as she walked away from him. The man with the rake stopped his work, glanced towards her. She was waiting, her hands loose by her side, feet close together. A cock crowed nearby. Soft breezes swished through the palms, hens squabbled over grain. A young girl feeding the hens saw George. Then she scampered off towards a house, her movements swift, silent. Should he stand further back? Moving sideways, he positioned himself behind a tree, watched Sarah as she made her way to a group of children sitting cross-legged in the shade. One of them stood, adjusting a sling as he gazed at Sarah. She crouched low, gave the boy a parcel. George could hear the murmur of her voice as she talked to the child, low, intimate. But he could not catch what she was saying. He scratched his leg and looked around at the maize seedlings sprouting, neat in a row. The sound of a baby cooing, gurgling, a woman singing a lullaby, drew his attention away.

A girl, older than the one feeding the chickens, came along the path carrying a pot on her head, keeping her eyes fixed on Sarah and the boy as she picked her way through the hens, past a munching goat. Laughter and chatter erupted from a house. George found himself wondering whether these villagers bickered and fought too. But all the doors and windows were open; there was no privacy, no seclusion to argue. George swallowed hard, realising how thirsty he was. Taking his hat off, he wiped his brow with the back of his palm, rewound his watch. It was taking a long time. He wanted to go home, have a whisky and cigarette on his veranda. What were they talking about? He put his hand to his mouth and coughed. The boy ran off towards a house, skirted round it and disappeared. Surely they had been there long enough.

Sarah was coming towards George. She looked relieved. "He's fine," Sarah said. Sweat shone on her cheeks. Time to go.

George felt a fool. Why had he been so frightened? Why would a bunch of local farmers want to harm him?

"Really," he said. "You are very kind." A fly kept landing on his neck. He swatted it again. Again, he missed.

"Are you being sarcastic?" She paused as if deliberating on her next sentence: "Dick is full of sarcasm whenever the subject turns to the native Malays."

This confidence in her marital disagreements felt wrong. "I didn't mean anything bad." He put his hands in his pockets, shook his loose change.

The cicadas had started up, bringing the forest to life. Heading back along the path he started to walk faster. He was already hours late. What would he say to Dorothy? It would be supper time by the time he got back; he would have to produce a good explanation.

He stopped and waited for Sarah. He started to call out to her, to hurry, but she was already walking towards him, swinging her arms, a broad smile on her face. They reached the car, and leaning against it, he fanned his face.

"So you've done your good deed," he said. Strange how these words came out so sarcastically. Quite the opposite to what he felt.

"You don't like them, do you?" she said. "The native Malays."

He took a sharp intake of breath. "No," he said. "You've got me wrong. In a way I envy them. The way they seem to take everything as it is. You never see them fretting, worrying. Like we all do?"

"You think they don't have their own concerns, just because they live a simple life?"

Could he say nothing right? "But they appear content. Not like us. Always wanting more, a better life. Things were much easier before. So many changes, so many demands and expectations, now." He opened the door. "My uncle had a small farm years ago. In Lancashire. With goats and chickens. Sheep. That kind of thing." A glance of a memory flittered in his mind. Of summer holidays in the lambing shed, cuddling newborns, in awe at their helplessness.

Sarah slammed her door to and smoothed down her hair, pulled a bottle out of her bag and dabbed her neck with the cologne. It smelt of freshly-cut irises. As she wiped it round her neck, she peered at him, then returned it to her bag, put the car into gear.

"You all right?" she asked.

"It's just the heat. It's nothing." He watched a lizard dart under a stone. "Well, anyway," he said. "The boy's fine. No harm done."

He pushed the window open and put his face to the breeze, eyes closed, only opening them when he heard the sound of another car coming in the opposite direction. The other driver waved to them and peeped the horn.

"So will you tell Dick how I came to your rescue?" he asked.

"He won't approve. He would have sent a note to the village via a servant." She leaned forward over the wheel. He thinks the Malays are lazy and incompetent. One of our little disagreements."

He did not press her. Best not to interfere. A whiff of her cologne swept past him in a soft breeze.

"He'll be back later on this evening." But he often stays over in Kuala Lumpur." She glanced at George quickly.

"You must miss him," he said.

She pinched her lips together, and drove a little faster. "We've been married a long time. You know how it is. Habits of a lifetime."

The car slowed and she pulled up outside the Palfreys' house. "You've been very helpful." She leaned across and kissed him on the cheek. Irises again, lilac-blue, with bright yellow stamens.

Heat rushed to his face. "See you in the Club then. Give Dick my regards." He got out of the car, waved to her through the open window and waited on the road until he lost all trace of her car. The shadows were getting longer; the air was buzzing. He watched as two Chinese women looked towards the Palfreys' house, pointing, exclaiming, their heads nodding, hands flitting across their faces.

The shade of the tree in which he had parked his car had moved round, exposing the leather seats to the heat of the day. He drove homewards, stopping on the way to watch the setting sun. The orange and red glow in the sky turned to deep purples, streaks of pink. He would remember this, when he returned to England. He would write to Emma, describe it; tell her how much he wished for her to see it too. As he stared at the sky, her picture rose before him. Her hand was resting along the curve of her naked hip, her hair falling across her breasts.

A serein was starting just as he arrived home. The fine rain moistened his face, playing on his skin. He ambled up the path, enjoying the sensation. It was strange that the front door was locked. And it was unusually quiet except for the ominous creaking of wood as it contracted and shifted in the changing temperature.

Unlocking the door, he pushed it open. "Dorothy," he called out. "I'm home."

No reply.

He rushed into the sitting room. She was in the rattan chair close to the window, rocking backwards and forwards, hugging herself tightly. Her lips were pale and frown lines were etched across her forehead. On a table in front of her, a set of cards lay, scattered in disarray, the game abandoned.

"Sorry I'm late. Got delayed." He took her hand in his. She had been crying. "What's wrong? What's happened?"

"I thought you might have got yourself caught up in all the commotion. I heard there was trouble this morning." She straightened the cards, drummed the pack on the table and flicked through them with a wetted finger. "I sent Liam home. It was he who told me about the demonstration."

"Nothing's going to happen to me. To us."

"I couldn't trust Liam anymore. The way he stared at me. Waiting behind doors sometimes, eavesdropping on us. Didn't you ever notice? I keep remembering what happened to that other family. I think he hates us, the Brits. Me. He had to go." She lit a cigarette, hand trembling.

He stroked her hair. "Ted Palfrey worked for the government. The Chinese terrorists are not going to be interested in us." He patted her shoulder. It felt skinny and slight. "You really mustn't get yourself into a state about it all. It's really not that bad. Not for the likes of us." He poured out two large whiskies. "So, you haven't actually sacked Liam have you?" He handed her a glass, waited for her to take a sip.

"That's what I just said." She was staring at her cards, her finger tapping the end of her nose. "You've no idea what it's like for me. Sitting at home waiting for you. Terrified. I hate it here. I wish I'd stayed at home. Never come out here." Her hand knocked the table, then flew to her mouth; the whisky sloshed in its glass, then settled.

Crouching on the floor beside her, he took her hand, felt the tremor until she snatched it away. It was as if he was consoling a needy child. "Don't say things like that. You don't mean it. I'm really sorry I'm late. Sorry you got so frightened. But I'm back now." He should have come home earlier. "Come and sit outside on the veranda. Get some air." But he did not move. "We'll find a replacement for Liam. Maybe you'd prefer a woman. Would that be better?"

"Yes, yes. A woman maid would be better. Why are you so late? You haven't told me."

"I will. Come outside." Walking to the door, he saw his reflection in the glass, his face gaunt, tie loose. He was surprised that Dorothy had not commented on his dishevelled appearance. At least she found consolation in reading. He settled onto the veranda, and picked up one of her books. *Northanger Abbey.* Seemingly abandoned now, her detective stories, the tales of murder and revenge she had preferred before.

Some frogs were applauding in the distance, their call united, in harmony. It would be better if Dorothy did not know about his visit to the village. But another lie was too much, unnecessary. And surely she would understand the concern, the dilemma in which he had found himself. He thought of Sarah swinging her bag, striding through the forest, fearless, full of the eagerness of an explorer. Difficult not to compare that to Dorothy's wild paranoia, her agitation and surety that she would be the next victim of a Communist attack. That was unfair. Dorothy had no experience of living abroad. But she was so unadaptable, unwilling to accommodate herself into new surroundings. A thought nagged at him like a bothersome mosquito bite. Would it have been better if Dorothy had indeed stayed in England without him? Always before, this prospect had seemed abominable; he could not contemplate a life on his own. But time here alone, now he had made friends and was gaining some understanding of the natives, the prospect did not appear so unattractive, as abhorrent as before. All the same, Dorothy would never leave, did not possess the courage. Of that he was certain.

The night air was thick, moonless, the insects droning in their secret lairs. The garden was shortened by the limit of light from the house. He heard the tinkle of liquid filling a glass and Dorothy stepped out onto the veranda.

"So why were you so late? You were in the middle of telling me."

The diffused lamplight made her look younger, reminiscent of the time when he had first met her. Now he felt a brute for wishing her away. He recounted the day, omitting the lunch at Sarah's house, assuming the role of the driver who ran into the Malay boy. As briefly as possible he recalled a solitary walk through the jungle, the villagers, the boy in the bloodied sling.

"I can't believe you did that," she said. "Why are you so stupid? Don't you realise the risk you took?"

"They're Malays," he said. "No danger. Just farmers cultivating the land. You have to believe me."

Resting her back against the railings, she looked at him, drew hard on her cigarette. "You're not going back though, are you? No need for you to return. His family will look after him now. And you didn't hurt him badly, did you?" She wound a coil of hair round her finger, dropped her hand to a string of beads round her neck.

"No, no need for me to return. But you would have done the same, wouldn't you?"

A pause, the smoke drifted out from her open mouth. "Yes," she said at last. "I would have wanted to know he wasn't hurt."

And for a minute he felt comfortable in her company, her approval won. A light switched on in a neighbouring house, patches of garden hidden before, were suddenly illuminated. He realised how the fabrication of the day must have sounded to Dorothy, his story of bravery, his tale of resourcefulness. He wondered how much she believed him. But she showed no sign that she had seen through his version. He sighed, took a sip of whisky and followed her through to the dining room.

Chapter 11

Dorothy's concentration was disturbed by the sound of branches crashing to the ground as Babiya pruned the trees. Resting her book on her lap, she looked up and watched him. His feet barely touched the trunk as he climbed to the top of the jacaranda tree. He leaned across and cut a branch, then cut another, before slipping round out of sight behind the tree trunk. She picked up her book again, conjured up the ballroom, the men in their ruffled shirts, the women in their lace and satin dresses; a pianist's fingers flying across the keyboard. The rhythms stepped out from the words, waltzes ran across the page. She read and read; the match-making, the flirtatious comments blocking out the concerns, her worries of the day.

Already the heat was becoming oppressive; the cooler morning lightness never lasted long. And the shade from the balcony made no difference to the force of the sun. It would be so easy just to sleep all the time, to sit and doze in the shade. But today she wanted to buy a new dress for the dinner that night. Her choice would be flamboyant, fancy, made of Chinese silk, closely woven, more luxurious than the thin silk of the sari George had bought for her. Perhaps he would notice. Would he be proud of her, want to show her off to the other guests? Or would he remain aloof, barely aware of her presence? Lifting her hair from the back of her neck, she gazed at Babiya, at his muscles, taut, his narrow back, as he carried the cut branches to the end of the garden.

She went indoors, sat at her dressing table and brushed her hair. Before she left her bedroom, she took a long look at the dragon which sprawled across her bed. The embroidery was a work of art. An emblem of strength and power so George had told her. Still she recalled the innocent look in his eye. As if this gift would be enough, could eradicate the past. Remembering, the verbal blows, the locking of her bedroom door, she wondered now whether she had taken her anger too far. Had the line been overstepped, was there no returning to base camp? She picked up a photo of Susan. There she was, laughing on the pier again, her hair making wisps in the wind, a hand reaching up to push a strand out of her eyes. The photo was starting to fade. It would be only a few weeks and Susan would be there. Perhaps she could try out the camera, take some replacements. No salty breeze in Malaya to make Susan's eyes water, no chance of her hair blowing haphazardly in a north-easterly wind.

A smell of baking filled the hall, and a high-pitched singing voice was clear above the clanking and crashing of pans. Then silence and Feng was standing in the doorway.

"Mrs Johnson," Feng said. "You ready? We go now before sun get too hot."

It was hard for Dorothy to hide her nervousness. She was aware that her face must have gone pale, that the sweat on her throat and brow was from more than the moisture-laden air. Her stomach rolled. Light-headed, she put her hand to her head. She wanted reassurance from Feng, but it was easier to treat this outing as if it were a weekly occurrence. Or had Liam told Feng of Dorothy's reclusiveness, warned her of her solitary ways? After all, the local Chinese must all know each other. Outsiders too, settlers, congregating in enclaves of gossip, not dissimilar to the gathering of Brits.

Feng was staring at her, waiting for an answer. Face moon-shaped, eyes dark, lidless. A faint smile showed tiny lines in her cheeks. "You never been before Mrs Johnson?" she asked.

Should Dorothy somehow avoid the question? She turned it round in her head, thought about ignoring it. Better not to give too much away. She told Feng that she was right in her assumption, waited for the surprised response. But Feng's features stayed the same.

It took them half an hour to get to the centre of Ipoh. All the way Dorothy kept close to Feng. Over the bridge and through the crowds they went, Feng pushing a clearway for her. The market stalls were scattered without order along the streets. Chinese filled every corner, crowds wound round the stalls, fed the main street from alleyways, towards the horizon as far as Dorothy could see. Dorothy followed Feng into the shade of a canopy. The bright sunshine stayed in her eyes, black spots danced, blinding her momentarily. Beneath a canopy the light was dim, fused with a choking cloud from meat being turned and tossed in flames. From a point somewhere across the street, a man's voice, deep and resounding, was repeating the same sounds, louder each time. Dorothy felt her breath come with difficulty. Searching across the black-haired heads, she looked out for another British face.

"We go there." Feng was pointing through the crowd, towards a domed building, not so far away. "Pretty dresses there. You like."

Dorothy was aware of the gaze from a group of men as she tripped her way round a tethered pig. Sucking on their cigarettes, they watched her, their eyes impassive. Someone gripped her arm. It was Feng driving her straight. Carefully, Dorothy avoided the rotting vegetables floating in slimy puddles. Steam rose from vast pots of noodles; sharp smells, like fish on the turn. Putting her hand to her mouth she saw a haze of heat over the giant woks; watched as browned chicken pieces were ladled onto plates. Chopsticks moved fast, picking, feeding. A woman, face worn and heavy, muttered, tried to push Dorothy out of her path. Angry words, fierce gestures as Feng led Dorothy on.

Eventually, the rancid smells, the coarse tones of the market traders faded, folding into themselves. They reached the domed building and entered an indoor market.

Here at least, was relative calm and the serenity of incense. No displayed animals prepared for slaughter, no smell of entrails boiling to catch the throat.

"Look, pretty boxes, lacquered and painted with hand." Feng led her across the cavernous room and stopped in front of a large table.

Picking up a box, Dorothy admired the strokes of bamboo, the opulence of painted gilt. The stall holder indicated to her to open it and as she chattered to Feng, pushed towards Dorothy first a feather fan, then a bowl, red and black with matching saucer. Three pairs of chopsticks, painted with flowers were lined up on the tablecloth. Other congeries of a similar kind were laid out and shown to Dorothy, the meanings of Chinese characters explained.

"You want buy?" asked Feng. "I get good price."

As Dorothy cooled herself with the fan, and opened a silk lined box, the pain at her temple subsided, the juddering of her pulse slowed. She pictured the artists at their tables, deftly sewing or dipping brushes into ink, their fingers tiny, hands steady. A carved wooden jewellery box caught her eye. Birds flew across the lid, their wings large, graceful. She told Feng what she would like to buy and waited for the two women to settle on a price. The purchases were wrapped in folded newspaper, handed to her. And for a second, Dorothy was reminded of fish and chips in Acton, Friday nights when the shop was closed.

"Silk dresses over there. Look pretty for tonight. Good quality." Feng was smiling, showing her gold-capped tooth as she slipped some notes into her pocket.

Dorothy turned to where Feng was looking. An English woman was sifting through a rail of blouses, her mousey hair looked washed out, faded amongst the bobbing black heads. Dorothy followed Feng to the stall. Silk head scarves wafted in the breeze of the fan, colours mingling, floating.

Dorothy ran her fingers down a silk shift, felt Feng's eyes on her. The green was emerald with embroidered flowers bordering a side slit. No need to wait for long; Feng extracted it from the rail, held it up against Dorothy's cotton dress. The cut was simple, the colour bold; it would flatter her, conceal her thinness. But her reflection in the mottled mirror showed every blemish on her face, all the months of humidity, skin drained of moisture, now showing sallow in the pinkish glow of the indoor market light. But she decided to buy the dress; she would wear it that night, make herself feel more worthy, a delectable version of herself.

The trip back through the market took longer; the shoppers had increased in number, their voices louder, shrieking to be heard.

They arrived home. Dorothy felt dishevelled, dirty.

"Sorry, Mrs Johnson," Feng said. "Street market very busy today. We go Monday to buy more dresses for you? No street market Mondays."

Dorothy swept her hair back from her face while she remained standing in the hall. She rested her head against the wall, felt the coolness of the fan as it dried the perspiration. "I'll have to think about it. Plan my day."

Feng nodded and went into the kitchen. Her mop was out, carbolic soap splashed onto the floor; the smell rising, carried through into the hall. Dorothy took her purchases upstairs and ran a bath. While she waited for the water to fill the tub, she unwrapped her boxes, placing them on her dressing table. Her amber beads hung over the mirror, untouched since the day before. They rattled on the glass as she lifted them and squeezed, caressed the resin; cool on her fingers, calming for her mind. Voices drifted from the garden. She walked over to the balcony, watched Babiya talking to his son. They wandered off together, out through the back gate, their laughter rapid, their saunter trouble free.

***

Dorothy was looking forward to the evening dinner. Better that guests came here. No more venturing out; she would remain at home in future, find pleasure in her books. The world they offered of gentle flirting, of whispered humour along river banks was preferable, less complicated than the bustle of a Chinese market. She imagined the fierce blue sky of Malaya as pale, with tufts of white cloud dissolving in the distance.

In a way, this decision removed all responsibility for being here, took away all effort that was required. To allow George to continue to worry about her gave her satisfaction, a strange pleasure that surprised even her. Sometimes she would catch him looking at her, as he rubbed his left eye, where his twitch had lately returned. But that night she would put on a show. She relaxed herself into the reclining chair, chased the air round her face with her feathered fan and looked out through the branches of the chopped jacaranda tree.

Absorbed in her thoughts, she was unaware of the front door slamming shut. Unprepared, she heard George's footsteps crossing the room behind her; she quickly set her pack of cards straight, picked up her book, flicked a page over.

A brush of his hand on her hair. "Everything all right, dear?"

There was no comment about her new dress. "I went to the market today. With Feng."

He sat down beside her. "Glad to hear it." Swilling the ice round in his glass, he looked in the direction of the cannas bordering the lawn. "I said before, you should go out. Not good for you sitting alone in the house all day. And you prefer Feng to Liam. So it's all working out." A smile, distant, passed across his face.

"I bought a few things."

"Good, good."

"This dress."

A turn of his head. "Charming," he said. "I did notice. It suits you so well." He put his hand on her leg, momentarily. "It's very pretty." Looking at the buttons which fastened to her neck, he took a sudden intake of breath. "Dorothy," he said and scratched the bridge of his nose. He was staring at her now.

She moved her chair away from him, returned his look. "Yes?"

His brow crinkled as he dropped his gaze and he seemed to be examining his foot. Was he waiting for her to probe him into action, to lead him on to whatever he wanted to say? But she refused to dig, to help him out.

"What else did you buy?" Eyes closed, rubbing his nose again.

She told him, knowing that he was not really paying attention. Then they sat in silence. The shadows were starting to lengthen, the cicadas throbbed and rattled in the grass, biting insects came out from their hiding places. George at last said he must go and change, for their dinner guests would be there shortly.

"It should be an enjoyable evening," he said. "Henry and Matilda are looking forward to meeting you again."

Dorothy opened her book, delved into the text. Intricate pictures formed in her mind; girls gossiping, perched on their beds, hair pinned and adorned, ringlets bouncing.

Pausing, she watched the sun drop, the sky change to a deep purple. She remembered Henry, the way he was with his wife. Remembered the ease in which they communicated; the envy she had felt.

The doorbell rang. A last check in the mirror. She practised a warm and confident smile, ready for the guests.

Matilda was wearing a yellow chiffon dress, a tie belt pulling in her bulky waist. Greeting Dorothy like an old friend, she clasped both her hands.

"At long last," she said. "We thought George was hiding you away." A pleasant laugh, eyes focusing on George.

"Not at all," George said. He poured out the drinks, His left eye twitched rapidly. "Dorothy's fine. Taken you a while to adjust to the climate, the different ways, hasn't it? But never mind. All in good time."

"But you've settled in now?" Henry asked. He adjusted Matilda's stole on her shoulder, patting her bare arm. "Matilda was only saying the other day how much she would like to see you again. You're short of a bridge player aren't you, my dear?" Another light touch on his wife's arm. Then he and George walked to the edge of the veranda, their voices dropping as they talked together.

Dorothy told Matilda of her visit to the market. As she smoothed and parted each feather on her fan, she said how much she admired the Chinese handicrafts. "Feng has told me she will buy anything I want on my behalf. She knows my taste more or less. Saves me the trouble of going anymore."

"Then you'll have time to play bridge," Matilda said. She was watching Dorothy, flitting her eyes between the fan and Dorothy's face. "I can't stand those markets. So dirty. And the smells. They eat anything, you know, the Chinese. And I don't much like the gaudiness of their garments. Too much red and brocade. Much prefer to stick to our English clothes. Know what you're getting at least." She played her fingers on her lips, then returned them to her lap, her face reddening slightly. "Oh dear. I didn't mean to offend. Your dress looks delightful. Lucky you. You have the figure for it." A nervous cough, a sip of her whisky, a quick look in the direction of where Henry stood, then back to her study of Dorothy.

"And you must come to the Club on Saturday. Do you play tennis?" asked Matilda.

"I can, but..."

"Good. That's settled. I'll reserve a court. It'll be fun."

"I might not be able to on Saturday," Dorothy said. "Sometimes things crop up. I'll let you know."

The murmured conversation between George and Henry had stopped and George was looking at her. She heard him sigh and rub his left eye. But he said nothing, as Dorothy expected. Not in front of friends. But he would question her later, show his exasperation.

"Matilda plays a good game," said Henry. "Good teacher, too, if you're out of practise." He stroked his moustache and Dorothy saw a look of fondness, of understanding pass between Henry and Matilda. The exchange made her feel remote, alone sitting on the veranda with all of them. Could she and George ever recapture the tenderness they had once shared? She wondered whether she should make more of an effort. Should she call a truce, give in to his need for forgiveness? But the brush of his lips every night on her hair was all she could take from him. The routine of a good-night gesture, an acknowledgement of their married state. No more, no more, not yet, she could not bear the thought. Nearby, some croaking frogs broke Dorothy's thoughts, their call sounding like rapid hand clapping.

Matilda was offering her a cigarette from a silver case. "We have a laugh when we play tennis, you know. We don't take it too seriously. But bridge. Now that's another matter."

Dorothy said. "I haven't played for years."

"You must get out. We're not that bad." Matilda chuckled then allowed her smile to fade. "You can't sit around on your own all day. It's not good for anyone." She patted her hair. "It's quite safe, you know. Nothing is going to happen."

"There was another ambush last week. It's dangerous out there. Besides..."

"But one can't let these things interfere with your everyday life." Sitting upright, Matilda lifted her foot, brought it down heavily on a patch of dithering ants. "I knew a woman once, a wife of a man in the colonial services. Hated it here, but it was more dangerous a few years ago. Turned into a total recluse. Not good. Now I know you're not like that." She handed Dorothy's drink to her. "You must try to get as much out of it as you can."

So Dorothy acknowledged Matilda's concern, agreed that she was most probably right.

"I can't this Saturday or the next, though. I'll let you know through George." She wound the beads in between her fingers. What would Matilda think if she knew the reason for their transfer out there? Would she have been so keen to play tennis with her?

Dinner was ready, and George was at her side. She felt his touch on her elbow. Instinctively she withdrew.

"I'll just pick up the glasses, then I'll come through," she said.

"Feng will...," he started to say, then stopped and led the others across the veranda threshold, their shoes squeaking across the polished wooden floor.

Alone on the veranda, Dorothy looked out at the jacaranda tree, silhouetted now against the light from a neighbour's house. A gecko to the right of her was making its presence known, its call rhythmic, regular. It was a comforting sound for Dorothy. She followed the others into the dining room, took her place opposite George with Henry on her right.

Chapter 12

George considered the letter he was about to dictate. Idly, he stared out of his office window and saw Henry below, leaving the building. With the intention of calling out to him, George lent out of the window. But he changed his mind, thought it might appear childish, as if he had nothing better to do. He thought back to the dinner, how well Dorothy got on with Henry and Matilda. Maybe soon, she would join the bridge club. Still, he had not put the question to Dorothy, asked her whether she would prefer to return to England. But the longer he left it, the more difficult the task appeared. And she seemed more relaxed of late, apparently captivated by her books. Though, frequently he would catch her staring out at the garden, a puzzled expression on her face.

Sitting back in the chair, so that he would receive the full impact of the fan, he apologised to Miss Hall, the secretary, for keeping her waiting. He cleared his throat:

"In our estimation, the goods should be..." the phone rang, startling him. Miss Hall stopped writing and moved her legs to one side, ankles together, her pen held daintily between finger and thumb.

"George. It's Sarah."

George nodded at Miss Hall, lifted his hand, and indicated five minutes with his splayed fingers. She nodded and left the room.

"Sarah. How nice..." the line crackled.

"I'm phoning from Kuala Lumpur. Can you hear me?"

"Yes, loud and clear, but what's the matter?"

"Can you meet me off the train in Ipoh at 4.15?"

"Meet you? Where's Dick?"

"Please, George. I'll explain."

The line hissed, "Sarah?" he said, "Hello?"

He looked at the phone, put it to his ear. Nothing but the dialling tone. Should he contact the operator, ask to be reconnected? Alternatively, he could just meet her, wait till then to speak to her further. He called Miss Hall back, nodded towards her chair. She looked up at him expectantly. She had, George noticed, replenished her lipstick.

"Where were we?" he asked.

She handed him a letter. "I forgot to give you this earlier. Got caught up with some invoices." The handwriting on the envelope belonged to Emma. "Sorry," she said.

He observed her watching him as he took it from her, following his hand as he slipped it into his shirt pocket. But she said nothing, merely smiled at him and tapped her pen on her notepad.

Drawn by the sound of laughter, he looked out of the window again. But it was only a group of Chinese men passing the building. He rattled off a letter, resumed staring out of the window.

"Is that all?" Miss Hall asked.

"For now. Thank you," George said. He needed to be alone. Lightly, he touched his pocket where the letter was sitting. "No hurry, I'll dictate the rest of the letters in the morning."

He unfolded the letter, feeling foolish for checking behind him. Did he really think anybody cared that he still kept in touch with Emma? Apart from Dorothy. But then sometimes he could feel her eyes on him when she was not there.

Taking the letter to the window, he read it. He read it quickly the first time, missing words, scanning it like an X-ray machine. Then he reread it slowly. An ache at his centre spread downwards. So now she had married the Lieutenant, her fiancé, the husband her father approved of. How could she marry a man she maintained she did not love? But what left him bewildered was the tone in which she relayed the news. As if he were a distant relative, to whom she was writing out of obligation. Throwing the letter on the desk, he sat, put his head in his hands. He thought of Moorcroft escorting her down the aisle. He pictured the wedding reception, the speeches, and the congratulations. Then Emma on her wedding night, the army man making love to her. Had she wept with emotion, the way she did with him? Had she touched her new husband the same way she touched him?

He pulled open a drawer in his desk, extracted a bottle of whisky. As he poured himself a large measure, he slumped in his chair. A giddiness swamped him. He could have arranged a divorce with Dorothy, if the opportunity had not been snatched away so soon. But how could he have supported Emma? He remembered Moorcroft's innuendos. And he was indeed a powerful man, had contacts throughout the City. But should he have defied the rule of authority, pursued his dream with Emma? Was it true that love conquered all? He swallowed the whisky fast and felt the liquor flood his mind. It took effect and a surface numbness set in. He withdrew a bundle of letters from his desk. Fumbling with the thin sheets of paper, he slid this latest letter onto the pile. He felt like burning them, watching the papers disintegrate into ashes. But for the time being he would put them away in his usual hiding place.

***

115

George left his office in plenty of time to meet Sarah, so when he arrived at the station, he was early. There was opportunity to loiter in the gardens opposite, in the shade of the palms, amongst the fragrant flowers and the poisonous Ipoh tree. Pulling his hat down to shade his eyes from the glare, he looked towards the station exit. He did not feel like making conversation. If only Sarah had rung later, he could have made his excuses, told her it was impossible to meet. But why was Dick not with her? Remembering the note of urgency in her voice, he wondered what had brought her back so suddenly on her own.

He had fifteen minutes to wait. He took advantage of the time. Casting his eyes over the Moorish style station with the reflective white roof, he strolled amongst the fan palms again, then sat on a bench in a patch of shade. Unfolding his paper, he turned to the crossword. But he could not focus his mind on the clues. Instead, he saw Emma's slanted hand writing. *Last week I married Christopher.* He thought of her, pictured her lying on a bed, eyes closed as she played with her hair, unravelling the auburn curls until they flowed loose on her shoulders. He stood again. Shoving his hands deep inside his pockets, he marched up and down the lawn opposite the station.

Finally, his eyes returned to the station exit. Men and women were streaming out into the sunlight, eyes squinting, some taking out sunglasses, others adjusting hats or removing jackets. He watched the other English men in their Oxford bags and brogues, their house colours displayed on their ties. Then he crossed the road and entered the coolness of the stone interior. Walking to the end of the platform, he glanced along an empty track, lonely, desolate without a puffing train to ride on its rails. Taking up position at the Kuala Lumpur platform entrance, he took out his paper and turned once more to the crossword, anxious to complete a few clues in the time he had. A show of normality, a return to simple pleasures.

There was a bellow. The train was coming in. Steam belched, billowing down the track. The train chugged and strained to a standstill, the engine sighed and wheezed. A door opened from the nearest carriage and Sarah stepped down onto the platform. She was wearing a flame-coloured dress and the same white shoes she had worn to the Palfreys' house, the narrow ankle strap flattering her legs. A smile, warm, appealing, grew across her face as she neared George. He could not help but notice the shadows under her eyes.

He greeted her. She put her hand on his arm. "I had to come back early. Thank you for meeting me."

"No need to thank me," he said. "So when's Dick returning?"

"Tuesday or Wednesday. I had to come back without him. I didn't put you out, did I?" she asked.

He caught her eye as she looked at him briefly. Whatever it was that had happened between her and Dick had nothing to do with him.

He told her no. And that was quite right in a way. For what else would he be doing other than draining a whisky bottle?

The station was emptying. The other passengers had dispersed, leaving them behind, and George realised how slowly they had been walking. He adjusted his hat, walked a little faster, aware of Sarah's long strides beside him. They reached his car. The shade in which he had parked had veered to the left, leaving the Morris in the full glare of the sun.

As he drove, she sat with her hands on her lap and talked about the dinner that she had attended the night before with Dick, and the stickiness of Kuala Lumpur, and of the hotel in which they had stayed, where the Art Deco plasterwork had reminded her of the popular coffee shops in London. While she talked, George thought

117

of Emma and the last time they had met, her promise to him that she would wait for his return. Finally, when they were on the road out of town, she rummaged in her bag.

"I bought some chocolates for the boy," she said.

For a moment, George did not know who she meant.

"We'll be passing the village in a minute. We could stop off." She was looking at him, blinking, smiling. "He's probably the same age as my son."

George rested his elbow on the window frame. "Your son? He's at boarding school in England, isn't he?"

She locked her fingers together. Staring at the road ahead, as if she was trying to focus on a particular spot, she said, "At a school that specialises in children, sick children with polio." She unclasped her fingers, put her hands flat on her lap. Then from her bag, she withdrew a pair of sunglasses.

He thought of the time before when he had asked her about her son. The same eyes, he had said, pointing to the picture on her sitting room wall. And the same smile, he had added, as an afterthought. She had nodded, and looked away.

"I'm sorry," he said. "I should have realised. "I noticed…"

"His legs?"

"Well, yes."

"It's all right, George. You didn't know. I didn't explain." She touched his knee. "He's my only child."

Slowing the car down, he said, "Is that what you really want to do? See the boy again? Is that why you came back early, without Dick."

"No," she said. "Of course not. But you wouldn't mind stopping off, would you?" And she tilted her head sideways, so she could see his watch. "We've got time, haven't we?"

"So why did you?" he asked.

"I find Kuala Lumpur difficult. Sometimes the noise and heat is unbearable. It was built on marsh land. Did you know that?" She looked at him quizzically. "And I have business to attend to at home. Do you see?"

"Of course," he said.

The walk through the forest took longer than before. It seemed more overgrown and the ground was sodden; they had to negotiate a small stream at one point. It was as if the recent rain that had fallen had settled there, taken hold, unable to evaporate, to dry up in the scorching sun that drank and vanquished every drop elsewhere, as soon as the rain had stopped. A trailing creeper caught on his shirt, and like a claw, would not let go. Slowly he unhooked the spiky tendrils; they had ripped his shirt and scratched his skin.

Then he smelt wood smoke, heard voices. The village came into view. Intermittent wisps of smoke rose from the embers of a fire, and a homely smell of roast meat hung, caught in the surrounding air. A man was scattering seed on a small furrowed patch. Not looking up at George and Sarah, he continued sowing his crop.

"Hello there," George called out and walked towards him, then stopped as he realised he was stepping on tiny plants, new growths. Was his call too impertinent, too intrusive? He watched as a flock of small birds ascended from the patch of land.

"Rafi," the man called up to one of the houses. He smiled at George, showing his blackened front teeth. A boy galloped down the steep steps from a house, stopping a short distance away from

George and Sarah. Gradually he moved closer and took the chocolate with a shy smile. The gash on his shoulder was healing well.

A girl came down the same steps, and gave them tea in two jars. It was sweet, strong. Flies tried to settle on George's lips as he licked the sugar from his mouth. Looking up, he saw a woman, standing in the shadow of a doorway, her hand on her hip, a patch in her sarong lit up red by the sun. Was that the boy's mother? Clasping his torn shirt together, he felt transparent, as if she knew what thoughts passed through his head. As if she knew about Emma. Aware of invisible eyes watching him from other houses, he turned to look at hens squawking, squabbling in the dirt, a goat chewing on a frond. Two children squatted under a tree, munching some of the chocolate, too. They were silent, their brown eyes big and staring.

He looked up at the woman in the bright sarong, still standing there, though she had moved so that the sun now shone on her face. She was coming down the steps, offering them some more tea, a plate of neat parcels resembling sweat pastries, in her other hand. They were being welcomed, accepted. He had misread the look on the woman's face. He watched as Sarah tousled the boy's hair and spoke with ease to the mother. He noticed a girl, of maybe Susan's age. She was crouching in the grass as she observed them with careful eyes. Sarah was smiling at the woman.

"We will visit you again," Sarah said. "I'd like to make sure Rafi's all right. I'll bring more clean bandages."

The man who was scattering seed called to the woman, said something in their language.

"No." the woman said to Sarah. "Rafi OK now."

"But I'd like to."

"No. We take care Rafi. You busy."

"Such a sweet boy. I'd like to come back and see him."

The woman glanced at the man sewing seeds. "Ok," she said. "If you want."

They left the village. Calls of childish voices singing out goodbye followed them through the jungle. Until finally they were out of earshot and Sarah linked her arm through his.

"That was all right. Wasn't it? Saying that we'll visit them again?"

Breathing deeply, he tried to place his thoughts in order. It was gratifying to see Sarah so happy; a welcome change from the dreary, speechless misery of Dorothy. And now Emma had removed his hopes, there remained no opportunity to rejoice with her. What harm could it possibly do to return to the village? He might as well at least please Sarah. He told her that, yes, he would accompany her again.

"Next week maybe," he said. "My daughter Susan will be over the week after that."

She dropped a careful kiss of thanks onto his brow. Her lips lingered. Dipping into her bag, she brought out a tiny bottle, the same perfume of English lilies that she had worn before.

He drove her to her house. She invited him in for a drink and without hesitation, he accepted her offer. After all, it would be foolish, childish to pretend. Following her into the house, he noticed the absence of servants; rooms unattended, a growing stuffiness from unopened windows, imprisoning the tropical humidity. The neat whisky she poured for him, the third one that afternoon, slipped easily down his throat.

She insisted on washing the scratches made by the intrusive creeper. As she attended to the grazes, he felt her fingers, cool on his skin. She smoothed some ointment onto the tiny wounds. Hanging over him, she toiled; he saw the dip between her breasts. The tips of

121

her fingers gently stroked him and traced the birth mark stamped on his chest. An urge he had, possessed him again, to tie her hands behind her back, the sudden compulsion surprising him. Their eyes locked. He pulled her to him. Touching him tenderly on his face, she kissed him, then took his hand in hers. But all thoughts of gentleness had departed from his mind. He snatched her hand away. Lifting her dress, he felt her thighs beneath his hands. He heard her sharp intake of breath.

"Can't we go upstairs?" she whispered. She tried to take his hand again.

But he ignored her request. He tugged at her clothes. She fought him, tried to cover herself. Her dress slipped off her shoulders.

"Not here," she said. "Not here. Please."

He pushed her hard against the wall, pulled her dress up higher, forced the zip apart. Crushing her beneath his weight, he knew he was hurting her, knew he should not carry on. He heard her shout for him to stop as she tried to push him away. Grasping her shoulders, he leant into her, stopped her from moving, from getting away. He felt the force of her hand against him. Fragments of images flashed through his mind; Emma embracing the army man, Emma slowly undressing for him. Sarah was still struggling, trying to wriggle from beneath his hold. He put his lips to hers, his tongue pressing inside the softness of her mouth. Then he forced his way into her. Pictures cascaded through his mind: Emma making love to the army man, Emma calling out to him. His breathing was faster, noisy when he exhaled. Sarah's nails dug deep into his shoulders, she wrestled him, but images of Emma pervaded, blocking out her pleas, the beating of her fists, his focus was centred, his climax vociferous.

He held her closely, ran his fingers through her hair, kissed away her tears. She softened in his grasp and sunk her head down, resting against him. Gently he raised it. Green eyes stared back at him, the lashes long, lustrous. Taking her face in his hands, he played his mouth over her lips, to her throat where her perfume was strongest. Lilies. He surfaced; the green eyes faded; Emma disappeared.

He felt Sarah move away from him, saw her fixing her dress fumbling with the zip.

"I'm sorry," he said.

Glancing towards him, she said nothing, then continued straightening her dress.

"I didn't mean to be so rough."

"You hurt me." She was struggling with a hook and eye. She moved further away from him, leant on a chair. "Why did you do that? Don't you have any respect for me?"

On her neck, he saw an angry mark, pink and blooming. What had possessed him? How could he possibly justify how he had behaved? "It's best that I go. Better that I leave now," he said.

She turned to face him. "You must despise me. What you did just then." She was crying. "You hurt me," she said again.

"No..." He made as if to move towards her, then stopped as she drew back. "I didn't mean to. I'm not like that... I'm truly sorry."

He saw her hand move uncertainly, as she touched her hair into place, sweeping it back from her face. Although a part of him felt he should go now, he remained standing. For how could he leave her like this? She returned his gaze, but said nothing.

He excused himself and went upstairs to go to the bathroom. Dazed, miserable, he wandered into a bedroom by mistake. Was this the one Sarah shared with Dick? There were oil paintings of hunting scenes: African skies, pink and yellow, wide trees standing isolated on the plain. And beneath the scene lay a double bed, the pillows shaken and puffed, sheet tucked in, stretched tight across the mattress. His eyes dropped to a bedside table, to a delicate china bowl, pink roses painted on the outside, a fine gold bordering the rim. He heard Sarah climbing the stairs. What was he doing nosing around? Striding across the rug on the landing, he made a hazardous guess as to which door led to the bathroom.

"I think you should leave," he heard Sarah say. She was standing outside the door. Then he heard her footsteps hurry across the landing and a door nearby bang shut. As he washed his hands, he gazed at his reflection in the mirror. Did he look any different from that morning? Putting his hands to his face, he pressed his fingers into the flesh of his cheeks. The past half hour flicked through his mind. Malaya was changing him. This would not have happened in England. Of people losing their minds in the tropics, he had heard. Is that what was happening to him? He would have to be careful. But for what? What did anything matter now? Emma's voice came back to him. "I'll wait for you," she had said. She had lied to him. But he would get her back. Once he was in England, once they had met up again…

Taking to the stairs, he crept back down to the room where he had assaulted Sarah. The word sounded terrible and his mind trailed to clues he might find in a crossword puzzle. *To inflict harm. Nine letters.*

From the sitting room, he could hear her singing. Her voice was strong and powerful. The song was familiar. He remembered hearing it on the wireless in London:

Blow me a kiss across the room.

Say I look nice when I'm not.

Touch my hair as you pass my chair.

Little things mean a lot.

There was a half table with carved legs in the hall and it was here he stood as he listened.

He moved to the sitting room doorway, coughed. With the scrape of a needle on vinyl, the music, her singing stopped. Then she was standing in front of him, hands on hips. And he noticed she had changed her dress. It was blue with a wide white belt.

"I am sorry," What else was there to say?

"I am too."

"You? For what?"

"I am sorry that you thought I was cheap. There was no need to force me like that."

"No. You've got me wrong. I don't know how to explain. It was the whisky, the heat. Whatever I say, you'll never speak to me again. And... well... Can't say I blame you. But I don't go round doing this... to women. Please understand that."

"Please go now."

"Yes, yes, of course."

He walked down the drive. The cicadas were pop-popping and in the distance dogs barked. The sound of gravel crunching beneath his feet appeared magnified in the quiet of the formal garden. A man appeared, pushing a wheelbarrow round from the back, a squeak from the turning wheels intruding on George's thoughts. The gardener nodded at him and George wondered if he knew.

125

The inside of the car was stuffy and hot, the wheel scorching under his touch. George opened a window and saw Sarah standing at the threshold of her house. Neither a smile nor a frown appeared on her face. She was watching him, observing his movements as an onlooker watches the ebb and flow of the ocean.

Chapter 13

Susan wound an elastic band round the end of her plait and put her face close to the mirror. A spot was forming on the side of her nose. At the moment only a small red lump, but she knew that soon it would develop and change into one like the spot on her chin.

It was typical that a new one was sprouting, on today of all days. The day she wanted to look her best. She was looking forward to meeting her father's colleagues, could not wait to be paraded. *Daddy's daughter from England.* They would look at her, then at her father, say what a lucky man he was. She poked at the spot with her finger. Would she be able to sneak into her mother's room and pinch some of her make-up?

She heard her mother's bedroom door slam and footsteps go down the stairs. Kneading the spot on her nose she peered in the mirror for other offending blemishes. She tucked her blouse into her skirt and went into her mother's room, first knocking tentatively on the door. The room smelt of face cream, talcum powder. Perfume, light and flowery. Hesitating at a creaking floorboard, she continued tiptoeing to the dressing table. Half-empty scent bottles, a tortoise-shell brush and comb set, hair grips and safety pins were scattered on the glass. She searched among the lotion bottles and the boxes her mother collected. She counted seven: wooden, jade, woven, porcelain. A painted wooden one caught her eye. A Chinaman, long plaits to his waist, covered the lid, his kimono black and gold.

Smearing a daub of make-up onto both spots, she stared at herself in the mirror. The spots stood out even more, showed red through the beige foundation. Better to smooth it into her cheeks. She pushed a lipstick up out of its outer case, touched her lips with Petal Pink, while pouting at her reflection. Quickly, she strode to the door, started for the stairs.

Her father was in his study, slitting an envelope open. He put the paper knife down, and looked up, beckoning Susan over.

"All set?"

"Rather," she said. "Can't wait. Is Mummy coming?"

"I'll just finish these." He waved the letter. "She's out on the veranda. "Why don't you join her?" He looked down at the letter, pushed his glasses further up his nose. Then he turned to Susan, put his fingers to his lips. "Her headache's gone. So hopefully..." He took a drag of his cigarette and looked at a place beyond Susan, nodding his head.

As she walked through the house to the veranda, she stopped for a minute at a bookcase to read the spines of her mother's books: *Jane Eyre, Great Expectations, Rebecca.* She frowned and retrieved a book, splayed open on the table, its spine splitting: *Wuthering Heights.* What had happened to *Murder in the Mansion, Deadly Nightshade* and *Poirot*? She missed the recriminations from her mother when the murderer was caught, the way she used to retell the story. The two of them sitting in the kitchen, the kettle bubbling on the stove.

Now, she looked towards her mother's profile, sharp against the sunlight streaming in from the garden. As she stepped over the threshold, more detail became clear: the roll of her chignon, and the wisps of hair that had escaped the hair grips. Watching her mother flip her cards out on the table, Susan saw her raise a hand and wave as if they were a long distance apart.

"Darling," her mother said. "Are you looking forward to your day out?" She patted the seat beside her. "This is my favourite time of day." She smiled and raised her eyebrows at Susan. "Is it yours?"

Susan picked up the Jack of Clubs. The corner had a deep crease in it, ready to break off. She put it back in the line of cards. "Are you coming into town, Mummy?" she asked.

Her mother put her hand on hers, moved her thumb over her wrist, backwards and forwards, sliding over the bony bit.

"No. You go with Daddy. I'll come another day." She put her hand to her head.

"You said that on Saturday. And Sunday..."

"Susan..."

"Why won't you come out with Daddy and me?"

Her mother took her hand away, looked out towards the garden.

"It'll be getting hotter soon. Doesn't take long. Allows us a brief respite, then whoosh." She spread her hands out. "Like a furnace." She was laughing; a forced giggle, a bit rusty, as if unused. "I can't today." She lifted a stray hair from Susan's face, tucked it behind her ear. "I will another time. Promise. And go and wash that make-up off." Bending slightly, she put a kiss on Susan's cheek. "Go on. Off you go." Her head was resting against the chair back as she breathed deeply. "I want to hear all about it when you get back."

"I don't understand..." Susan started to say, then she saw her mother look behind her. A shadow fell across the floor and she caught a whiff of tobacco smoke. Susan turned round.

"What's the verdict? Are you coming with us, Dorothy?" Her father was standing at the door, rubbing his hands together.

There was an edge to his voice, as though he was nervous or tired. She had noticed it before. He was blowing smoke out through his nostrils and watching her. When he did that before, they used to laugh together. She thought of Carol back in England. How they yelled and screamed, clutching stomachs, bent in agonising bliss. Begging each other to stop the jokes.

"Not today, dear," her mother said. "I've explained to Susan."

Her father put his hat on and went through into the sitting room. As she followed him out to the car, she heard her mother behind, calling out to Feng for some more tea. Surely she got bored drinking tea, playing patience all day. And sleeping, having a rest, or sighing and closing her eyes as she rocked herself backwards and forwards in the swing seat. She *must* get tired of doing that. Looking back towards the house before she stepped into the car, she saw her mother's face at the window. She was waving, blowing a kiss. Susan waved back as the car jolted them forward. She watched her mother disappear into the shadows and wondered whether she was ill. Could it be something serious, something they did not want her to know about?

"Daddy," she asked. She wrapped the hem of her skirt round a finger. "What's wrong with Mummy?"

He glanced at her. "Nothing, nothing," he said. "She finds this heat difficult. That's all."

Her father was whistling through his teeth, drumming his fingers on the steering wheel as he drove.

"We'll have a splendid time," he said. He pointed to the sky. "Got the weather for it."

She stared out of the window at the thick blue sky, then at a woman on the other side of the road, pushing a pram, shade down, hiding the sun from the baby's face. Her haircut was the same as Feng's, short with bands. Four other women in pretty sarongs and headscarves were walking towards them. They progressed steadily, their hips moving gracefully, their bodies perfectly upright as if they

130

were balancing books on their heads. The houses flicked by, the sun darting between the trees. She watched a man carrying a striped bag, saw him look up at them briefly as they drove past. His dark face was wizened and old, his back crooked.

She looked on, memorising every detail she saw through the open window. She was looking forward to recalling her time here to Carol. She thought of her again, how she would put her head on one side as she listened.

Her father had stopped whistling. "I'll show you that temple today if you like," he said. "The one I told you about. Hewn out of rocks. They worship their ancestors you know, the Chinese. Did you know that?" He swiped at a fly that had been buzzing around his head. "Their deceased relatives." He turned towards her, watching, as she pulled her skirt down over her knees and batted the creases out.

Susan thought of her grandparents in Manchester, how her grandmother used to sit motionless at the dinner table and wait for her father, or her mother, her, anyone who was sharing the meal, to recognise what she needed next: more potatoes, another slice of meat, mustard, salt and pepper. Her tongue clicking as she waited.

She decided to tackle her father again. "Mummy always used to come out with us. Now she's always tired, or has a headache. If she is ill, you would tell me, wouldn't you?"

Her father was frowning. "We never keep things from you. Your mother's not ill." He changed gear, made the engine grate. "But we'll all go to the coast at the weekend. It's much cooler there." He patted her knee. "You worry too much. Just like your mother."

Susan nibbled at a nail as she turned away from her father. Head fixed, staring out of the window, she saw a woman in a white head dress; she was standing at the side of the road, a child holding each hand. The car stopped, engine wheezing, rattling as it idled. The woman was wearing an orange sarong, and smiled at Susan before she stepped in front of their waiting car. Susan turned to watch them as they drove away, returning the children's wave. And as she peered at them, she thought of her mother, how little she smiled now, as she passed her amber beads through her fingers. As if she were saying Hail Marys.

They were pulling up outside a long building with palm trees shading the other parked cars. A sign across the front of the building was beginning to peel:

"Rowland Smith Export Company Ltd," Susan read.

In her imagination she had seen a much grander office; something akin to the pillared white buildings they had passed before, with their ornate plaster work and recesses, black and mysterious in the shadows cast by the sun. She remembered the visit to his office in London; parquet floors, the reflections like puddles on a summer's day, the rhythmic sound of typewriters as they passed along the corridors.

"I won't be a minute," her father said. "Come in. Meet the crew." He opened the car door for her.

Her father was heading down a dimly-lit corridor lined with closed doors. He led her up a flight of stairs and finally opened a door right at the end. Summoning her in with a sweep of his hand, he pulled a chair out from under a table and lifted a pile of papers from the seat.

"Two minutes," he said. "Then we'll be off."

His office was airless and incredibly hot. He switched on a fan; it creaked and swayed, moving its head round the office, lifting papers in its breeze. The desk where her father sat was at right angles to the window. Heaps of papers, books and files were scattered on the desk top, piled topsy-turvy, the edges of papers fluttering in the flurry of brushed air. He lifted the blind and opened the window wide. His office looked out onto the street below. A couple of dark-skinned boys were kicking a ball around.

"So where do they live? The Malays?" she asked.

He followed her gaze. "Those are Indians," he said then pulled out a file from a tray on his desk.

She watched them for a minute, then someone in another office shouted out to them, told them to go and play somewhere else.

"But where do the Malays live?"

"Villages. Houses on stilts."

"Near here?"

Her father sighed. "Yes. I believe a couple are near here."

"So can we visit one?"

"Susan."

"Can we? Please."

He turned around to face her. "We made other plans for your day. You'll enjoy what you'll see." He moved the fan towards her. "Anyway it's rude to poke around people's houses."

Susan fingered the spot on her nose, trying to rub it away. She thought of the woman in the orange sarong. She looked so calm and carefree. Surely she would not think it rude to visit where they lived?

Her father was working his way through some forms, his fingers staining a deeper blue each time he lifted some carbon and slipped it under the sheet. He worked steadily, a cigarette smouldering to its tip in an ashtray at his elbow. Susan watched the ash drop off the filter, and the smoke slowly disintegrate as it wafted upwards towards the stained ceiling.

"Sorry about this," he said. "Nearly finished." He picked up a stamping machine and rolled the date mark round, colouring his fingers a deeper blue. Another pile of papers. Signature, stamp, signature, stamp. She could see the sweat collecting on the back of his neck, wetting his collar.

There was a knock at the door. A man with a black moustache stood in the doorway. He looked at Susan.

"Good morning Henry," Her father turned to Susan. "This is Mr Golding."

She held her hand out.

"Susan," he said. "My daughter."

Mr Golding coughed twice. He smiled at Susan quickly. Then he looked at her father, out through the window, back at her father. He cleared his throat noisily.

"I need to have a word with your father," he said to Susan as he held the door open. "A quick word."

They walked to the other end of the corridor so she could not hear what they were saying. It was the slamming of the building door which made her look out of the window. Her father was moving swiftly away out of her vision. A mosquito whined in her ear. She tried to catch it. Another one joined the first, then another.

She waited, watching the swing of the fan. And still he did not return. Running down the stairs, she saw a shaft of light, falling down the corridor from an open office. It was Mr Golding. He stood in a doorway, one hand on the handle, the other one held before him, in front of her.

"He won't be a minute," he said. "Best you wait in your father's office, heh?" With one hand, he was running his fingers through his hair, the other hand directed her back.

Back in his office, she looked out of the window again, searching the street. No sign of her father. Only a couple of minutes, he had said. It was ages now.

She stuck her head out of the window, screwed her eyes up in the glare of the sun. Her face grew hotter. Determined, she clung to the sill, stretched out as far as she dared. Her father was leaning into a car window. As he moved aside she saw a woman get out of the car. Tall and busty, she was wearing a blue dress. Susan could see her smiling at her father; put her hand to his face. He stepped back quickly, stumbled; the woman caught his arm, held on to it, touched his face again. Susan knew she should not be watching, spying. Snooping on her father. He was hurrying back now. She heard a car stall and scrape before driving away.

Her arm itched where a mosquito had bitten her. Furiously, she rubbed and scratched at it. Why did the woman touch him like that? Why was he taking so long? She wanted to get out of this building with its clamminess and hair cream smells.

The office door opened and her father stood there mopping his face and neck.

"Sorry," he said, "I had to go out and see someone." He switched the fan off. "Come on, I'll take you to that temple now." He cupped his hand to her elbow and led her down past other offices, their doors now open. She stood at the entrance of four offices, her father's arm round her shoulder. "This is Susan," he repeated each time.

And the men all turned and came towards her, took her hand and said "Delighted," or "Lovely to meet you," or "Charmed."

135

But her enthusiasm for being shown off had worn off, dwindled like a dying sun. Gone, the wish for admiring smiles, an opportunity to be the centre of attention; her father's daughter just arrived from England.

They drove in silence for a while. Her father gripped the wheel tightly, his Adam's apple bobbing up and down as he swallowed again and again.

"Daddy," she began. But how could she ask him who he had been talking to?

He glanced at her.

"Nothing."

There was something about the way that woman had looked at her father. It was wrong, she knew that. Out of the corner of her eye she watched him as he steered: as his hand kept rubbing his left eye. She stared out of her window, at a group of bare-footed children squatting by the roadside, throwing dust into the road. They waved to her and two of them chased their car, laughing and shouting, until the distance between them increased too much and they were tiny figures standing in the middle of the road, their arms still making arches in the air.

The town was behind them now; they were surrounded by towering trees on either side of the road. Three women walked in single file along the side of the road. Their sarongs were blue and green and orange, their feet dainty as they stepped between the stones. Her father had started whistling again. He pulled up.

"Here we are," he said as he opened her door. "This is a limestone cave temple. See through the trees?"

She followed him over a plank set across a ditch. Craning her neck towards the sky, she saw the gold and red top of a temple poking out above a long flight of steps.

"How did they build a temple out of rock?"

"I'm not exactly sure. But you'll see a magnificent view when we get to the top."

She smiled at him. "Can you take me to a Malay village after this?"

He sighed and tutted. "You'll like this. It's really beautiful." He put his arm round her.

There were a lot of steps. Susan climbed steadily ahead of her father. A creeper was growing along a wall and she tugged at a tendril, curious to see how long it was. A colony of ants, disturbed by her, headed upwards, away, along the stone wall. She waited for her father, heard him catching up with her, a few steps below.

"Hard work in these temperatures," he said.

It upset her to see him like that; panting, bending, holding his knees, his face the colour of rhubarb. She walked alongside him for the rest of the way. At the top, she gave him a hug as they looked out over the tree tops. She wanted to ask him who the woman was. But how would she explain her reasons for spying on him?

The walls of the temple were painted bright red, like the telephone boxes at home. And on one side of a gate a snake unwound itself up the wall, its jaws open, its tongue lashing. On the other side a tiger had been painted, ready to pounce.

It was cool and dark inside; the burning incense made her nose tickle and itch. But it was a pleasing smell, and she sniffed the air, taking in the sweetness, the musky drift. They were ignored by the monks in saffron robes who fiddled with offerings of honey, cakes and tins of condensed milk set before the statue of Buddha. And a woman intent on brushing the floor, did not look up at them once. She wore a navy dress, old and shapeless; her hair was scraped back in a wispy bun. Susan stared up at the golden Buddha, examining its pose, cross-legged, hands resting on his knees. She followed the curve of its face, fat lips, creased smile. A man lighting bundles of incense with dripping candles stared at them, muttering under his breath. She watched his face, shrivelled, ghoulish in the light from the flame and thought about the woman in the car again. The man's muttering became louder; the smell of melting candle wax grew stronger.

"Enough?" her father whispered after twenty minutes or so.

Linking arms they descended the steps.

"So." Susan turned to her father as they sat in the car. "Where now?"

"Spot of lunch," he said as he pulled at the gear stick. The car was turned around, and they headed back towards the town. But he drove slowly and, after five minutes, pointed to a clearing in the forest. "There's a Malay village down there," he said. He pulled up, leaving the engine running.

Susan peered at the path, followed it as far as she could see, through the jungle. How long would it take to reach the village? She thought of a delicious meal roasting on a fire, imagined pretty women sitting in their doorways, weaving baskets and matting. Girls in colourful clothes feeding grain to chickens, children playing in the stream. She looked up at her father.

"Can we visit it?"

"Not today. Maybe another time."

The brakes squealed as he reversed and sped back along the road.

Chapter 14

Her father was munching toast behind his newspaper, crumbs falling onto the white napkin spread on his knee. Susan pondered. Was this a good time to ask him about the woman she had seen with him last week? Or had she left it too long? But he was always so busy, no chance had arisen before. It was now or never.

"Daddy... Who was...? I was wondering..." she began.

"Spit it out." The newspaper crackled as he folded it into four. He glanced at the crossword, before he smiled at her encouragingly.

"Who was the woman you were talking to...?"

"Sorry?" He flicked his pen between finger and thumb.

"At your office on Friday?"

He was gazing out of the window. She followed where he was looking. Babiya was snipping the grass that bordered the path.

"You dashed out..."

"Oh her. A colleague's wife. Why?" he asked.

"Nothing. I just wondered." Picking up the sugar spoon, she began to scoop up sugar, watching the grains fall and settle.

"Right. I'll be off." Her father stood and brushed toast crumbs from his trousers. "Might be back a bit late this evening." He ruffled Susan's hair. "I'll just nip upstairs and tell your mother." He collected up his newspaper and crossed the hall. "Must dash."

Susan went outside to sit in the shade of the jacaranda tree. From there, she could see her mother's bedroom. She checked every now and again for a movement of the blind, listened out for a call from her balcony. Her father shouted goodbye. The front door slammed. She looked down the lawn, to the house beyond. Walking steadily, she positioned herself at the bottom of the garden. Yesterday she had heard music from a neighbouring house. Modern music, not the classical stuff her father played. But today there was no music, only the chirping of insects. Apart from that there was silence. She thought of the woman outside the office again; how she had stretched her hand out to touch her father's cheek.

There was no movement from her mother's room: the blinds remained firmly shut. It looked like she was going to have to provide her own entertainment again. Maybe she could hunt for clues about the woman she had seen. Her father's study was off-limits. One last look up towards her mother's window. Nothing. Not a flicker. How could she ignore such an opportunity?

Susan closed his study door behind her, walked carefully, quietly to his desk. The blotter with the images of his writing was curled at the edges. His paperknife lay next to it. She tried to open the top drawer to his desk. It was stuck. She began to rattle the handle, jiggling it around. Eventually the drawer opened; she pulled out some brown envelopes. Thumbing through them, she realised they were letters from his work in London. There was a knock on the door. She stuffed the letters back in the drawer, slammed it shut. Feng was standing in the doorway, a duster and a tin of polish in her hand. Face burning, Susan squeezed past her and hoped she would not be reported.

From the hall, she could hear the bath water draining upstairs. So her mother was out of bed. She must be feeling better now. Maybe they could go out together, to the shops, or to meet Mrs Golding's daughter, Jennifer, here for the holidays like her. It was an outing her mother had promised. Company of your own age she had said. A door upstairs banged shut and her mother came down the stairs. She was dressed in one of her long flowing dresses, the sleeves trailing from her arm as she reached out to the banister. Where could she possibly go dressed like that?

"Shall we sit on the veranda?" her mother asked.

Susan followed her mother outside. They both waited in silence as Feng brought out the tea tray.

"Right, young lady," her mother said as she replaced her teacup in the saucer. "How would you like to go to the market with Feng?"

"And you?"

"You like Feng, don't you?"

"Of course I do."

"There are lots of pretty clothes there. And it was Feng's idea to take you. She suggested it last night." She took a sip of her tea, added some more sugar. "You'd better get yourself ready. She'll be leaving soon. I'm sorry I can't come with you. But I really can't." Leaning over, she kissed Susan on her head. And Susan wondered again about the woman she had seen with her father.

"If you won't come out with me, why won't you let me go into town on my own?"

"No. Not on your own. With Feng."

"I'll be careful. After all, you left me behind on my own in England."

"It's dangerous on your own here. I would go with you..." Her mother's voice dwindled, faded.

Susan waited.

"You know I find it difficult here, outside," her mother continued.

141

"When I'm not in the car. I can't walk very far. The heat makes me feel ill. We'll all go to the coast at the weekend." She smiled. "I'm sorry, but we've had some nice times here, haven't we?"

"I may as well be in England."

"Don't be ridiculous."

"At least I would have been allowed out if I'd stayed in England instead of coming here."

"You're being impossible. You are allowed out." She closed her eyes for a minute. "Just not unaccompanied. It's for your own safety."

"I get so bored staying in the house all day."

"Why do you insist on arguing with me?" Her string of amber beads were lying on the table. She picked them up. "I've explained why you can't go out on your own."

"Just because you won't go out."

"Enough, Susan."

"Well, you don't."

Her mother picked up her cup and saucer. They rattled in her hand as she stood. "I don't know what's got into you" she said. "Now go and get yourself ready." She went back indoors.

Susan heard her close the sitting room door. Now, she was alone again. Tears were starting to form. She blinked fast and wiped her eyes fiercely with her hand, stepped back down into the garden. Carol's mother was not like this. She would try anything, go anywhere for a bit of fun. Susan thought of her turning the volume up on the radiogram, jiving round the sitting room. Why was her own mother not like that?

"Susan," Feng called.

She looked back at Feng. She was standing at the veranda door. Susan walked towards her. She had taken off her white housecoat. Now she was wearing a neat black dress.

"You come out with me?" Feng asked.

"Yes," Susan said. "Let's go now. I can't wait to see the market."

The walk to the market took longer than Susan had expected, over an hour; and although they were always in the shade, she was still soaked by the time they reached the town. She thought of her mother suffering in the heat, sighing as she pressed an ice cube to her head. Susan found the humidity a release; she liked to let it seep through her.

Feng did not say much, though she was always stopping to make sure Susan was still there, close behind. She would not let her stop and look at anything. But Susan observed her surroundings. Walls concealed some of the houses, others stood behind ornate iron railings, their gardens laid to lawns; houses, large, foreboding, beyond the swept driveways, kept clear of fallen leaves and dust. They passed two English looking women going the other way. They looked at ease, happy to be out. She followed Feng through the quietness of the expatriate compounds and crossed a river.

As they neared the Old Town, bicycles began to clog the road. Some were pushed with children on the seats, or leaning out of baskets. Most were battered with dirty string dangling from seats, with bent handle bars and squeaking wheels. Men in straw hats, yoked burdens on their shoulders, or pulling carts stacked with bales of hay, moved steadily along the road. Tendons on their necks bulged with the strain. Susan stared at one of the women. She was wheeling a bicycle; a torn umbrella held over her head, cardboard boxes piled high in a basket, a girl with pigtails was sitting astride the handle bars. Susan wondered about the girl, glanced towards the serious

143

face. Did she ever have new clothes? Were there toys for her at home? Watching the retreating bicycle, she noticed the girl's feet, bare, as they dangled. A thought crossed her mind, that it was unfair, unjust, that she should have so much to bring out here, while others owned so little.

Feng pointed to a building at the far end of the street. "There it is," she said and walked faster, holding on to Susan's arm.

Inside the covered market, a smell of unwashed clothing merged into the fragrance of incense. Feng led her to a stall selling the boxes her mother adored. Carved animals were displayed on a black cloth. She wanted to wander around on her own; there was a man selling paintings of mountains on scrolls. She pulled away. Feng pulled her back. Susan had no choice but to stand next to her, to look into the carved faces of goats, of tigers, of dancing bears with beads and coloured glass for eyes and noses.

"Luck charms," said Feng. "I buy one for Ma." She picked up a bird, its wings in full flight. She spoke to the stallholder.

Susan picked up a tiny statue of a Buddha. His legs were crossed, its eyes closed, a look of serene happiness on the painted golden face. Would her mother like this? Maybe she could sleep with him on her bedside table. She wondered whether lucky charms worked on headaches. She pictured her mother, her head in her hands, her face grey with pain.

She handed the Buddha to the stall holder, waited for the woman to wrap it then slipped it into her pocket. "I'm going to look at those scrolls" she said to Feng.

But Feng had tight hold of her. Susan watched her open a box with hibiscus painted in pink on the lid. With two fingers, Feng pinched the velvet lining; she seemed to know what her mother would like.

144

Now Feng was arguing with the stall holder, a woman whose face was wrinkled, like the fallen plums Susan used to pick off the ground in their garden in Golders Green. Suddenly, she spotted her moment and started to push her way through the crowd, elbowing her way to the stall with the painted scrolls. But even she could not see above the heads of black hair, could not watch the man who was painting. She checked behind her for Feng, then moved towards a stall selling hats. It was strange that the Chinese took so little notice of her, she had expected more curious looks.

She picked up a woven hat, the conical kind she had seen worn by women in rice paddies. As she watched the stall holder count on an abacus, she had an idea. She would go and visit the Malay village. It would be easy to find, as there was only one main road out of Ipoh. She could be back by teatime if she walked fast. And her father, apparently too busy, had not fulfilled his promise and taken her there.

Somebody took hold of her arm. It was Feng.

"Come on. I show you silk dresses Ma likes."

Reluctantly, Susan smiled at Feng. "OK," she said, "But I want to go to the lavatory first."

"I show you where," said Feng, She led the way, pushing through the crowds, always turning, her fringe bobbing. Then she indicated a door, told Susan she would wait.

The lavatories had no doors, no separate cubicles and were in a row, like troughs. The stink made her stomach heave as she squatted over the cleanest one she could see, one hand pinching her nose. A crack of daylight caught her eye as a door opposite the one she had come through, opened. Two women came in from the street. Without stopping to rinse her hands, she squeezed past them. Out through the door she hurried, heart thumping, and into the open air. She

145

found herself amidst an array of birds, cheeping and twittering in their tiny cages. Bird droppings carpeted the ground, thick and slippery. Ducking and stooping, she wove her way through the aviary. At last she saw the street before her. She walked quickly, though not running.

At a shop where brooms and brushes hung from the doorway, she stopped, looked back and saw Feng. To Susan's embarrassment, she realised her name was being called. She turned into another street, and then again into another.

Now there was no sign of Feng following her, but Susan knew Feng would not give up that easily, so she turned into an alleyway. Washing dangled from lines stretched across the cobbled passageway. Chinese women yelled exchanges to each other. Cooking odours of fried cabbage and boiled bones filled the small space. Running, leaping over drains and black puddles; she finally reached the alley end. Would she soon hear Feng running behind her, feel her pulling at her arm? But there was only a woman in blue and white overalls sweeping vegetable peelings into the gutters.

She began to swing her arms as she walked. It was such a relief to be out on her own. And what was the danger? What could happen to her? If her mother never went out, how could she possibly know? Then there was her father going to work every day and coming home safely every evening. Susan looked over her shoulder. It looked like she was well and truly on her own. She thought of the comments she would make to Carol, if only she were here. She would point out the temple and the library with its huge colonnades.

She was passing a cricket green and she watched a man wearing a piece of cloth wrapped round his middle, rolling the grass flat. There were a couple of English looking men standing in the shade of a tree, hands in pockets, legs apart. One of them was smoking a pipe. He reminded her of Uncle Tom, moving onto his heels then onto his toes, like a nursery rocking horse. He looked towards Susan, and took the pipe away from his mouth. Did he know who she was? Would he go and find her father and tell him? But he turned back to his friend and resumed his conversation. Susan hurried on. But now there was a tightness in her chest; it was getting difficult to expel the air after she had breathed in. She sat on a box outside a shop where sacks grouped round the entrance. If only she could control her breathing.

She went next door where people were sitting under an awning. A woman in a blue overall was pouring water from an oversized kettle into tiny bowls. Everyone was drinking tea. Susan licked her dry lips. If she stopped, Feng might catch up with her. For a few seconds, she battled with her desire for liquid; she listened out for Feng calling her name, the accent falling on the last syllable. With the sun washing over her face, her breathing eased and she started to feel better.

But she had been dawdling too long; she continued, this time at a faster pace while keeping the dome of the station to her left. A good landmark her father had told her. Pleased with herself for not getting lost, she saw a glint of gold in the sun and recognised that it was a temple at the end of the street. The road out of Ipoh lay just ahead. And with that clear direction in her mind, her pace became deliberate, steadied. She wondered what Feng would do. Was she running around the stalls, perhaps asking the man selling the caged birds if he had seen her? Glancing at her watch, she gave herself an hour. Best not to push her luck.

There were not many buildings along the road now, and the station dome had merged into the townscape behind her. Voices approaching her made her turn and she watched as three women passed her carrying pots on their heads and wearing long pretty sarongs tied at the waist, with matching tops. They greeted her as they passed and she wondered if they lived in the village she planned to visit. Should she stop them and ask, gain their permission? But she was only going to have a peep, she would not stay. She thought of what her father had said about the villagers, about invading their privacy, their way of life. How would she like it, he had asked? Now, she remembered the Jewish boys in Golders Green, returning from synagogue. How they would stop and stare at her as she sat at the window playing cards with her mother.

She admired the gracefulness of the Malay women's movements, but they had the effect of making her feel clumsy and uncomfortable. Her underarms were chafing against the tightness of her sleeves. The polka dot dress felt sticky, clammy; the belt was too tight in the heat. She slowed down. Soon the women were specks in the distance ahead of her. No cars passed by her, only goats and the odd scrawny cow herded by men in bare feet. Some were wearing sarongs not dissimilar to the women's. They too greeted Susan.

She was beginning to doubt the wisdom of coming out this far. She had been walking for over two hours now. The resolution to teach her mother a lesson was beginning to fade. She looked backwards at the empty road, at the short shadows cast by the trees. The afternoon was at its hottest now and a new thirst was making her feel dizzy. It was just as she was about to turn round and start back, when, half-hidden though it was by encroaching foliage, she caught sight of a parked car up ahead. She quickened her pace despite the temperature, despite the difficulty she was having in breathing again. As she neared the car, she saw the familiar shape appear from the gloom of the shading tree; she thought how lucky she was. It was her father's car that was parked under a tree. Opening the door, she searched the interior, as if she expected to find him hidden inside. She leant against the closed door and looked around her. The realisation came slowly. It was where they had pulled up before; she now recognised the clearing. But why had he parked in that particular place; near the path to the village he had pointed out last week? She remembered his insistence that they should not pry into other people's lives. As she rubbed the dust from her eyes, she tried to work out reasons as to why he might be there. A path led through the forest. She decided she would find him and ask all the questions that had nagged her for so long.

Chapter 15

Dorothy woke gradually as the rumble of a lawnmower entered her dream: she was searching for Susan in the ruins of the blitz. Picking her way through rubble, she discovered a burning crater, and was staggering back from the heat. As she surfaced, the rasp of the mower sounded like the wheeze of Susan's mucous-filled chest. For a minute she thought she was back in a London destroyed by war, was waking from the nightmare there.

Switching the bedside light on, she looked at her watch. She had been asleep for three hours. It was late afternoon now, but still the air was as sticky as it had been that morning when she had taken to her bed. No cooling down, no release. Shaking a pillow, then giving it a punch, she sat back, resting her head on the soft down. In that position, the fan was now cooling her torso, but the flurries of cool air ruffling her silk nightdress were sensual, and she closed her eyes, allowing herself to drift momentarily. Picking up the other pillow, she hugged it to herself. She thought of Henry. Casting her mind back to the dinner, she remembered him stroking his moustache as he watched her pass round the box of Milk Tray. His choice had been of nougat. He had bitten into it, keeping his eyes fixed on her face. Had she imagined his look of admiration as he picked out a chocolate for her; a soft-centred strawberry cream?

She considered their meeting. It had to be destiny, a movement of the planets. Why else would her fortune have led her out there? There had to be a reason for everything. Dorothy longed to see Henry on her own. At least then she would know for sure. But it would be best to bump into him accidentally and, of course, it would be a doomed affair, shrouded in guilt and despair at their impossible future together. He would hold her, and allow her to sob onto his shoulder. They would meet at lunch times. He would come to the house when George was at work, sneaking out of the office, on an invented errand. She would play slow waltzes on the radiogram and they would dance on the veranda with the flutter of butterflies in the afternoon sun. He would hold her and whisper into her ear, tell her how beautiful she was and how much he wanted to be with her. She cuddled her pillow, fought off the idea that perhaps she was fantasising his desire for her. How else could she explain his watchful eyes, observing every move she made?

She sat up and moved the fan so it blew directly onto her face, cooling her intermittently as it alternated between her and the foot of the bed; she closed her eyes and listened to the drone of insects. The lawnmower sounded further away now, like the fading of Susan's attack as the catarrh thinned in her lungs.

Moving to the window she drew the curtains. She would never get used to the thickness of the air outside, the way it hung in heavy drapes and lingered, unmoving, as if a thunderstorm was brewing, ready to crash. After all these months, she still expected, a refreshing touch, a wind from an open window, to cool her down. She decided to take a bath. Then Susan would be home. Their argument of before would be forgotten. They would have tea and cakes. Just as they used to. Perhaps Susan would play a game of cards with her. Or maybe they would sit and talk. Mother and daughter at peace, opening the packets Feng brought back; the chosen artefacts from the market. She was looking forward to this too; the slow unwrapping of the paper which would reveal a neat cardboard box. And then? What had Feng chosen for her today? A shawl with swallows migrating across a sunset sky, or a velvet pouch, small and delicate? Perhaps a box, ivory with mother-of-pearl encrusted in the lid.

A couple of flies had found their way into the bathroom and she watched as they buzzed and chased each other around the room. She wondered what Susan was doing. She should have gone to the market with her, looked after her, taken her to a coffee shop, bought her cakes, shared a table with another family. All laughing together. Was she a terrible mother; a mother to be despised, ridiculed, less competent than the others? Was it possible that Susan preferred the boarding school, the teachers, the matrons who cared for her?

She emptied some bath salts into the running water and remembered Susan giving them to her when she first arrived. She had changed so much in the few months that had passed. With moods that were impossible to foresee, sometimes she presented softness, smooth as cats' fur, or else an explosion of anger like this morning. And her face too had altered, it was more angular, her chin with a defiant point, like her father's, more apparent with the loss of her plumpish cheeks.

Dorothy reached up for the soap and lathered herself slowly, luxuriously. Imagining Henry's fingers sliding over her skin, she lay back in the bath. Would he massage her shoulders, kiss the nape of her neck? As she stepped out of the bath and wrapped a towel round herself, she wondered what it would be like making love with him. Would he be forceful, lifting her limbs, holding her high as George used to after a couple of neat whiskies? Or would he be gentle, caressing her, murmuring softly into her ear, as did the heroes in romances, or, like the boys at the dance halls during the war, always pushing their luck, trying to get her to succumb to their jostling? No, not this either; she longed to be courted, won, placed on a pedestal as a Queen. And that is precisely how Henry would behave. But, reluctantly, as if taunting, her mind slipped to the dinner that evening; she remembered his arm around Matilda, as he adjusted her stole. Had he looked at Matilda with fondness? Or was the action merely habitual, like George brushing her hair with a touch of his lips every night?

She chose her clothes with care. Even George had noticed the effort she had been making of late. Of course, for a while, he thought

152

it was for his benefit, considered it to be a come on, and that she would welcome having him ruffling her hair, touching her breasts. She slammed the wardrobe door. It did not take her long to put him straight on that point. No more Friday night tumbles. She remembered the last time she had obliged, how she had lain there rigid, while she stared at geckos catching tiny flies, willing him to finish, to get it over and done with. And now even his light kiss on her head made her shudder; the nightly performance, as if they were married in every sense of the word. So it suited her that he spent so much time at the Club. And she had got used to putting on a show; pretending everything was normal. Of course the time spent on picking out the most flattering dresses, the matching bracelet, and necklace, maybe an extra ring, a hint of contrasting eye shadow; it was all for Henry. And she knew Henry noticed such efforts, understood him to be an appreciative man.

Finally, she chose a dress brought over from England, pink with a large bow at the front, and full skirt: simple, but elegant. She could always change later, there was plenty of time to muse. In the sitting room, she looked up at the clock on the wall, glanced at her reflection in the oval mirror. She was pale; a stroll around the garden would do her good, despite the air never feeling fresh. And Susan and Feng would be here soon. She paused at the veranda steps, looking out. Strolling to the hibiscus bush, she took in the aroma of newly-mown grass, reminding her of walks in the park with Susan; the plop of tennis balls, of calls, straining, from the players as they served.

She followed a trail of grass cuttings to where the jacaranda tree stood, then rested under a fan palm and surveyed the garden. She turned her gaze in the direction of the orange and yellow cannas bordering the boundary wall, their flower heads stretching vertically towards the sun. She thought how peaceful the garden was. Then she heard a sound from the house. Was that Susan? She waited for the familiar voice, a greeting followed by leaps down the steps and a call to show what she had bought. But there was only silence; she had imagined the footsteps. Or had she? Was someone waiting for her, ready to pounce? A sense of panic seized her. Jean Palfrey had been in their garden when the attack had happened. Cutting roses, so she had been told - no one else in the house. Glancing towards a cluster of roses, planted by her as a reminder of Golders Green, Dorothy tried to imagine how Jean Palfrey had reacted to the invader. Had she been speechless with fright? Or perhaps she had chastised the man, told him to put the knife away, as one would tell a child to stop running up and down the stairs. She could picture this woman she had been told so much about, admonishing the terrorists, using her clipped tones to remind them who she was. Dorothy would not have the courage for that.

Back in the sitting room she sank into the rocking chair. She lifted her fan, waved it in front of her face, cooling herself and drying the tears which had sprung so suddenly; taking her by surprise. Once they started, they poured, as if from a leaking gutter. She rocked herself backwards and forwards. Why had she allowed herself to imagine Henry occupied his mind with thoughts of her? She started to sob. Picking up her book, she tried to read. Although the print was distorted and blurred through her tears, like a mirage in a heat haze, she blinked and blinked, concentrating, willing herself to stop the tears. Eventually, she managed to stem the flow and her breathing calmed. After a few pages, she put the book face down on her lap and picked up her amber beads, sliding them from one finger to the next. Susan should be home soon, then George. And Henry here for dinner again with his tiresome wife, Matilda and her oversized frame, candy floss lipstick caught on her front tooth. Dorothy snapped her book closed and stood. At least there would be company for Susan, a surprise, a girl of her own age; Henry and Matilda had said they would bring Jennifer over for the evening. Looking through the veranda doors, she watched the shadows take over the garden, moving across the lawn, ready to engulf the house; the grass stripes created by Babiya, glistening like phantoms in the bluish light. It would be dark soon; already the moon was visible, slipping upwards and away through the trees. Susan and Feng were very late. Maybe Susan was still angry, had persuaded Feng to allow her to stay out longer than arranged. She could be very insistent, demanding, wilful like her father. But it was unusual for Feng to stay in the market so long.

Staring into the gloom of the garden, she passed her amber beads along each finger as she crossed then uncrossed her legs.

Chapter 16

Susan stepped over a log and onto the path. The determination to visit a Malay village had faded into second place; her priority now was to find her father. She stopped for a minute and thought carefully. Should she wait for him in the car? That would be sensible, but why should she always do the right thing when her father and mother did not play by the rules? Her father must be here somewhere. But why had he said nothing to her about his visit this morning? It was unusual for him to go back on his word, though she had had an inkling he did not intend to stick to his promise this time. Always so busy, so distracted with his job.

Although large boulders partly blocked her view, she could see how the path meandered and turned through the forest. The ground felt springy and soft, squishy under her feet. Moss was growing on tangled roots, camouflaging them, so they looked like green tendrils winding along the path, half burying themselves under new growths. Swiping at an ant making its way up her shin, she followed the path downwards through the trees. She stopped for a minute and listened hard, feeling goose pimples prickling her arms; never before had she known such quietness, a silence that was audible in its stillness; she had expected parrots and hornbills to cackle and whoop above her head, animals to scuttle through the undergrowth. Her father must be further down the track. She started to walk again, tip-toeing as best she could across the stony ground, as if she were frightened of waking some peculiar beast dozing in the lazy heat. Why was her father here? With a fist, she wiped her face, scrubbed the tear away which was falling onto her cheek.

Now that she was surrounded by curtains of green growth, the heat was more intense. Intermittently, the sunlight flashed through the tree tops high above in the canopy. The road had disappeared when she looked behind her, and she toyed with the idea of turning back, of returning to the market and finding Feng. At least then she would be able to get something to drink. But she had to go on; she had to find her father and half expected him to jump out at her from behind a tree, to tell her everything would be all right, that it was only a joke. But she was alone in the forest. The path began to get steeper.

At first she barely noticed the smell of wood smoke: it merged with the scents of dripping vegetation and sodden soil. Then it became stronger and she knew she must be near the village. Excitement at the prospect of seeing her father; his surprise, his delight at her independence; gave her a renewed energy. She picked up speed, jumping over boulders, leaping over the strange lettuce-like growths that protruded from tree roots. Voices drifted towards her; they sounded angry, as if they were shouting commands. She trod more carefully, slowing down again. As she neared and saw the smoke drifting high into the canopy, she realised the voices were Chinese. Puzzled, she stopped and listened. Her father had told her this was where the native Malays lived, not the Chinese. As she arrived at the top of an incline, the voices faded away into the jungle and she heard the sound of heavy feet running into the distance. The shouting was replaced by the silence of before. She started downhill. Thatched roofs rose through the trees; she saw houses on stilts surrounding a fire. It hissed and spluttered with smoke wavering, meandering in gentle air currents. Two men in red and orange sarongs poked at the flames. It was just as she imagined, a homely scene with the meal cooked on an open fire. Her mouth started to water as she smelt the roasted meat. Her stomach growled. Hunger, forgotten before, produced sudden longings for a roast dinner: potatoes and Yorkshire pudding, thick gravy with apple sauce. She licked her lips. But, she should not be there. What would these villagers think of her snooping around? Her father had been right.

Maybe his car was parked there for a different reason. Had it broken down. Did he walk to find help? Why had she not considered that as a possibility before?

Apprehension made her falter, uncertain whether to go on. She gazed ahead. A curtain of smoke in front of her cleared and her father came into view. He looked up and she saw his dishevelled hair, his shirt dirty and torn. He stared at her without moving. Not even a wave. Surely he was not cross with her? It was then she saw the ropes.

"Daddy," she called out. Her throat contracted. "Daddy," she yelled again.

She ran down the slope. Her eyes fixed on the sight of her father lashed to a tree, dirt smeared across his face. Blood was everywhere, on the ground, staining the grass, colouring a man's sarong as he freed her father from the ropes.

Her father came towards her, his arms outstretched, his palms turned upwards. There was a thin line of blood down his cheek. Putting her hand to her mouth, she tried to scream. No sound came, her voice was paralysed, her tongue stuck to the roof of her mouth. She saw him wipe his face with his shirt sleeve before a fog came across her vision, before she felt herself falling, collapsing like a tent in the wind. His voice was familiar but the sound was wavering, a distant rumble, floating away, then back. Just like in a dream, the thatched houses wavered and swung, they merged with trees and sunlight, with spots which played in front of her eyes.

"Susan. Are you all right?" Her father was turning her over, rubbing her cheek.

She was lifted high above the ground. Her face was turned upwards and she opened her eyes: trees revolved round her as she was carried, her legs loose, flapping while the sky peeped through the canopy, clear and shining. A rose-coloured cloud was tearing itself apart in the blue and the moon was bright, almost as bright as the dipping sun.

"Susan." Her father's voice.

"Drink this." He was holding her, putting a cup to her mouth. She could see the hair poking through the top of his shirt as he leaned over her. Trickles of sweat, grey with dust stained his neck where his shirt was unbuttoned. A cut on his cheekbone was black where the blood had congealed and dried in the heat. The water was cold. She looked around her, at the brown faces crowding, at the dying fire, the red embers glowing. An acrid smell, sickly and dense filled the air. Her eyes became heavy, she wanted to sleep, but she forced them to stay open. Her father was speaking to her. His voice still sounded faraway, fading then returning. A bloody object caught her eye. Flies were buzzing and swooping on a butchered goat's head, settling on its jaw, its bloody face. One eye was turned into the dust, the other open, glowering at red-stained hen feathers scattered on the ground nearby. A man picked up the head, threw it onto the fire; the flames soared, orange and angry, spitting sparks towards her. Instinctively, she jerked her head away, saw a white woman sitting on the ground, hugging her knees. There was dirt on her blue dress, staining the rumpled skirt, and ropes were being loosened from round her waist, by a native woman. Her father's face was close to Susan's his breathing short and rasping. She sat upright, tried to stand again.

"What's happened? Daddy? What? Tell me?"

Her father had his arm round her.

"How long was she there?" she heard him ask someone. "Did you see her when the Chinese were here?"

"I see her come through the trees." A boy was standing in front of her.

159

Susan started to sob uncontrollably.

Her father gripped her shoulders. "Shh," he whispered as he cradled her head in his arms. He lifted her face. "Did they harm you? Susan, did you see them, the Chinese? We must get you away from here. They didn't harm you, did they?" he asked again.

"I saw your car," she heard herself say. She tried to stand, but her legs folded, containing a will of their own.

The top of Susan's arm was nudged, and the boy held half a coconut out to her. The white flesh looked succulent, but she moved away until her father, crouching next to her, putting his arm round her, holding her firmly, put the coconut to her lips. "Drink," he said. "Drink. Good for you."

The boy moved nearer to her. "No, don't touch me," she scream-ed. This time she managed to stand. She had to escape. She shoved her father away with her fist and began to run. She had to get away, escape.

Everyone was shouting, yelling at her to come back. Somebody grabbed her shoulder. It was the boy again.

She fought him, kicking, spitting, biting his hand. "Leave me alone," she yelled. "Daddy get him off me."

But the boy held on. "No go out there." He waved with his hand beyond, pointing to where the jungle was dense beyond the village, in the other direction from where she had come.

"That's enough," her father said. He grabbed Susan's arm, pulled her away from the boy's grasp. "Don't you think you've done enough?" He started to walk away from him. "We're going home *now*, Susan."

She saw him glance back at the boy as he led her away. "We trusted you all," he called over his shoulder. "We were your friends. How could you side with those bullies?"

The boy darted away, climbed the steps up to a house. Halfway, he turned round and looked at Susan for a minute then disappeared inside.

"Come on, Sarah." her father said to the woman. "We must go. Now." He started to make for the path.

Soon, the village was behind them and they were back in the thick of the trees. He tugged at Susan's hand, hauling her along, half-dragging her, ignoring her stumbles on slippery rocks, pulling at her arm with such ferocity she felt it would dislodge from the socket. The sunlight was vanishing fast and sometimes she could not see where she was putting her feet, but she could hear the sniffs from the woman as she followed, close behind. Susan whimpered. Her legs were trembling so much; it was difficult to climb through the forest, back over the tree roots, through clinging creepers catching at her hair.

"Come on," her father hissed when she slowed, exhausted, almost too weak to be frightened, to care anymore.

He was glancing back at the woman who had stopped, eyes wide open, hand clamped to her mouth. There was a noise to Susan's left, of a branch falling and she felt her father's grip tighten. She half-ran to keep up with him, heard the panting of the woman close behind. Gradually, the overhanging canopy thinned then they were out in the open; a large red sun was sitting on the horizon.

The car was parked where she had first seen it. Her father fumbled in his pockets for his keys, opened the passenger door for her, helped her in, bent and kissed her on her cheek. She could see the blood from his cut, smell his breath, familiar, homely, of tobacco and

161

aftershave, reminding her of bedtime stories from long ago. The woman got into the back seat. The car jolted into action. He drove with both hands gripping the wheel, his eyes flicking between the road and her. Frequently, he searched to the right, then to the left, over his shoulder, driving faster and faster.

"You all right?" he asked. "Be home soon." A glance in her direction. His breathing was noisy. "No one behind us is there, Sarah? Is there?" he repeated when she did not answer immediately.

"No," the woman said. "Can you drive faster?"

He did not reply, but the car sped along the road, screeching as they rounded a bend. "Be home soon," he said again to Susan. The only noise was the accelerating engine, no more talk; they continued in silence. The sky had darkened, as if a blind had been pulled down.

She closed her eyes, but the images of the village returned. So she stared out through the window. Trees and bushes rushed past her, some shapes tall and looming, others squat, their branches reaching out and scraping the car. Above her, a curved moon hung, lighting a patch in the sky. As she fixed on it, she tried to dispel the images in her head.

She felt sick and told her father to stop the car. The woman got out with her and stroked her back, making cooing sounds as Susan strained and threw up on the grassy verge. Refusing the woman's hand to help her into the car, Susan slammed her door shut. Her right leg was juddering. She held it down with her hand. But it kept on twitching and shaking, her heel hammering on the floor of the car.

"Who were those men?" she burst out suddenly. "And why had they tied you up? Why did they cut your face?"

"The villagers were sympathisers." It was the woman who answered. "Maybe we should have realised. But the boy..." she broke off. Susan could hear the break in her breath, as if she were trying not to cry.

Her father glanced at Susan. "I'll explain later. At home."

But there was an uncertain tone to his voice and she did not believe him; he was a liar. Her father would lie to her as he had done before.

She stared at the road in front of them, at the tunnels of light from the car headlights. Her jaws were clamped tight to stop her teeth chattering. She felt in her pocket for the Buddha, wrapping her fingers round it. She wanted to be with her mother. She wanted to go back home to England.

She closed her eyes; thoughts and questions revolved in her head. Pictures of her father, dried blood on his shirt, terror marking his face, flashed in her mind. Nausea rippled through her. The rumble of the engine stopped and she forced her eyes open.

"Where are we?" she asked. They had stopped at a wide gate, a palm tree stood at either side dwarfing the railings; an eerie light silhouetted the fronds.

Her father opened his door. "Just a minute, Susan," he said. "We'll be home soon." Hurriedly, he swung the gate open, drove onto bumpy ground, stopped again in front of a long building. She recognised the sign above the door at the front, illuminated in a glow that came from inside. This was where her father worked.

The back door of the car opened; she heard the woman get out, close the door, felt her presence at her father's window. Susan did not want to look up, acknowledge that she had seen her, have to say goodbye.

"I'll go to the police tomorrow. First thing," she heard her father say, then he turned to Susan, rested his hand on her knee. "Two ticks," he said to Susan. He went to open the door, hesitated, as if uncertain what to do next. "I'll wait until you're in your car. I'll watch you," he said in a low voice. "I don't want to leave Susan alone in the car."

The woman said something that Susan could not catch and she snatched a look at her, noticed her face shiny with tears, glistening in the low light. Susan stared out of her window, heard the woman's footsteps as she ran towards a car nearby. A light went out in one of the offices on the ground floor, she looked up and saw a figure appearing in the doorway to the building.

"Hey, George," the man shouted. "George, had you forgotten?"

"Damn and blast," her father muttered. "I'd forgotten about Henry."

Mr Golding poked his head through her window and Susan heard another car door slam shut nearby. "Oh, hello," he said to Susan. "Nice to meet you again. Are you all right? You look very pale."

She did not answer, but she turned to her father. "I want to go home."

"Get in, Henry. Please. Be quick," her father said.

The man glanced over towards the other car, with the woman in front, barely visible in the muted light; its engine stuttered and choked before turning round, tail lights glowing. Susan saw the man look across at her father, raise his eyebrows.

"You're later than I expected," he said. "Everyone else has gone home."

"Come on. Get in," her father said.

As soon as the door was shut, he accelerated into the road. "I must get Susan home. And Dorothy will be at her wit's end."

Chapter 17

The hum of the cicadas was becoming louder, like the crescendo of an orchestra as it reaches the finale. Perhaps a storm was preparing, gathering moisture into huge rain clouds, their darkness encouraged by nightfall. Dorothy was staring up at the sky, watching the moon as it became lost, fading into mist. Night time appeared so suddenly there, without warning; without the preparation of twilight, or a slow lowering sun.

Still there was no sign of Susan and Feng; they were hours late now. Surely Feng realised how concerned she would be, even if they were having fun, bartering, then slowly returning, idling along, chit-chattering, not caring about her, not considering, not realising the time. But, although Susan was quite capable of delay, especially in her rebellious mood of that morning, it was not in Feng's character; she was duty-bound, calculating in her every move.

Dorothy came in from the veranda, stared at the clock, started to pace the room. Moving swiftly, she walked through the hall into the dining room and lifted the blinds as a shiver passed through her, running up her spine, the back of her head; her hair feeling as if it were standing on end. Upstairs, she wandered into Susan's room, casting her eyes round, as if she were looking for clues. But there were only heaps of clothes, abandoned on the chair, disrespectful in their untidy heap, and the ticking of Susan's clock on her bedside table. Holding Susan's dress to her face, she inhaled deeply. Where was she? Where was her little girl? Something had happened to her, she knew it, felt the truth sink into her, as blotting paper soaks up ink.

Through the open door, she heard a key turning in the front door.

"Madam, Madam," Feng called.

Dorothy ran to the top of the stairs, looked down at Feng, waited expectantly for Susan's voice to call to her. But there was only one figure standing in the hall.

"Where's Susan?" she said. Running down the stairs, she looked beyond Feng, to the front door. It was shut.

"She not here?"

The question seemed ridiculous. Why did Feng think Susan was here? Perhaps she had misheard, misunderstood the amah. "Of course she's not." Her heart beat fast, breath captured in her lungs "What are you talking about?"

"She run off." Feng frowned.

"Ran off? Where to?"

"I look for her everywhere. Maybe she see friend in market. Maybe she with friend now."

"What friend? She doesn't have any friends here. What are you talking about?" She was aware that her voice was shrill, the volume moving out of control.

"I thought she here." Eyes narrowed, her face turned to a frown.

"I told you to look after her." Dorothy stood face to face with Feng. "What have you done with her?"

"I go back."

"Go and find her. If you can't, go to the police." She was shouting while she squeezed her hands together and the nails dug into her flesh. She wanted to scream, to beat Feng's chest with her fists. She flung the front door open. "Now," she said. "Go and find her." Suddenly, she stopped, turned to look at Feng. "I told you to keep an eye on her. I warned you what she can be like." She fought an impulse to shove Feng down the steps.

"I find her now." Feng put her hand on Dorothy's arm. "I very sorry, but I find her now." She started to hurry along the path.

Dorothy watched her.

At the gate, Feng turned to Dorothy. "Not worry, Mrs Johnson. I bring her back now."

"You do that."

Dorothy thought how easy it would be for Susan to get lost in the market, to merge into the pressing crowd and become part of the noisy swell. Could Feng possibly have a harsher side, kept hidden from Dorothy? Did she have friends, or was there a family connection with the Chinese Terrorists? But what about the herbal remedies, her pleasing companionship, the forays on her behalf to the market? Surely all this was not a front for a more sinister motive?

Was Feng to be trusted? Susan would be frightened on her own.

Pacing the sitting room, she wound her amber beads round her wrist, pulling at the string. She must go and find her. Grabbing a scarf, she threw it over her head and ran down the front steps, through the gate and into the street.

The poor street lighting disorientated Dorothy, and she could not remember which way to turn for the direction of the market. She looked to the left, then right. Which way? In the distance a dog barked. Decision made, she stepped right, anxiety mounting as she saw images of Susan, tears dribbling down her face, trying to find her way home, or worse, lying injured, in a street, a victim of an attack, left there to suffer and agonize alone.

She broke into a run, passing other expatriate homes she had not visited; she should have taken up the coffee morning offers, for now

167

she needed some comfort, a demonstration of hope from someone familiar. Unused to running, she slowed, to regain her breath. But there was no time for dawdling; she set off again at a fast walking pace. Voices meandered across the lawns and through open windows: Laughter, English chatter, she imagined discussions, about the weather, or the latest office gossip, perhaps news from home, the conversations ordinary, so uncomplicated. She turned a corner. Was this the route to the market? Unsure, she looked around her, trying to remember which road to take. Fifteen minutes must have passed since she left the house; it would be foolhardy, pointless if she were to get lost, if Susan returned to an empty house. Dorothy ran back, panting in the sticky heat, unaware of the rain which had started to drench her dress.

She arrived home, the house was lit up, car in the drive, engine still popping, doors left swung open as if it had been deserted in an emergency.

Susan was standing in the doorway with George's arm round her. He looked up at Dorothy quickly, as if startled.

"Dorothy," he said. "I didn't know where you were... thought for a minute... Christ. It's good to be home."

"Where have you been?" she asked Susan. Then to George "Why is she with you? What's going on?"

Susan was shivering, teeth chattering, her expression fixed, mask-like as though trying to control the involuntary movements of her jaw. She staggered from George's hold, down the steps towards her and Dorothy saw leaves in her hair, her dress smeared with dirt, her face so pale, almost diaphanous.

She threw herself at Dorothy, into her arms. Sobs kept breaking out from deep in her chest. Dorothy, bewildered, hung onto her. She stroked Susan's neck as she buried her head under her chin, just as she used to when she was small. She soothed her, trying to make her more tranquil, half-carrying her back into the house. Susan was mumbling incoherently, moaning, clinging on to Dorothy as she shook. But no tears were shed. Every nerve in Dorothy's body was alert, tingling, ready for action against the person who was responsible for whatever had happened, as she whispered into Susan's ear, told her to be calm, that nothing would harm her. She kissed Susan on her hair. It smelt of bonfires and the lemon shampoo she used. They all trooped through to the hall.

"Susan," she said and looked at George. "You must tell me. Who's done this to you?" She felt dizzy with terror. "Thank God you're safe. I was so worried..." She saw for the first time, the cut across George's cheek, making the rest of his face look drained of colour, the tan faded, a puffiness concealing the Roman-like features.

"Will somebody tell me what's going on" she said. Immediately, she regretted her raised voice when she felt Susan go rigid in her arms as she started to cry.

Then she saw Henry, behind George; he must have been in the dining room and she remembered the invite. Had he been in there waiting patiently for the promised dinner? But his face was stern, his body stiff as he walked into the hall and stood before her, stifling a cough, then staring down at his shoes. But no one was talking; it was as if whatever had happened had removed the power of speech from them all.

George's touch startled her as he steered both her and Susan into the sitting room. "I'll explain," he said. "Need a drink first." He gripped her shoulder tighter than usual, alarming her even more, then let his arm drop loose to his side when he had guided them towards the sofa near the veranda. He poured three whiskies out, picked one up and folded himself carefully into the chair opposite the sofa.

169

Henry hesitated at the door. "Won't stay long," he said. "Just wanted to make sure they got back all right." He was looking directly at Dorothy as he spoke.

She returned his stare for a second, recalling her longings of the morning. She lowered her eyes, then directed her gaze towards Susan.

"Susan," she said. "Please. Where have you been? What's happened?"

"I didn't mean it," she said. "I was only…" she stopped and drew away, sat slightly apart, ignoring Dorothy's attempt to keep her close. "I just wanted to look around on my own." She was holding herself upright, hands folded on her lap, with her eyes fixed on to the night beyond, out past the veranda, her mood, changed so quickly from the neediness of before. "I didn't mean to go all that way."

She grabbed Susan's hand. "Where didn't you mean to go?" She looked up at George then to Henry who was standing, his hands in his pocket, jangling change. "What the bloody hell is going on?"

George looked up sharply and Henry left the room, murmuring his apologies, his goodbyes. The front door closed softly just as a cloudburst descended.

"I was visiting the…" George started, then pulled a packet of cigarettes from his pocket. His hand was shaking as he lit one. "Just a minute," he said. "I was just…" he said again, then looked over to Susan. "Christ, I don't know where to start. I had no idea that Susan… It was awful, Dorothy, terrible. You've no idea…" He stopped speaking, put his hand to his head.

"What was?" She thumped her knee.

His feet played with the rug, turning the fringe over, pulling it back. "I was visiting a young boy, I told you about him…" He took

170

three drags of his cigarette, no pause in-between, then noisily exhaled a cloud of smoke towards the ceiling. "In that village. They came out of nowhere and attacked." Now he was holding his stomach. "The Communists. I had no idea," He slid his eyes over to the corner of the room, groaning, holding his stomach. "I feel sick."

She heard Susan sniff, saw her wipe her face with the back of her hand. Dorothy pointed her finger at George.

"What did they do to Susan?"

"Nothing," he said. "Nobody touched her."

"I don't believe you. Look at her." She was yelling at him now. "I don't believe you. Tell me what happened."

"It's true, Mummy. They didn't know I was there." Susan said. Her tone was one level, robotic. "They'd captured Daddy. There was a huge fire." Her shoulders began to shake, her face screwed up and tight. "Then a boy tried to give me some coconut..."

"Who?" Dorothy's breathing became rapid, her vision more acute: every object in the room was brighter, the hues more vivid "Why? What are you talking about?" She stared across the room at George. "What does she mean?" She pulled Susan to her, burying her face in her daughter's hair. But Susan sidled away from her again, squashed into the end of the sofa, and resumed staring out into the garden. Dorothy was bereft; as if she was being deprived of the last glimmer of light.

George was mopping his face with a handkerchief. "I had no idea you'd be there." He put his hands together as if he were praying, banged them against his head. "Thank God you didn't come earlier. I'd have never forgiven myself. Never. But the boy meant no harm." He reached over towards Susan, slowly, but she did not make any sign that she wanted his touch; he withdrew his hand from where it had been hanging mid-air and let it flop on the arm of the chair. "The Malays. The villagers. They were sympathisers. Giving food to the Chinese, the Communists, the guerrillas. We didn't know, had no idea, they seemed so kind, peaceful." Rubbing his eye with a fist, he paused. "I thought they were going to kill us, the Chinese tied us to a tree, put guns to our heads. They had bayonets, knives..." He touched the wound on his cheek. "Then Susan arrived. After the Communists had fled back into the jungle. I think the Malays stopped them killing us..."

"No more. I don't want to hear any more." Dorothy clamped her hands to her head.

But George continued, his voice now steady, under control. Relentlessly, he went on, as if he were practising the recall of memory for the police, or maybe he needed to re-enact the events for cathartic reasons. He lifted himself off the chair and described how they had been visiting a boy called Rafi in the Malay village. "The Chinese told us they would kill us. Running Dogs they said we were. I honestly thought we would be thrown on the fire too." A shaking hand was run through his hair. "Then Susan appeared, just as the Chinese had left. You just appeared out of nowhere." He gripped his whisky glass, knuckles white, then sat back. "Luckily you didn't see the worst. Only what they'd left, after they'd gone."

A coldness spread through Dorothy. "You said *we*. Who else were you with?" she asked. She repeated the question, noticed Susan clenching and unclenching her fists as she stared straight ahead. So Susan knew something. She was protecting her father, keeping the truth from her, her mother. Suddenly, she felt heavy, listless. Rain was slashing at the windows. An earthy smell of composting vegetation slithered in from the garden. She leant forward, waited for him to reply, watching him, recognising the spontaneous twitching of his left eye. He glanced towards Susan, made a miniscule movement of his head. Was he only just realising the reference he had made to the other person he was with? Susan, she saw, out of the outer edge of her eye, sitting very still, her breath quiet, as if she were holding it. She was watching her father. The whirr of a mosquito close to Dorothy's ear got louder, more insistent.

George ran his tongue across his lips, then finished his whisky. In a quiet voice, he said, "I was with Sarah. You met her once. It was her idea to visit the village, to see the boy, Rafi, who…"

But Dorothy did not want to hear anymore. Taking Susan's hand firmly, she led her upstairs and ran a bath for her. Chattering lightly, she emptied the entire packet of bath salts into the steaming water. She talked all the time, though what subjects she touched on, she was mostly unaware. Maybe she spoke of the ruined dinner congealing on the cold slab in the larder, or the absence of Matilda and her daughter Jennifer. Were they both ill? Or was there a different, less worrying reason for them not visiting that evening? She should have enquired of Henry. And what had happened to Feng?

"Mummy. Stop," Susan half screamed, and she slammed the bathroom door.

Dorothy stood for a while on the landing. The lock on the bathroom door clicked into place and she heard the slopping of water, the echo of Susan's sneeze round the tiled room. She knocked on the door, pleaded with Susan to allow her in.

"Go away."

Abruptly, Dorothy turned round and headed across the landing.

Singing softly to herself, Dorothy sat on the balcony of her bedroom and stared out across the garden. She rocked in her chair and slipped her new bracelet up her arm as far as it would go, then downwards to her wrist bone. The action was repeated at an increasing pace again, then again. Thunder was booming in the far distance and an occasional slash of lightning illuminated the hills on the horizon.

Chapter 18

The wind was bending the jacaranda tree, sending its blossom across the garden like unruly confetti. A branch staggered across the lawn, bouncing, twitching in blasts of air as it lay on the ground. Susan had her nose pressed to the glass in the door. A rattan chair blew over onto its side then clattered down the steps. She opened the door, just a fraction; she wanted a clearer view of the storm. A palm tree shook and swayed. Gusts whistled and thumped around the house. There was a bang from the end of the garden as a pot blew over and crashed onto the path.

"Susan, don't, there's a terrible draught."

She closed the door gently. Her mother was playing cards. With tears in her eyes, Susan watched her. She wanted everything to be normal again. She wanted comfort from her mother. But she maintained such an ordered presence; the dealing of cards, clicking them into suits, her actions precise, meticulous. Another crash drew Susan's eyes back to the garden, but her mother remained still, unperturbed by the violent Sumatra.

"Do you know?" said her mother, "I'm actually cold. Most extraordinary." She looked at Susan, smiled. "Be a dear and get my shawl." She added a card to a line, turned another one over. Ace of hearts. "I'm winning" she said. "Look." She turned her face towards Susan, pulled out a card from the set in her hand. She stopped the movement in mid-air. "You've got more colour in your face today," she said. "But you need to eat more. Help you get your strength back."

Susan looked at her mother's lips, pinched together in silence as she concentrated on her hand. She saw the plaster wound round her finger. She recalled the row. She saw her mother throwing the ashtray at her father, remembered the hush after the smash of glass.

"Susan, I thought you were at the library with Feng?" her father had said when he saw her standing on the veranda, looking on. "Go to your room." It was as Susan turned at the door she saw her mother crouching to pick up glass fragments, splinters from the shattered mirror. But Susan had heard it all, and now she understood even less.

"What are you going to do about that woman?" Susan blurted out.

Her mother put her hand to her head. A squall of wind blasted the house and the door to the veranda swung open. The cards scattered, blowing this way and that, landing without order on the rug, the floor.

"Now look what's happened." Her mother got up and slammed the door shut.

Kicking at the edge of the rug Susan listened to the wind rebelling against the house, trying to disrupt the afternoon. Her mother was shuffling the cards, her fingers expertly playing the pack.

"Now then. Let's start again," said her mother as she dealt the cards out, deliberately, slowly. "You must try not to worry. The police will put them away or deport the terrorists." She took Susan's hand, stroked her fingers. "They won't be allowed to go free." She looked up at Susan. "And you, just a child having to see what they did to your father... But I'm glad you're not dwelling on it too much. You have to put it out of your mind or you'll make yourself ill. And the police will deal with them."

She noticed her mother's eyes were pinkish, a little swollen round the edges. Everyone shed tears in this house now, but they were hidden, spilt in secret, concealing a conspiracy. Like her father creeping to the bathroom last night, stifling his cries, the wretched sobs, making her curl into a ball, cover her ears with her pillow.

"I still have nightmares," said Susan.

"They'll stop in time."

"I'll go and get your shawl."

"If only you'd stayed close to Feng."

"I didn't mean to. Not completely lose her." How many times had she re-routed her steps, turned back to the market to find Feng? Biting off a shard of her nail, she watched the blood slowly ooze from the tear. It tasted metallic: the flow was reassuring. And if she had returned to the market, or if she had not run off in the first place... her mind drifted, making up scenarios, concocting events. She left the room and went up the staircase. She trod lightly, straining her ears in case Feng came out into the hall. She wanted to renew their friendship, but Feng avoided her, spoke only when spoken to; it was clear she was still angry with her. Susan heard the clatter of saucepans from behind the kitchen door, and a smell of treacle slid into the air. A sense of homeliness brought solace, reminded her of the preparation of cake tins and biscuit trays in readiness for a baking session.

She fetched her mother's shawl and returned downstairs. Now, there was no sound from the kitchen. Her mother's cards lay on the table; her hands were clasped on her lap, as she dozed in a pool of light with the miniature Buddha looking on. The time Susan had spent picking it out, filtering it from the other more opulent and garish carvings felt like another era, a previous existence.

The wind had dropped now. It was as if it had never been. The sun was bright, and the sweat started to dribble down her back again; insects droned, singing in the solid heat. She draped the shawl over a chair, so the dragon would face her mother when she woke.

177

"Going to the market. Buy fish."

Susan had not heard Feng come in. She swung round to face her. "I hope," she began. "I didn't mean to get you into trouble…"

"Shh," Feng said and nodded towards the form of her mother, leant her head sideways on two hands, mimicking her mother's gentle slumber, and left. The front door clicked behind her. Susan glanced over towards her mother, at the empty whisky glass, the mark of pink lipstick imprinted on the side. She stepped out onto the veranda and down the steps into the garden. Someone was playing *Rock Around the Clock.* A sudden longing for Carol to be there, hit her, totally unawares. She wanted to talk to her, giggle in helpless waves, listen to her advice, for she would know what Susan should do next. There was a whoop of laughter from the neighbour's house before *Rock around the Clock* finished; it was not replaced with another song. The air hummed instead. Images of the week before flashed again through her mind as she stood under the jacaranda tree and waited, though for what she was not sure. Eventually, she made her way back to the house. Would she be able to talk to her mother now? As she entered the sitting room, she saw her, head rolled to one side, her mouth slightly open. Susan bent over her mother's face. Fast asleep.

The study door was open. Sitting down at the desk, she picked up the paper knife. It was really just like a sword, with its fancy shamrock handle. She prodded the back of her hand with it, slowly, gently at first, before she pressed harder, then pulled it away. She pushed the knife in harder, whipped it away when it started to hurt, when she knew it was about to pierce her flesh.

Opening the desk drawer, she lifted papers and pens, lined them up on the desk, carefully searched through sheets of Basildon Bond notepaper. Every page was blank, except for the blotter with its hundreds of mirrored images of her father's curled writing. She recognised the bundle of brown envelopes from her father's London job. Creeping to the door, she opened it as quietly as possible, biting her lip at the whine of its hinges. Her mother's soft snores were just audible, in matching time to the ticking of the clock.

The first letter was about travel arrangements to get to Malaya, with lists and counter-lists. And she was just about to discard the next one when the word *daughter* caught her eye:

I am sorry to hear about your daughter's bad reaction to your posting abroad, and your wife's illness, but I am not able to delay your transfer. Your position here has already been filled with a young man who is eager to get on. It is a pity your wife and daughter have to suffer so much for your actions. It is even more of a pity you didn't think of this before interfering with my daughter, my precious Emma.

Yours sincerely

D. Moorcroft

"Emma," she said out loud. What bad reaction? When was her mother ill? Susan reread it: *It is even more of a pity you didn't think of this before interfering with my daughter, my precious Emma.*

Susan could feel her face flushing. A finger was lifted to her mouth; she nibbled on a nail, as she tried to work out the meaning of the letter. A posting to Malaya would be good for her father's career prospects, her mother had explained, the morning after she had first told her: she remembered her father gazing at the Christmas tree as he whistled through his teeth.

Susan folded the letter into four and put it in her pocket.

"Susan," Dorothy called out from the sitting room. "Where are you?"

Closing the study door softly behind her, Susan stood in the hall, called to her mother.

"There you are." Her mother stood in the sitting room doorway, hands on hips, hair askew.

Susan swallowed twice. Her mouth was dry. She had difficulty forming words. As if she had suddenly developed a stutter, or been struck dumb she stumbled over the question. "Why did you and Daddy move out here?" She saw her mother frown, her face change colour slightly.

Flicking at something on her skirt, her mother said, "That's all been explained to you. Why are you suddenly asking me, now? I told you, your father was promoted." She glanced over at the study door.

She felt her mother's arm brush against hers as she hurriedly walked past her. She followed her into the sitting room. Standing with the back of her legs against the sofa, Susan felt the coolness of the leatherette. "So who's Emma?" she asked.

"What?"

"Emma. Who's Emma?"

"What are you talking about?" Dorothy put her hand to her face. "What on earth are you talking about?" she repeated.

"Mummy, I just want to know who Emma is." She spoke fast.

"Susan, I'm sorry but I don't know who you're talking about. You're getting all worked up again. Come and sit with me. I'll make us some tea in a minute."

Susan looked up at the broken mirror, at the decanter with half an inch of sherry. She followed her mother onto the veranda, picked up a chair thrown on its side by the wind.

"You must try and calm yourself. You had a dreadful shock last week. I worry about you so much." Dorothy touched Susan's hair, pushed a lock back from her forehead. "Everything will be fine."

"I hate it when you and Daddy don't tell me everything." Susan picked up a playing card and rolled it into a tube. "I saw her before, you know. I saw that woman before with Daddy."

"What woman?"

"The Sarah woman. I saw her with Daddy. Where he works. I saw her when he took me to his office."

"And?"

"Who's Emma?" Susan persisted. "Tell me who Emma is."

Dorothy grabbed her wrist. "No, you tell me." She tightened her grip around Susan's hand.

"Let go, you're hurting me."

"So what if Sarah was at his work? So what? Why are you telling me?"

Susan pulled her wrist away. Straightening out the playing card, she replaced it on the table, in line with its suit. "It wasn't right, that's all. The way she touched him on the cheek. Then when I saw her..." She rubbed her wrist, looked at her mother accusingly.

"Go on."

"He'd been to that village... with her before." She hesitated. "He told me about the car accident."

"He told me about that when it happened a few months ago." Shrugging her shoulders, her mother stared out down the garden. "I don't know why you're telling me all this."

She went indoors and Susan heard the plop of a bottle being opened, the glug of sherry topping up the glass. Susan massaged her wrist again, watched a beetle crawl across the floor of the veranda and disappear down a crack. She picked up her mother's book from

181

where it had fallen before, put it on her chair. Glancing over her shoulder, she could see her mother rocking, as she dealt out from another pack of cards onto the table in front of her. Susan went down the steps and into the garden, stood under the jacaranda tree. Strains of rock and roll drifted from the neighbouring house.

"Susan," her mother called out. "I want to ask you something." Her arm was outstretched, beckoning. "When you first saw your father with that woman," she said. "What happened?"

Susan slowly moved towards her mother. "Nothing, but..." How could she explain? "It was just the way she looked at him, and held onto him. For too long. And then..." She remembered the woman reaching out to her father as they left the village. "It's just the way she was with him."

It was as her mother bent and kissed her, that Susan regretted the illicit foraging in her father's study. Better that she had left things as they were. Now there would be more arguments late into the night. Taking Susan's wrist in her hand, gently, her mother slid her thumb over the mark she had made earlier. "Shall we have a cup of tea?" she asked. "I'll make it. You sit here." She pointed to her chair and removed the book from the seat. "And I'll tell you about your father."

She watched her mother as she stood in front of the broken mirror to retouch her lipstick and comb her hair. Looking upwards at the sky, Susan saw a flock of yellow-tipped birds making their way higher and higher into the blue.

***

Susan's mother came into her bedroom.

"Aren't you dressed yet?" she said in a whisper. She tapped her watch. "Five minutes. We have to leave now."

182

Bed covers thrown back, Susan stretched her arms above her head, groaned and turned over. She tried to recapture her dream, but it had fragmented, dispersed, gone for ever. She kept her eyes tight shut, willing it to return, then heard the blinds rattle as her mother raised them. She opened her eyes. It was still dark, far too early to get up. Her mother's lips, cool, smooth on her cheek, brushed her gently, then she pulled back the bed sheet, told her again to hurry, that they had to go. Then she left, her dress rustling in the quiet.

Still trying to catch her dream, Susan dressed, choosing her coral skirt with the large wide belt and a matching white blouse. She sat at the dressing table, combed her hair, weaving it into one thick plait that she threw over her shoulder in a nonchalant fashion. She thought of what her mother had told her the day before about the Emma woman, about the real reason for them coming out here.

The door handle turned and her mother was standing there again. Susan noticed her hair remained unbrushed, the curls damp, flattened against her scalp. A tortoiseshell comb had been shoved into the side, tugging her hair away from her temple.

She took Susan's arm. "Let's go. Now."

She closed the door behind them and looked across the landing, put her finger to her lips. Hesitating, drawing her arm away from her mother, Susan remained on the top step, uncertain. She heard a cough from the direction of her father's room, then a sigh of a spring in his bed as he turned over. If she strained her ears, she could just make out the whistle on his breath.

"I want to say goodbye…"

"Shh," Dorothy interrupted. She beckoned Susan down the stairs. "We have no time. Come on."

Slowly, Susan descended the stairs behind her mother. Halfway down, she stopped, looked behind her, then remembered the letter

183

she had found, her mother's tears as she related the affair. She reached the bottom of the stairs, saw Feng with a small case at her feet. She wore a grey dress; it made her look older, more severe, like the Chinese women she had seen guarding the temples, polishing the gold. Feng nodded to Susan and opened the door, guiding her down the steps as though she were blind.

The sun was just starting to rise now, the sky pink like the flamingos she had seen in London Zoo. And the air was fresh, with a keen silence which hung over the resting trees and clung to the bright petals of the cannas. The crunching of her feet on the stones made Susan feel like a thief leaving the house, trying not to disturb the sleeping occupants. Feng followed behind Susan, her tiny feet treading more lightly on the coarse gravel.

"Best you get into the back, Susan," her mother said as she opened the car door. Then in a softer voice. "Feng knows the way."

Her mother was breathing quickly, making little sounds like a trapped animal as she started the car. She turned and looked at Feng.

"No bad men here," Feng said. "They stay in jungle." She swept her arm in an arc. Not here. Not now."

Bad men? Is that what she called them? Men who left rope marks on her father's wrists? And Feng called them bad men, as if they were the culprits in one of those Westerns she used to watch on wet Sunday afternoons at Carol's. The images returned again, and she threw them out, tugging at a thread on the seat.

"Are we coming back?" she asked. "Won't Daddy need his car for work?" Maybe she could talk her mother into turning the car round, and making it all up with him. Instead of running away, not facing up to problems, as she had always told Susan she should do.

"He can get a lift in," her mother said. "From Henry." And she said the word 'Henry' in a kinder tone, a softer note.

"How long are we going for?" Then in a louder voice. "When are we coming back?"

But Feng and Dorothy were talking together now, excluding her. Although she tried, Susan could not hear the words over the motor. She repeated her question, tugged at the loose thread, wound it round and round her hand. It broke, ripped free of the leather, fraying at one end. Feng and her mother still chatted, their voices low, deliberately hushed. She looked out through her window as she sucked and chewed on the worn thread.

The sun was higher in the sky, the pinkness had disappeared, replaced by a deep blue with streaks the colour of sherbet. A tall man carrying a pair of shears came into Susan's view. The car slowed down and he crossed the road, glancing towards them. He looked like Babiya, face criss-crossed with furrows and lines, deep, encrusted, like the footprints of tiny birds across sand. Her father would not be totally alone, Babiya would be some company. She thought of him, sitting alone at his single place setting, waiting for them to return, Babiya's mournful singing painting a backdrop to his sorrow.

Her mother turned so that her profile was visible to Susan. "To answer your question," she said. "I'm not sure how long we're going for, but you'll like it there. Where we're going."

"But where? Where is it we're going? You never tell me anything. It's not fair." She thumped her seat with her fist.

"Stop that right now." Her mother pulled up at the side of the road. Taking her hands off the wheel she pressed them together. "I think you're the guilty party when it comes to not telling, Susan." She released her hands from their lock, and Susan noticed how much they trembled as she slipped her wedding ring over the knuckle and back again. "You must try to understand. I just need to get away for a while. To think. You know everything that's happened now. Everything. You're old enough to understand," she said, turning round. Touching the top of Susan's head, she smoothed a lock of hair, tucked it into place. "You'll like where we're going," she said. "Away from all this."

Swallowing hard, Susan apologised. So her mother thought she was old enough to understand. This was new. And it was odd how much she had been longing for this day to be confided in as an adult. But now it had happened it frightened her. She longed to be protected, to be cuddled, guarded, kept close to her mother. She turned her head away from her mother's searching look. A cat sat by the road, the tip of its tail dipped in a murky puddle. It was licking its paws and whiskers, then it stared at the car, got up and stalked off, leaving behind the remains of a tiny bird, feathers tangled and dusty.

"You mustn't make such a fuss about everything," her mother continued. Susan saw her look across at Feng. "I told you we're visiting a friend for a while." She met Susan's eyes in the mirror, then started the engine and swung into the narrow street.

They were driving along a cobbled road. Unused to motor cars, it ground and shook the car and they slowed down to crawling pace. Tall houses leaned together, shutters closed, wood unpainted or peeling. Trees were hunched up close to the houses, providing shade to doorways and upper balconies. Scrawny dogs lay in the shadows of the tree trunks, their tails beating off the flies, ears twitching. Some were poking their noses into rubbish, ribs visible through their scanty coats. Susan fretted. Who lived in these closed houses? Were they waiting with ropes and guns? She slid down into her seat and watched, half covering her face with her hands. A stench of rotting flesh, of decaying vegetables, broke into the car. Susan eased herself up, took a peep out of the window, saw a woman aiming the contents of a bucket into the gutter, a greyish brown stream flowing outwards across the cobbles. Closing her eyes and holding her breath, she touched the Buddha in her pocket. Her father would be in the bathroom by now, getting ready for work. How long would it take him to realise they had gone? Or would he not miss her at all? Perhaps he would send for the police, lead a search party in his quest to track them down. But he knew more than Susan, knew exactly where they were going – she had seen the letter from her mother propped up against the pot plant in the hall, heard her mother explain the contents to Feng.

Soon they were passing the clearing which led to the village. It looked smaller than she remembered, the charred remains of a fire was centred in the middle. An army truck was parked nearby, empty; a squashed cigarette packet lay on the ground by the front tyre, papers piled high on the dashboard. She heard Feng mutter to her mother and indicate towards the jungle with her hand.

Susan kept her foot pressed to the floor, leaning forward clinging to the back of Feng's seat as if she had the power to force the car along. And only when she knew they had left it behind, that the trees which surrounded the opening would have vanished from sight, did Susan release her hold.

They drove for three hours along a deserted highway, and eventually Susan slept. When she woke she was startled not to find herself in the place she had been dreaming of: there were no humpbacked bridges over meandering streams; the water she had heard was the swish of the tyres as they drove through a flooded road. She stared out of the window at the mountains that surrounded them. And still they drove further for another hour until the landscape changed; the trees on either side of the road were denser, cutting out the light. Susan was hungry now and she asked how much longer it would take them to get there. Not long, she was told; they would be there in half an hour.

People started to crowd the road, carrying parcels, boxes, pots on their heads and staring at the car, at them. Some of them turned to follow the car as it crept up a hill. But Susan was fretting again. What if she did not like where they were going? The car stopped and her mother pushed open her window to buy a bunch of bananas from a boy who looked like the one she had met in the village. Startled, she sprang up from her seat, told her mother not to stop.

"You no worry, Susan," Feng said. "We long way now."

"Nothing's going to happen," her mother added. "You're safe now."

But the boy had the same solemn eyes, the same hair, smooth-looking, so black, a blue tinge showing in the shadow cast by their car. Another boy joined the banana boy with a basket full of melons. He swatted the flies away with a palm leaf, kept swiping at them as they landed on the melons or his face.

"Where you go?" he asked.

Her mother did not reply, but closed the window and started to drive away.

They drove past houses on stilts with chickens wandering, circling the yard, pecking at grain. For a minute Susan had a rush of excitement; she was going somewhere new; another experience lay in store for her. But then she thought of her father sitting alone at the dining room table, untouched food on his plate, the empty decanter at his side, Babiya's song streaming in from the garden.

A sign nailed to a tree caught her attention: *McPherson's Rubber Plantation*. Her mother started to hum as they turned left in the direction of the sign. The car rumbled and shook over a track where small huts had been built along the verge. Washing; blue, red, green, brown, white, hung from lines supported by trees, tiny naked children played in the mud, their mothers watchful, as they crouched over pots. They stumbled and shook for a mile or so along the track, until eventually a bungalow came into view. On its vast veranda a woman reclined on a long chair; her hair was white blonde, and her dress bright red. She stood, waved and ran down the steps towards them.

Chapter 19

George kept his eyes closed as he listened to the dawn chorus. There was no point in trying to sleep, not now. And he had got used to the daze his over active mind had brought, the oblivion he sank into when the night birds hooted, hunting their prey.

The sheet that he lay on was damp and tangled, tossed about in the night, as if it were a fisherman's net bobbing in a stormy sea. Throwing off the top sheet he lay there, naked, stretching his legs and twiddling his toes.

The stupidity of the agreement he had made with Sarah to visit the boy in the kampong popped to his surface thoughts again. The idea of going with her was supposed to be part of a truce, his payment to her for his brutish performance. But her need for comfort had overridden her hurt after the day of his assault. She wanted, no, needed an affair with him. He still found it hard to believe he had acted in such a cruel way and since then had been tender towards her. He thought of Sarah clinging to him after they made love. But he could no more control his fantasies as he lay next to Sarah than his physical reaction to her as he watched her step out of her clothes. Sometimes, it was as if she had actually become Emma, as if somehow their beings had merged. Certainly, the affair helped him deal with the disappointment, the anger he felt towards Emma. But to get Susan involved. He would never forgive himself for that. More to the point would she ever forgive him?

He lay like this for a while, gazing through the open curtains, mulling over his feeling of isolation, watching the sky lighten as the sun rose. This at least brought pleasure.

Still he expected to hear Dorothy's foot on the stair, her voice calling him, telling him how long she had been awake. It was as if she had left a presence behind, had only taken the outer shell of her body. Except for the letter sent to keep him alert. To prevent him drifting into a state of amnesia. That is what she had said in so many words. But missing Dorothy was a surprise; he had not expected to feel sad about her going. And even though he quite liked the peace and quiet her absence brought, it was a bit like having a piece of him removed, though a part of his anatomy he could easily do without, like his tonsils or a spare rib. He touched the indent in his side where his infected appendix had been scooped out all those years ago.

He peeled the letter from underneath the whisky glass. Straightening out the creases, he reread it. The rounded, precise letters, the formal explanation, it was all so familiar. He could almost hear her repeating the words; see the impatience on her face. He put it back in the envelope; the ring left by the whisky remained stubborn, a stain on the otherwise white paper.

The cicadas had just started their morning chorus. They were deafening today. A butterfly, orange like the sun rise he had just seen, flew near the window, its tiny wings whirring, hovering. It fluttered out across the garden again, disappeared into the blue. He got out of bed, threw his dressing gown on and took a peek into Susan's room.

Everything had been tidied and put away. Not a trace of her remained. But she would be back soon. He would take her to the beach, a chance to recapture their former relationship. Combing his hair briskly from his face, he wondered whether solitude was driving him mad.

He heard the rattle of the front door and silently thanked Dorothy, glancing at her blue and gold kimono hanging from his door, for allowing Feng back. The smell of frying bacon made his mouth water and drew him downstairs. As he landed on the bottom stair, he glanced over at the hall table. A few bills, a letter for Dorothy from England, nothing else. But then why would Dorothy write again? She had made her plan quite clear.

Sitting at his place at the table he waited for Feng and glanced at the newspaper she had placed next to his fork. But he had no interest in reading the article about the Suez Canal crisis, instead he picked up the pen he had left on the table the night before, turned to the back page and started the crossword. Dorothy never approved of him doing crosswords at breakfast. Ink got into the butter, she always said. Better do three a day until she returned.

"Thank you," he said as Feng presented him with a steaming plate. He coughed into his clenched fist. "Bit strange for you is it, cooking for one, cleaning for one?" He lifted his fork and prodded the bacon. "They'll be back next week. You must miss them. Mrs Johnson especially."

"Yes, sahib," Feng said. No sign of surprise.

"Susan is due to return to England you know, next week."

"Yes, sahib."

"So I'll go and fetch her back in a couple of days."

"Yes, sahib."

"So Susan likes it out there does she?" How many times had he asked Feng this question? But there was always a chance he had missed a point, or Feng would remember something new.

There was a hint of a twitch on Feng's upper lip. "It very lonely there, Mr Johnson. But she happy. A holiday."

"Indeed." A two-week stay on a rubber plantation did not sound like a holiday to him. He wondered whether Feng was being entirely truthful.

192

"Mr McPherson play cards too."

"So I believe." George cut up his toast into four pieces. "Or maybe you'd like to go and collect them? Bit difficult for me without the car."

"Very far from town. Very lonely for Mrs Johnson," Feng continued. "But she have good time too."

George stared at the place where Dorothy usually sat. The picture of Dorothy enjoying the wilds did not fit, from whatever perspective he looked. Like dropping Constable into the East End of London. "Probably better you go. Never been much good on buses." he said. "Shall we say next Tuesday?"

"I check with my husband."

He looked up at her. He had not thought of that. Feng for him was here in his home, the other more personal side to her was unknown to him, never spoken of. "Susan will be catching the boat on Friday."

"I let you know, sahib." She waited.

"Thank you Feng," he said. "I expect you'll enjoy the bus ride." His knife scraped on the plate.

She nodded and pattered from the room, the scent of carbolic soap in her wake.

George dipped his toast in his tea, and thought of the remarkable speed in which he had regressed into his bachelor ways. He studied the crossword clue again. *Perfectly sweet. (Seven letters.)*

Not for the first time, he wondered what Feng thought of him, and popped a sausage into his mouth. In England he would not have cared what a maid thought, but here it was different. He could never fully accept the fact that he was living in someone else's country, employing them to wait on him. And Dorothy had become surpris-

193

ingly close to Feng. What had they talked about as he slogged away in his office, stamping export papers and drinking tea by the gallon? Had she revealed this side to Feng, this aptitude for travel, for enjoying herself away from the city, from him? A piece of scrambled egg fell off his fork. Globules of yellow and white splashed on his sock. He bent to pick the egg, and saw a butterfly struggling on the floor. Its wings fluttering hopelessly. Carrying it to the window on the palm of his hand, he blew on the wings, watched it drop on the path to continue its battle.

He thought of the first time he had visited the village. How ridiculously clumsy he had felt, and humble. As if he owed them an apology for being British, for the way he dressed, for treading on their seedlings in his size twelves. He had actually envied their simple life. His views on living off the land had been recounted to Dorothy. He remembered questioning this constant need to get on, to better oneself. And she had given him one of her withering looks, so he had said no more. Now there she was, happy to stay in a house with intermittent electricity and water that would trickle to a stop without warning. That is what Feng had said, or implied. A rampant imagination was not always a virtue. He put down his knife and fork, rested his head in his hands and watched the remains of his eggs congealing on his plate. Out of the window he could see Babiya arriving, his son running along beside him. Just as he was turning to follow the path behind the house, Babiya swung his head round and looked directly at George, though he could not have actually seen him sitting at that angle to the window. Perhaps he had sensed George watching him, like a rabbit is aware of a stoat.

It was hard for him to admit he had been duped by the Malays so very badly. Why had he not realised they were friendly with the Chinese Communists? Was there something gullible in his nature that had prevented him smelling out the treachery in time? If only he had kept his wits about him, instead of being taken in by their hospitable smiles.

He chewed on some cold toast. He wrote *angelic* with his marmalade encrusted pen, on three across. He stared at the empty chair to his right for a minute before returning his gaze to the crossword.

The door bell rang. He looked at the clock on the wall. Henry was early. He shoved the remainder of the tea soaked toast in his mouth and chewed briskly, swallowing more than he should. He heard Feng cross the hall and unlock the latch as he wiped the butter from his fingers. To his embarrassment, Feng opened the dining room door just as he was choking on some crumbs that had caught in his windpipe. He gasped for breath as he coughed and spluttered. If Dorothy were here, she would have fetched him a glass of water, patted his back, then admonished him for being greedy, for eating too fast.

There was no indication that Feng had noticed the difficulty he was having with his toast. "There's a man from the army in the sitting room," she said.

He felt a rise of panic. What had happened now? Snatching the napkin from the table, he stood, still struggling to regain a normal rate of breath and walked past Feng. He felt her eyes on him as he turned into the sitting room.

A man in military dress was standing under the mirror on the wall, his hat clasped to his stomach with both hands.

"Mr Johnson?" he said. "Officer Burrows." He put his hand out. "From the Intelligence Unit."

"What's happened?" George asked. "Why are you here?"

"Sir, I'm here to inform you that the Chinese Communists who attacked you have been caught."

"Good," George said and mopped his brow with the napkin. "Thank you for letting me know," he said.

"And that the settlement has been destroyed, sir."

"Destroyed?"

"We had been watching it for a while. There were suspicions about the occupants, sir."

George noticed the deep comb marks on the officer's sand colour-ed hair, the hair cream making it look unwashed and greasy, his eyebrows and eyelashes bleached white by the sun.

"It would have been better, sir, if you had not befriended them. They have different ways…"

"Yes, yes. I realise that now," George interrupted. "So what's happened to them, the occupants?"

"As I said, the settlement has been destroyed."

"Pulled down?"

"We use fire, sir. So the huts can't be reoccupied. And the villagers have been incarcerated."

"I see," said George. He wondered whether razing the village to the ground was a bit harsh.

The officer sniffed and removed a packet of cigarettes from his pocket, offered one to George, who shook his head. "We would request that this…" He flicked his lighter open and looked at George's feet. "We hope this doesn't happen again, sir."

George laughed. "Christ. So do I! Do you think I enjoyed being tied up, having my life threatened? I thought they were going to kill us." He noticed the officer pucker his lips slightly. "Do you think I'd want it to happen again? But if we hadn't made friends with the

Malays, the Chinese would have slaughtered us, like they slaughtered the goats and God knows what else. The villagers saved our life. Did you realise that?"

"But sir, if you hadn't been at the village in the first place." He sucked noisily on his cigarette. "We had our suspicions already that they were insurgents, providing sustenance, food and the like for the Communists."

"So why didn't you arrest them before?"

The officer did not reply. George waited. He listened to the house creaking as the day heated up. The cicadas were continuing with their mating calls. "So why didn't you arrest them before?" he repeated.

"We were watching them."

"But not that day obviously. Not when they attacked us."

"No, unfortunately not, sir."

"I see," said George again. "Where are they incarcerated?"

The Officer raised his eyebrows, then brushed some ash from his trousers. "I don't have any information about their location, sir."

George felt an idiot for asking where they were. What did it matter to him? But they had stopped the Communists killing them, hadn't they?

"And what happens to them when they are released?" George said. "If they can't return to their village?"

Officer Burrows looked puzzled.

"How do you make sure... How do you stop them siding with the Communists again, I mean?" He was asking all the wrong questions, as if some meddler were sitting on his shoulder, sifting his words.

Would the man now be suspicious of his motives, think he was supporting them. But that was not the case; he just did not wish them harm. As he glanced up at the officer, who was passing the time looking over the room, he felt a sense of relief that the smashed glass in the mirror had been replaced.

"We disperse them, move them to other areas. Surely you know Government policy, Mr Johnson. I realise you've not been out here as long as some, but..."

"Yes, I'd heard that. I just wanted to make sure."

Officer Burrows' mouth turned into a smile, but the eyes did not show any change of mood. "I must be going now," he said. "I'll see myself out. And try to remember what I said about... Well I'm sure you will, after everything that happened, sir." He put his hat on and nodded. His sunburnt face glowed red against the pale hairs on his upper lip.

George turned the handle on the door for the other man and heard Feng's feet scurrying away. Who could blame her for eavesdropping? He most likely would have done the same. He went over the conversation in his head. He should have handled it better, could have done without the growing embarrassment that now glowed in his face. Feng stared at him, questioning, surmising, disapproving.

As he went through to the veranda, he wondered how the boy Rafi was surviving in a prison camp. Did they chain them up, lock them in tiny cells? Were they left in solitary confinement, mistreated? He realised how little he knew about this country and how it was run. And now he felt much the same as he had when Moorcroft had handed him that letter, like a lesser being that deserved everything that befell him. The villagers would be punished in the same way; moved to another destination when they were eventually released, perhaps a place not known to them. There was a peculiar justice about this turn of events; a chance irony.

Henry was late, half an hour. George started to pace up and down the veranda. But he was not sure he wanted to go to the club again even though it would get him out of the house, away from himself. He stepped down into the garden and walked beyond the pergola. *Love letters in the Sand* drifted across from his neighbour's house. A woman's voice sang along with the tune. It was soothing, an easy tune to listen to. Nice people, he thought. Strange that he had only got to know them, after all those months. At least their enthusiastic talk of Hong Kong had caused him some distraction from his maudlin recollections.

And how many times had he noticed Susan standing there, looking out over the fence? The day he had seen her standing at the veranda door after Dorothy had aimed an ashtray at his head, he thought it could get no worse. Or that she could witness no worse. Her face, white and drawn, too old looking for the youngster that she was, had revealed a kind of satisfaction, that made his mouth go dry. Why did he give in to the waves of lust for Sarah? Respect from Susan would take months to regain. Years even, possibly never. But he could not contemplate that; like trying to work out the distance of infinity. Returning to the pergola, he put his nose to the climbing bougainvillea, but there was no scent in the opening buds.

George heard Henry call out to him as he stood on the veranda steps, and he looked up at the familiar greeting. The sound of the doorbell had evaded him, as had the salutations that Feng and Henry must have exchanged. Understanding why Susan liked to stand there, protected by the hidden archway and purple sprays, he blinked away the wet in his eyes and waved to Henry, then rubbed his face on his sleeve.

"George," Henry held his hand out. "Hot, isn't it?" He stood with George in the shade of the hanging flora.

"Indeed."

George led the way back to the veranda and stood looking out at the garden. It was comforting how the weather was still such a reliable form of communication. "Good of you to pop round," he said.

"No trouble," Henry said as he removed his panama.

"I've just had a visit from a representative of the army."

Henry turned to look at him. There was, George noticed, genuine concern in his expression. "I heard they caught some CT members," he said. "The army have their own ways of dealing with them." He put his hands in his pockets. "The less we know what they do with them the better."

"I suppose they know best. Who are we to question their ways? And the Malays have been dealt with too."

"A prison in Penang. Best place for them. You were lucky. But then you don't need me to tell you that."

"Strange that you know so much," George said. And that he knew so little he thought to himself.

Henry put his foot on the railing and retied his shoe laces. "I have a friend in the army out here. Went to school with him. Good chap."

"I never knew that," George said. He wondered whether the manner in which he had dealt with Officer Burrows would get back to Henry. He had been foolish to behave that way, to allow the officer to think he disrespected him. Spending too much time alone in the house was causing his perspective to move out of kilter. He found himself sympathising with Dorothy, understanding the relationship she had formed with her playing cards.

Henry was repeating the lace tying exercise on his other shoe. George watched as his friend hoisted his sock up to his knee and turned the top over with a precision that was almost feminine. Then standing up straight, Henry resumed his habit of pushing his fingers through his hair. "And Dorothy," he asked. "When will she be returning from her visit?"

"Soon. Next week I hope."

He lifted his face to the sky at some birds cackling as they flew overhead. "Safer down there," Henry said. "In Selangor. Not so many trouble makers." Looking at George as he stroked his chin, he said, "and what are your plans for the future?"

"I'm waiting for news of my request for a transfer," he said. "To get away from here will please Dorothy. So many bad memories here in Ipoh. I'd like to make amends with her. We haven't been seeing eye to eye recently." A spider was nipping along the railing. "As you know," he added. He decided not to say anything about Susan. It was too hard to put into words, the loss he felt, always feeding his guilt. He watched the spider's progress down the wrought iron support.

Henry was looking at him curiously; his eyes kept rolling up to the sky, and back to George's collar." Shall we have a swift drink then?" Henry asked and picked his hat up from the table. "There's something you should know, but it's better to talk about it away from here." He expanded his chest as he took a deep breath. "I know just the place. A bit out of town. With a pleasant breeze from the mountains" He gave a short laugh. "Well sometimes there is, if the wind is blowing in the right direction."

"Not the club then?"

"Somewhere else. Just for a change. Shall we?"

And George did not ask what it was that Henry wanted to tell him. For him, a decision had been reached; he would make use of Henry's knowledge of the firm, find out about a transfer to Hong

Kong. He needed a fresh start, was willing to try another British colony, provided Dorothy approved.

Chapter 20

Dorothy was sitting on a chair by Susan's bed underneath the window. Quietly, she got up, drew the curtains closer together. She listened to the drone of the generator, the humming of the night insects. Outside, there was nothing but darkness, not a glimmer of light. Susan was sleeping. A quiet slumber, without the usual asthmatic wheeze. Strange, that it had vanished so rapidly, as if the catarrh had been squeezed from her lungs for good. She strained her ears, ever ready for the rasp of her mucous-filled breath. Nothing. Not a murmur.

The room Hannah had given Susan was small, with a window looking out onto a kitchen garden, with the mass of rubber trees in the distance. Dorothy hoped the house would remain lit that night, unlike the previous two. But the sudden cut of electricity did not frighten Susan; in fact she'd taken it more easily than Dorothy. To Dorothy, it was blitz blackouts all over again.

Dorothy watched Susan's face. Her mouth was moving as if she were commenting on a dream, or a nightmare. If only Dorothy could erase them for her. As well as her own guilt about removing her from Ipoh - it persisted so obstinately, like a stubborn stain.

Leaning forward she kissed Susan on the forehead, first lifting a stray hair. Then she adjusted the mosquito net round the top of Susan's bed and turned out the light.

The door clicked behind her and she trod quietly down the short corridor. The dining room light was on and the door ajar, but there was the unmistakeable sound of snapping of cards, the slamming of a glass on a table, and a particular smell of bourbon, and beery clamminess, that Dorothy had become familiar with in the few days she had been there. Still she felt, raw, vulnerable, threatened by the presence of these men, these giants with their large hands and muscular legs sprouting from their khaki shorts.

"Have a drink," a voice called out to her.

"Play poker do you?" another asked as he pushed the door open with his boot. A wink accompanied his question as he stood and waved her into his seat. The man belched.

A quick smile. Averted eyes. "No," she said. "No, thank you."

Patrick McPherson said nothing, just shuffled his hand of cards, rolling his blue eyes towards her momentarily, his interest in her lost when she shook her head, to emphasise the refusal. She watched a man with dark eyes and a ruddy complexion. He opened his legs and patted his lap.

"You're not going to sit on my knee?" he laughed.

She saw Patrick glare at the man.

"Leave her be," he said and kicked the door shut. Despite the closed door, she kept to the far wall, away from the slant of light slithering down the narrow hallway. Just in case they pursued the idea, took it to ridiculous lengths, as they had done the night before. Her breath was held and she felt her pulse racing. That night, though they were too absorbed in their game and she ticked herself off for allowing a group of men to disturb her so. After all they meant no harm, did they?

She entered the sitting room at the end of the bungalow where Hannah was waiting, two glasses of gin and tonic on the table beside her.

"Asleep, is she?" Hannah asked as she handed Dorothy her drink.

Dorothy nodded, eased herself into the chair opposite Hannah, lifted her feet onto a stool and studied the photo on the wall of Patrick McPherson standing, one foot resting on a bulky snake, the intricate pattern on the reptile's skin reduced to grey in the fading picture.

"Hannah," she started. "The men with your husband?"

Hannah looked up. "Harmless. Bark worse than their bite. Only a bunch of planters. Nothing for you to worry about. Not used to seeing another woman about the place." She patted her hair. "Starved, they are, of the feminine touch. And a couple of them aren't married at all." She coughed delicately, her hand to her mouth. "Not to one of us at any rate." Then she changed her expression. Smiling, she waved to the door. "But what about Susan. Is she all right? Such a nervous child." Hannah got up, locked the veranda door, drew the blind down.

"As right as you would expect after what her father put her through," Dorothy said.

"Couldn't help noticing her nails. Bitten to the quick." Hannah studied her own, painted, pink ovals. "You don't mind me saying, do you?"

Dorothy hoped Hannah had not noticed the cut on Susan's arm, where, according to Susan, the source of a mole had been investigated. But her eyes had been dull, a plait twisted round her finger, as she explained her motive; her need to explore what lay under her skin.

"She's always bitten her nails," Dorothy said as she picked up a magazine. It was *Woman's Weekly*, folded back to the fashion page with a drawing of a woman in an off-the-shoulder dress and an impossibly narrow waist.

"Let's have some music," Hannah said. "Then we can talk without disturbance." She jerked her head towards the closed door. "We don't want the boys' play time interrupting us, do we?" Moving over to the gramophone, she flicked through the record selection leaning against its side. "Something suitable for the occasion," she said. She turned round and grinned at Dorothy. "You're feeling a bit better now, aren't you?"

Perry Como's voice was a distraction. Dorothy floated, the muscles in her shoulders eased, her jaw relaxed. The music reminded her of another time; a different phase, a former life in a cooler clime.

There was a series of cheers from the other end of the house.

"Somebody's won something," Hannah commented. "Feeling better now, aren't you?" she said again. "Now you've had a few days to settle in. Gather your thoughts as it were."

Dorothy did not like to offend her host by telling her the truth that in fact she felt an impostor, as if she had duped herself into coming here to seek comfort in this house, this lonely outpost full of leering men and rough laughter. But the choice had been hers, as she reminded herself. Where else could she have gone? Impossible to stay in Ipoh. But the image she had kept close, of Hannah's home, of her surroundings, the servants, the genteelness of a lady-like existence, bore little resemblance to the reality which Dorothy now faced. And there in front of her, on the table where her drink stood, was the photograph Hannah had shown her on the boat. Slowly, Hannah picked it up. She must have seen Dorothy looking at it; maybe she had read her mind too.

"Such a shame those times are over," Hannah said.

"Yes," said Dorothy. She knew she would have to allow Hannah some reminiscences. Like the habit of drinking brandy after dinner, the same memories were churned out every evening. Still, she liked

Hannah. There was an understanding between them, a loyalty between friends that was new to Dorothy. Easier to put on one side the exaggeration, the move aside from the truth, the enhancement that Hannah had created.

"We were doing well then. Rubber was in great demand, before the discovery of a cheaper substitute."

Hannah replaced the photo by her glass, and Dorothy waited a few minutes. Maybe there would be something else, a previously unrelated memory. At least there was no pressing her about Susan.

"I do hope Patrick doesn't mind us staying. In these troubled times. You know if business is a problem. Maybe he would rather we weren't here." She thought of him kicking the door shut with his boot.

"Patrick?" Hannah said. "I told you before. Of course he doesn't mind. He's too busy to mind. He's not a man of many words. As you've probably gathered. No need to concern yourself about him." She looked behind her as the blind chafed against the sill. "It's all much harder than it used to be. With all the problems of the flagging rubber industry. As I've explained. But of course he's got all his other pastimes to occupy his mind. No time to concern himself with you." She took a deep breath. "But it's just lovely to see you again." She smiled and hummed along with: *Some Enchanted Evening,* swinging her head in time to the melody. "Too bad," she said and closed her eyes, "that we had to lose most of the servants." Opening one eye and looking at Dorothy, she said, "It's different for you. You can go back to England any time. Not me. I'm stuck out here, all alone. Think of that. You're the lucky one. At least you've got choices. More than I'll ever have." Both eyes were open now, and she leant forward.

A sensation that Dorothy had been slapped in the face, or reprimanded for being an ungrateful girl came across her. She wriggled in her seat. The chair supporting her creaked as she moved to cross her legs. It was an old leather chair. There were two, and a matching sofa on which Hannah sat. Even though the leather was worn, patchy, like an over-loved teddy bear, it still bore the mark of expense and fashion, of finer times. "Why can't you leave? If that's what you want?" she asked.

Ignoring her question Hannah stared at the blind as it knocked against the woodwork again. Her mouth was open, eyes narrowed. She tied the blind down, came and stood next to Dorothy. Two cigarettes were eased out of a packet. "Have you decided what you're going to do about George?" She reached over for the bottle of gin and topped up both their glasses, then lit the cigarettes. "As I said, I'm not going to say I told you so, but I knew he'd do it again. They always do." She inhaled deeply, sank back into the sofa.

"I don't know what to do," Dorothy said. "I miss him, now we're apart." And she did. Though she ridiculed herself for seeking out his shadow lengthening before her, for listening out for the tap-tap of his pen on the table, the rustling of paper as he completed the cross-word. It was the routine of their existence together, that she missed.

Hannah put her hand on Dorothy's. "You're bound to at first. You haven't been here very long."

"I'll have to go back soon though."

Some enchanted Evening, when you find your true love, sang Perry Como. Tears came to Dorothy's eyes. This was not what she wanted. Hannah was starting to sniff too. Covering her face with her hand, Hannah removed the stylus, scratching the record on the way.

"Enough of that," Hannah said. Smoke billowed out of her nostrils. "Is he still writing to her?"

"Emma?"

Hannah nodded. "The girl in England. Have you found any more letters?"

"No. That doesn't mean he's not still writing, of course."

"Have you asked him?"

Dorothy watched the ice move round the glass as she stirred her drink. "Yes," she said. "He says not." The memory of the letter she had found on the boat flickered through her mind.

"Who was she anyway?"

As she tapped her cigarette, watching the ash fall into the brass ashtray, Dorothy pondered. Now Hannah knew all about Sarah, she wanted the entirety of George's unfaithfulness, the history of her failure. She glanced at Hannah. So why would she want to leave Patrick? But Hannah was watching her, waiting for a response.

"George decided to have an affair with the Chairman's daughter. That was Emma. Already engaged, probably married by now to a Lieutenant." Not for the first time Dorothy wondered how she would have dealt with an affair with a less prominent person, like his secretary, or a neighbour, a friend. Perhaps it would have all been forgotten by now. Perhaps it would have been worse.

Hannah tutted. "An army man's fiancée."

"He was posted to Germany apparently." Dorothy put her hand to her head. "Out of the country. So he had no idea either." A familiar throbbing had started again over her eye. She tried to sink into the heat, let it take over, not to fight it, as Hannah had advised.

Closing her eyes, she tried to wish the pain away. She did not want to say anything for a while. Talking about George, discussing her plans for the future, remembering how she discovered the affair with Emma, was all too much. She deserved a little quietness, a portion of peace.

"So how did you find out about it?" Hannah asked. As if on cue. "Men never cover their tracks. That's what I've learnt. No self-discipline. They get careless when carnal thoughts have got the upper hand."

"Has your husband ever then? I mean did he have an affair once?" Try as she could, Dorothy could not imagine Mr McPherson entertaining another woman, declaring his love for her, as George had with Emma. "Patrick!" Hannah laughed. "No. Not Patrick. He's not interested in other women. As far as I know."

Dorothy said nothing. No need to pry any more. Perhaps she really was lucky, as Hannah said.

There was a commotion in the corridor of the bungalow. A bitter sweet smell of tobacco drifted through as the men stood for a minute talking outside the room, before they passed by on their way to the front porch. Try as much as she could, Dorothy could not make out what the men said. Their voices were low, and their accents broad, compared to the clear vowel sounds of George and his contemporaries.

"So how did you find out?" Hannah said again.

"I was supposed to meet him for lunch one day, after I got off the train at Victoria. I had been to visit my sister. He didn't turn up, so I phoned his office. His secretary left me waiting… then his boss came on the phone. He told me that I should have a chat to George, that night, that I should get him to tell me everything. He was very angry. It made me frightened; I couldn't think what George could have possibly done. I had no idea. Always trusted him. I was made to look a total fool. Me, his wife, the last one to find out."

Hannah said nothing, just nodded as if she too had known.

"He denied it at first."

"Naturally."

"It was awful, terrible. The shame. "

"So you thought it better to make out he'd been promoted here. That's understandable. I would have done the same."

"Would you?" She waited a minute, while Hannah finished her drink. "So would you prefer to be without Patrick?"

"Yes, yes I would. What do you think I was doing in England?"

"Your sick mother. Weren't you seeing her?"

Hannah shook her head. "You're lucky," she said again. "You should take the opportunity and go."

The door was pushed open and Patrick McPherson was there. His large frame blocked out the light from the standard lamp in the corner. Dorothy uncrossed her legs and pulled the skirt of her dress down over her shins so the hem nearly covered her ankles. His brick coloured hair stood out from his scalp like a frayed wire brush.

"Can I have a word?" Mr McPherson twisted his body round and quickly looked at Dorothy. A murmur of a smile. "You don't mind, do you?"

"Of course not," Dorothy stood and started to make her way towards the veranda door. She felt his hand on her shoulder. An insistent grip.

"No, you stay in here. No need for you to move."

"Put some music on. Your choice. Back in a mo'," said Hannah.

The choice was limited. But Dorothy picked out Alma Cogan. Cheery music, a reduced risk of increasing her sadness. She had to think straight. Work out her next move. No good relying on someone else to provide her with the answer. Though Hannah's advice was worth listening to.

She tried to make out what Hannah and Patrick were saying, considered for a minute the idea of standing near the door. She could always pretend she was admiring the painting hung nearby. It was of a snow scene in Edinburgh. A blue tint of frost on the castle walls, a whitish grey covering the road. Men with tartan scarves wrapped round their necks, tucked into their overcoats. If she stood near enough its effect was to cool her, to lessen the ache in her head.

An urge to go into Susan's room, to watch over her while she slept appeared abruptly. She would have to talk to her, put a stop to this self inflicted harm. What would George do if he knew? She tried to imagine his reaction. But he would not believe her, would tell her to stop finding things to worry about.

Again, she had to pass the dining room where Hannah and Patrick were, with the door closed. There was the whine of a mosquito in Susan's room, and the sound of her breathing, a regular reverberation that consoled Dorothy, made her feel sleepy. The outline of the chair where she had sat before was just visible after she stood for a while allowing her eyes to adjust to the darkness. She sat. It was good to be alone again, quiet with Susan slumbering nearby. She stayed like this for a while willing the beat at her temple to go. At last it began to subside.

She heard Hannah and Patrick in the hall. The heaviest step halted, a door handle turned, a door slammed. The other lighter steps continued down the corridor. Time to go.

"There you are," said Hannah, when Dorothy returned to the sitting room. "I'm really sorry about that. I hope you didn't think us rude. Only business. Boring really. Patrick said you didn't come here to listen to his tales of woe." She laughed, a little nervously, Hannah thought.

Of course she did not believe Hannah. But listening to Susan's steady breathing had made her long for sleep. She stifled a yawn. "I think I'll go to bed, if you don't mind," Dorothy said.

"You must be exhausted." Hannah patted Dorothy on the hand. "We'll talk tomorrow. We can go to the Club." She took hold of Dorothy's hand, touched it lightly with her fingers. "You must leave him," she said. "You'll never be happy with him. A man like that."

Withdrawing her hand in a movement to tug at a curl, Dorothy said, "You're probably right. You keep telling me I'm lucky. I can't think why. My husband is a womaniser, and Susan... she's not very well…"

Hannah interrupted her. "You don't have a religion to stop you doing what you want. Do you?"

Dorothy thought of Grace and her constant praying. But Hannah?

"Remember the nuns?" Hannah said. She opened her eyes wide. "They knew. That's why they despised me." She licked her lips, clenched her fist. "The feelings were mutual. Believe me."

"They knew what?"

Hannah's laugh was raucous, as she raised her eyebrows, threw her head back and Dorothy was reminded of the first time she met her. "I can't divorce Patrick. Ever. But you can divorce George." She tugged at Dorothy's sleeve. "I'm Catholic, don't you see? Lapsed. Naturally. But once a Catholic always a Catholic." She raised her eyes to the ceiling. "According to Him, anyway."

Dorothy was aware of her face reddening. So that was what lay beneath Hannah's scorn of the nuns. All this time, she had thought it a joke, that Hannah was poking fun at them to relieve the boredom of the trip, to entertain Dorothy, keep her spirits up. "Why on earth do you want to divorce him? You said before he doesn't bother with

213

women. And you have..." She stopped suddenly. Hannah was, after all, her host. These late night confessions were too much. All she wanted to do was to check on Susan again. There was a nagging fear that was chipping away at her conscience.

"I make sure I have a good time. If that's what you mean."

"No. I didn't mean that. Your husband, Patrick. The servants, the man on the boat, the one from Kuala Lumpur. You remember? George would never let me..." She stopped, thought quickly. "I don't see why you would want to leave him," she repeated.

"Maybe mine isn't a real marriage. Have you thought of that?"

Now Dorothy was even more puzzled. Furthermore, she had an uneasy feeling about the way the conversation was going. She stepped backwards.

Hannah flopped back on the sofa. "Sorry," she said. "You go to bed. We'll talk tomorrow." Grabbing the gin bottle she pointed it at Dorothy. "Or a wee nightcap, as Patrick would say?"

But Dorothy shook her head, said goodnight again. She felt as if a clamp was being tightened, crushing any hopes of tranquillity. The venom behind Hannah's talk was as unexpected as the peeling paint, the weeds in the garden.

Once more, Dorothy sat by Susan's bed and listened to her exhale and inhale. As regular as the cicada's call. Impossible, while Susan was at peace like this to think that she would want to hurt herself. It was as if she wanted to punish herself. But why would she want to do that? Nothing wrong had been committed by her. Readily, Dorothy would exchange the asthma for this new affliction; there was a remedy, knowledge of that at least. She watched Susan's face, remaining like that for a while until the house was silent, apart from Patrick's reverberating snores from across the hall.

Chapter 21

Dorothy opened her eyes, waking to a change in the sounds of the night. The quietness in this house was somehow different, more intense than in Ipoh. As if the fabric of the building was in deep slumber. A slow plopping sound of the insects was the only backdrop to the thick night air: this time of night created a sense of pleasure, of stillness and peace, a respite before the punitive heat. She reached out with her hand to switch the light on, but there was no illumination. And she realised how she had grown accustomed to the drone of the generator, and that she had been awoken by its sudden absence. She drew the curtains back and waited for the hint of pink to seep upwards from the horizon and above the tree line. After a while, the sky became lighter and a red glow split the clouds like scissors cutting through a bolt of blue cloth. A cockerel made its call to the new day, and she heard the front door open and the pat-pat of bare feet hurrying along the hall, into the kitchen. There was a clatter of opening and closing of doors, then the sound of a brush nudging lino, the knocking of cupboard corners, as the boy swept the floors and batted the matting. In a flash, Dorothy missed Feng, wanted to talk to her, to regain the trust which had saved her from a madness she knew had been hovering, waiting to take her over in Ipoh.

Dorothy wondered whether Susan would be awake. Gently, she turned the handle to her door and stepped out into the corridor. A faint glow from the early morning sun provided a weak light in the hallway, just enough for her to see the boy standing, leaning his head on the broom handle. He was slight in build, wearing an oversized shirt over a sarong, brown, red and orange. Their eyes met momentarily; his, dark, large, sombre. Snatching her night dress at the throat, she returned his nod, hurried along towards Susan's room.

There was an unhealthy, stale odour in Susan's room. Dorothy pulled the mosquito net back and wound the ends over the frame. At first, she could not place the sour smell and instinctively walked towards the window to let some air into the room. Standing by the window, she inspected Susan's sleeping face. Angelic, pale, like marble, it looked young, untouched. A plait curled under an ear like a pillow, her head resting on it. A cup of milk was on the floor, the contents on the turn. It was as though Susan had regressed, was reliving her younger days with hot milk at bedtime, a cuddly bear on her pillow. It was then that Dorothy noticed the pins on the chair where she had sat the night before. Only a few, but how many did Susan need to pierce her skin? Dorothy sat on the bed and stroked Susan's brow, taking her arm in her hand, licking her finger, brushing the pin pricks and wiping a smear of blood away.

"Why do you do this to yourself?" she asked. Susan was awake. Dorothy knew that, had seen Susan's eyelids flutter open when she had tied back the mosquito net.

Susan opened her eyes wide. She withdrew her arm from Dorothy's hold, hid it under the sheet. "What's the time?" she asked. "Is it time to get up?" A look of feigned surprise passed over her features.

"I simply don't understand why you do this." Dorothy lifted Susan's arm out from under the sheet, pointed to the marks, moving her finger to a cut; tiny and precise, the healing process already beginning.

"It was a mosquito bite. That's all. Don't make such a fuss," Susan said. Then she leant over and kissed Dorothy on the cheek. "They itch so. Drive me mad."

"And the pins?" Dorothy persisted. Picking one up, she held it up to Susan. "Why?"

Susan grimaced, picked up the pins, one by one, and stuck them in her felt-covered pin cushion. She climbed out of bed then opened a drawer and pushed the pin cushion to the back. "There," she said. "No more pins." Her face, pale as milk, gazed at Dorothy as she stretched her arm out. "No more scratching. Sorry Mummy." Opening the wardrobe door, she pulled out her green and white checked dress. "When are we going to see Daddy again?"

Always this question. Always the uncertainty of the correct answer to give. "Soon," Dorothy said. "But things will be different."

Hands on hips, Susan looked up to the ceiling, an expression on her face showing an impatience, a superiority; as if Dorothy were the child, the one to whom everything had to be explained.

"I know that, Mummy," she said and stretched her plait, slowly unwinding it, pulling her fingers through the strands. "What are we doing today?"

"Something special," Dorothy said.

Susan turned and stared out of the window, her dress hanging over her arm. "Can I get dressed now?"

"Yes. Of course. We're going to the Club this afternoon."

Turning round, Susan said, "You might develop a headache." Her tone was calm, and Dorothy could feel Susan's eyes on her as she slipped her wedding ring off her finger and rolled it in her palm.

"No, I'm fine today." Replacing her ring on her finger, Dorothy stood. "You shouldn't talk to your mother like that," she added, and immediately regretted saying this. She wanted to soothe Susan, to understand her, to allow her to divulge her inner thoughts to her. "I'm going to sit on the veranda, while away the morning with a book."

***

Dorothy stretched out on a long chair waiting for the others. She arched her back and looked over the wooden rails of the veranda. The sounds of men working, machines whirring, distant shouts intermingling with the chirping from the cicadas, the squawking of the occasional bird lulled her, encouraging her to stay put, cool in the shade of the canopy. Little use in trying to relax though, an overspill of considerations, of concerns, and regrets occupied her mind. There was a need to talk with someone about Susan; the absence of a confidante made her feel alone, abandoned. But she was ashamed to talk to Hannah about it, frightened of George's reaction, also embarrassed, unsure what to do about this habit, and Susan's refusal to acknowledge its existence. Dorothy had never heard of such strange behaviour. Could it be a result of witnessing her father as a victim and of seeing him for the man he truly was?

Patrick was making his way up the path. Nodding to her briefly, he disappeared round the corner. They would be leaving for the Club soon. Dorothy's stomach was beginning to turn over. All those times when she had refused George's urges to accompany him to the Club in Ipoh. She remembered Matilda's words about rotting in the tropics without the support of other Brits. Is that what had happened to her? Had she been more willing to accompany Susan to the market... she stopped herself here. It was useless trying to remake history. Now, though, Hannah's efforts in persuasion had succeeded where George's had failed. And a decision to please Susan, not to let her down again, was feeding her determination to go.

She could hear Patrick in the bathroom, singing his usual bathing routine: *My Bonnie Lies over the Ocean*. A soothing baritone that made her smile. Would she have been happier with a husband who sang in the bath? And again, she wondered about Hannah's bitterness the night before. Out of character, Dorothy thought. Or was it a hidden side, usually concealed with perfection?

The singing had stopped, but Dorothy continued with the ballad in her head for a while as she waited and watched the afternoon haze rise lazily over the plantation. Hannah stepped out onto the veranda. Her white dress swung and rippled at the hem.

"We'll be off in a minute," she said. "I've just seen Susan. Quite excited about it." She looked at Dorothy, tapped a finger on her red lips. "Poor child. She hasn't had much fun at all since she came out here, has she?"

They took Patrick's jeep, he drove with elbow and knee stuck out of the vehicle, in much the same manner he sat at the dining room table playing cards or eating. Dorothy sat with Hannah at the back on freshly laid blankets which made her legs itch through her thin cotton voile dress. She watched Patrick turn to say something to Susan, as she sat upright, alert, pointing, asking questions, her hair loose, flowing in the breeze.

The fuscous rubber plantation seemed to go on for ever. Patrick was pointing to the taps on the trunks, explaining to Susan.

"The latex," he said, "flows from the trees."

"Like sap?" Dorothy heard Susan ask.

"That's right. They have to tap it very early in the morning, before dawn. The heat of the day stops it flowing so easily." He was pointing at the trees, at the tappers sitting cross-legged in the shade.

Dorothy felt herself smiling in spite of the trepidation she felt for the afternoon ahead.

They were passing the worker's huts, thatched and on stilts. Smoke wove its way upwards from the houses, hens pecked in the dirt and a man chopped logs. Dorothy stretched forward and put her hand on Susan's shoulder. The girl's muscles were tense, her breathing fast. The man looked up, wiped his brow with his shirt sleeve and lifted the axe high in the air. Then they were out on the road, and she saw Susan turn to Patrick as if she was going to ask him another question. The association forgotten, for the moment anyway. Dorothy again touched Susan on the shoulder, but was shrugged off, Susan's attention now drawn to Patrick.

"We'll have a good time," Hannah shouted above the noise of the motor. "All the locals come out today. All the planters and their wives, children..."

As the vehicle stuttered over a pot hole, Dorothy missed the rest of what Hannah said.

After an hour they arrived at the Club. It was a large barn-like building, with a cricket ground in front, where some children were playing rounders. Susan was already out of the jeep and watching the other children.

"Come on," Hannah said to Susan. "I'll introduce you to Miss Talbot. Then you can join in." She turned and winked at Dorothy. "Back in a mo'."

Now, left alone in Patrick's company, Dorothy felt embarrassed, at a loss for words. He was looking out across the lawn towards Miss Talbot who had lifted a whistle from where it rested on her shelf-like bosom. She blew it three times and the children gathered round. Dorothy looked on, at Susan, arms swinging in a show of bravado, while Miss Talbot turned to Hannah, laughing loudly, contented in her role.

"I'll be off to the snooker room," Patrick said as Hannah started walking back towards them. "Not a dancer, like my wife." He lifted a hairy arm to his hat, raised it a fraction. "See you when we start back for supper," he said.

Two small patches of freshly mown grass, bordered with cannas of yellow, blue and red, stretched out on either side of the steps leading up to the building. A group of orchids struggled in a pot; pastel colours, and delicate shapes. Dorothy heard strains of brass and piano which grew louder, made her long for a previous existence, an easier time, even though the melody was unknown to her. But as she and Hannah drew nearer, it became apparent that what she had assumed was the low beat of a drum, was in fact the throb of the generator, reminding her again of the temporary state in which this part of Malaya existed. A couple, the woman wearing a yellow swing dress, the man in tuxedo, were fox trotting around the bare floorboards, carefully avoiding the bulbous rug which lay rolled up at the far end. The couple were watched by a few people sitting round the room. All faces turned to Dorothy and Hannah; Dorothy felt herself redden, her palms began to sweat.

"Come on, let's sit down," Hannah said and took Dorothy's arm. "I know it's a bit basic, but we'll have some fun. Not much else we can do, living miles from anywhere. These are all planters, managers. Rubber, that's all we know about down here."

It was true; there was no resemblance to the Club in Ipoh, with its cushioned rattan chairs, and Indian waiters, always ready to serve, perpetually smiling, constantly vigilant. This room was painted a light brown with a faded photograph of a moustached man against a backdrop of mountains on one wall and, on another, a picture of the Queen wearing a glittering tiara. The Chinese waiters leant against the bar, idly cleaning glasses and talking amongst themselves. Another record was put on, and more couples took to the floor.

"Are you going to have a dance?" Dorothy asked Hannah. She remembered Hannah jiving to whistles of encouragement on the ship.

"I might, but my priority is to make sure you have a good time," Hannah said.

Focusing her eyes on the folds of the blue dress on the painting of the Queen, Dorothy thought how delightful it would be if Henry were there. If he was asking her for a dance, instead of the man wearing an old school tie who stood over her right then, his arm outstretched, waiting. But the picture of Henry that Dorothy conjured up did not come so easily to her mind these days; she was unable to maintain his image in her eye, dream up his touch on her hair.

Hannah was looking at her, as was the man in the red striped tie.

"Of course," Dorothy said, and she took the man's offered hand, hoping he was not aware how slippery they were, and the extent to which they shook.

He told her his name and, at first, Dorothy thought he said Palfrey.

"No, Hartley," he said. "Hartley's the name."

Briefly, Dorothy wondered what had happened to the Palfrey family, then asked him if he was in rubber.

"Tea," he said. "Fairly new to the area. I took over the management of an estate six months ago." They turned on the dance floor. "Lucky for me really. Step in the right direction." He glanced down at her face. "It gets lonely out there, these weekly dances keep me sane. Most men have wives to keep them company. Unfortunately for me…" He whisked her round.

Deliberately, she turned her head away for him, waiting patiently for the record to finish, listening politely to his comments. Occasionally asking questions. Mostly getting no satisfactory reply. Eventually, the music finished, he escorted her back to where Hannah was sitting.

"Nice chap," Hannah said. "Fresh blood." She stirred her drink slowly.

"What happened to his predecessor? He wouldn't tell me."

Hannah stared at a knot of wood in the flooring, rubbed the toe of her shoe over the unpolished surface. Backwards and forwards it went, up and down as if trying to erase the curling pattern. "Another drink?" she finally said.

"I am guessing it's something to do with the Communists." Dorothy recognised the closed look, the unwillingness to speak of the enemy. As if by doing so, she would tempt fate to repeat itself.

A long pause, while Hannah polished the floor with her foot. "You guess right," she mumbled. "The whole family shot. It was just after I arrived back from England. After you and I met." She looked towards Mr Hartley who was leaning on the bar. "They got them though. They always do."

Dorothy's breath faltered momentarily. The music had stopped. As if waiting for her reaction. Slowly, Dorothy rose and walked to the door.

"His plantation is up in the mountains. Not here. Not here," Hannah was at her side, pulling her arm. "Christ, I shouldn't have told you. But there is nothing anyone can do. Not us. Not people like us. But it's safe down here on the plains. Nothing's going to happen."

Dorothy watched the game of rounders. The white in Susan's dress was catching the light, her voice shrill, distinct to Dorothy. Safe under Miss Talbot's watchful eye.

"That's what everyone said to me in Ipoh," Dorothy said. "Nothing's going to happen to people such as yourselves, I was told. The Emergency's nearly over, they said."

"Sometimes you just have to get on with it."

"So will you ever leave?"

"Patrick's been here twenty years. What would he go back to? He'll never leave, even though he knows his days are numbered by continuing to stay in the tropics. It pickles the brain, wears out the lungs, the heart. He's seen men fall in mid-step and expire on the spot. Men in their fifties. But he has everything here. His cards, his whisky, his precious trees. Like babies they are to him. He's thrilled as a boy with a new train set, when a new batch is planted. But lots of the tappers are moving out, going back to their kampongs. Frightened of the Communists, or waiting for Independence."

"It's not just me then, who's frightened."

"No, not just you."

Susan was the runner now, her legs moved swiftly, blurred against the hazy field. The late afternoon air was inert, the flowers on the orchids drooped as if fatigued, in need of an afternoon nap. Strains of Perry Como floated towards them. Hannah took in a deep breath. Again, Dorothy tried to imagine the scene that Susan had witnessed in the jungle, and watched her clap with the other children.

"They're playing my favourite song. Come on," Hannah said.

The floor was packed with dancing couples, the women's flowery dresses spreading out like waves as they twirled and twisted, the men austere, proud, as they led the dance. Hannah ordered more drinks.

"So why do you want to leave Patrick?" Dorothy asked.

"Sometimes a marriage is not really a marriage."

Dorothy fiddled with a strand of damp hair that had fallen across her cheek, but said nothing.

"Our marriage was only a marriage for the first year. Unusual for a man of his age."

Blood rose from Dorothy's neck to her face. She should have realised, recognised the signs; the lack of physical closeness, the sibling-like relationship of understanding. She caught Hannah staring at her, an amused look on her face.

"I get by," Hannah continued "Take up opportunities as they arise. We - Patrick and I have an understanding." She took Mr Hartley's hand and allowed him to guide her onto the dance floor.

Watching them glide across the floor, Dorothy felt envious of Hannah, of her ability to pretend, to cope, to make do. And of Mr Hartley, his only concern to find a mate to keep house for him while he watched over the tea pickers, not knowing, and seemingly not caring, which ones would turn on him with guns and bayonets. Dorothy hugged herself and walked to the doorway, stepping out onto the pathway where she could follow Susan's every move.

For the drive back, Susan sat with Dorothy on the back seat, her head lolling against hers as she dozed fitfully, an unruly plait brushing against Dorothy's shoulder. The moon was just coming up, as they arrived at the bungalow, a full moon, perfectly round, unblemished. The thoughts that had been rumbling at the back of her mind all day like trains chugging in the distance became uppermost. A decision had to be made, the weighing up was complete.

She would leave George, take Susan with her back to England, start afresh without him.

In her room, Dorothy sat at her table. She had twenty minutes before supper would be served. She picked up her pen and started a letter to George. It was time she and Susan returned to Ipoh. Now she had made a decision about him, she wanted to move on to the next stage. She decided she would write to her sister Grace in the morning. The wording for that particular letter required a clear mind and careful thought.

Chapter 22

It was hardly a club that Henry took George to, more like a pub of the kind to be found in the sleazier parts of London. The drinkers were mostly Chinese business men. Trading in tin, Henry said. Four British men sat under the only fan that worked, their faces red and shiny. One with a dark moustache and a few strands of hair pulled across his balding head glanced up at them as they walked across the room. A smile creased his face, and he lifted his rolled newspaper in greeting.

George looked around while Henry ordered the drinks. The wallpaper was embossed, but peeling in parts and faded, as if tired of putting on a show. And the carpet was deep crimson, stained black at the edges where some buff lino had been laid bordering the bar. Despite the dilapidation of the building, there was an atmosphere of geniality amongst the customers; unrestrained laughter broke out from round the small tables.

"Gone to the dogs, this place," Henry said to George as they settled at a table near the window. George reached up and pushed the window stay to the next notch. Henry carried on. "Used to be a grand spot. An escape from the city." He glanced towards the bar. "Changed hands, so they told me."

George took a look at Henry, waiting.

Henry continued. "The Chinese used to hack the tin out by hand. Then the British brought in the dredgers before the First World War. Wholesale exploration. Broke the monopoly of the Chinese. This used to be a watering hole for the Brits." He looked across the room. "I suppose everything has to come round again."

George had not expected a history lesson. Clasping his hand round his drink, he felt the coolness of the ice on his fingers, thought of the Chinese who had tied him up. He closed his eyes for a minute and felt his left eye start to shudder.

"Well, I'm afraid I've got bad news for you," said Henry. Smacking his lips together after taking a sip of whisky, he dug in one pocket, then the other, patted his jacket and pulled out his pipe. "Can't think why I put it in there," he muttered. He leant forward as if intent on passing a secret to George, then sighed. "The firm is being sold," he said.

"Sold?"

"Yes, to a Chinese gentleman with a keen interest in the export business."

It was not too often that George found himself speechless. If he had been confronted with the telling off he had been expecting... well there were a couple of responses, explanations, he had planned on the journey there.

Staring at his hands, he noticed some blue ink embedded in his thumbnail. Instinctively, he put his hand away, shoved it into his pocket.

Henry was taking his time, lighting his pipe, making a great to-do of it, puffing and blowing, examining the tobacco in the bowl as if it were a disobedient child. At last he held his pipe to one side, cleared his throat. "So there'll be a few changes."

"Naturally."

"The thing is, the Director," Henry paused. "Mr Harding. Well, he thought it a good idea if I told you." He turned to follow the progress of a fly after it landed on the table. "With everything you've been through." He stopped talking, sucked on his pipe. "Rather than him calling you into his office on Monday, making you worry."

George waited as Henry puffed, noticed a man in the corner laughing, unable to restrain the peels of mirth as he explained an event to his companions; his face blotchy, and burnt from the unyielding sun, his guffaw whisky-filled, throaty. Turning to Henry, George saw him lower his eyes suddenly and knew Henry had been observing him, saw the instinctual glance away, protecting his thoughts, his inner-most abstractions.

"Good of him to consider my feelings," George said.

"He's sending one or two people out. Unfortunately you are to be one of them," Henry said.

"Out...?

"A branch of the firm. Another opening. Similar interests. You'll be looked after back in England, of course."

"England? Sorry, Henry. Not sure if I get your drift."

"Unfortunately... At least Dorothy will be pleased. Never really settled here. Has she?" Carefully resting his pipe in the ashtray, he said, "You'll be fine back in England, won't you? I mean the decision to come here wasn't exactly made by you. Was it, old chap?"

The hidden reference to Emma, the first Henry had ever made, startled George. He wished he had confided in Henry earlier, wished he had not conformed to the norm of pretence. "And does this... this transfer back... does it have anything to do with the business in..." his voice trailed off and he coughed. "Do I have any choice, any say in the matter?"

Henry said nothing at first, leaving ample time for George to wonder what menial job the Director had in mind for him; the old boy's network, their punitive methodology, spread right round the globe.

"It would appear not," Henry at last said. He was watching the fly sup his beer as it crawled round the rim of his glass. It was swatted with a discarded newspaper. "This is as difficult for me as it is for you... The posting might not be... how can I put it... you may well have to tighten your belt."

Perversely, George wondered if he had been demoted to a menial clerk, or perhaps he was to be a messenger boy. On the way here, George had rehearsed his speech: his regrets about the recent turn of events, and his wish to move on, to change direction, providing Dorothy agreed of course. Hong Kong sounded like the perfect location for his purpose. He had been looking forward to telling Dorothy about his plans. So certain that Henry would have a word on his behalf, he had not allowed himself to consider that the Director had other plans for him. But England, back to England, and for a reason outside his control - if he was to believe Henry.

"The firm is being taken over," Henry repeated. "Something similar in London, or possibly Portsmouth. Yes, I believe he said there's an opening in Portsmouth. I expect he'll fix it up for you."

"Of course."

"Naturally, you'll be given time to get yourself ready."

George visualised a map of southern England. Portsmouth, he recalled, had been badly bombed in the war. With great annoyance, he recognised a sensation in his nose, of tears being formed. Covering his nose and eyes with a hand he pretended some grit had been caught up in his eye and rubbed it with rapid movements. "And this has nothing to do with Dick. You know, with his influence and..."

Henry ignored him again. "Jim Price and John Drummond are going too. It's not just you that's being picked out."

"I understand."

Henry's pipe was giving him trouble again, the tobacco refusing to give the required satisfaction, failing miserably to stay lit. Finally, he succeeded in lighting it again and sat back, his drink in his hand. "Of course Dick is, as you can imagine, not a little upset at your escapades with his wife."

Preparing himself for the sermon, George knocked back his drink in one go.

"But he's dealing with it in his own way." Henry tapped a rhythm out on the table with one hand and fiddled with his moustache between finger and thumb with the other. "Unfortunate business," he said. "But no need for you to go to the office on Monday. Easier that way."

It appeared the Director was uncomfortable knowing George was still working for him. The little chat with Henry, the changeover at the top was a useful excuse for his removal. Not good for business, getting mixed up with the natives. He thought of all the letters from Emma, neatly bound in an elastic band, the papers well thumbed, damp with the mildew and the sweat from his hands. But he had not reread them for a few weeks now – it was months since the last letter had been delivered to him by Miss Hall, a demure smile flitting across her face. And now he would not be given the chance to clear his desk; the letters would be thrown out, discarded, never to be read again.

"I was going to ask you your views on my putting in a transfer to Hong Kong," George said. Surely, Henry would be able to persuade the Director. What difference to them would it make whether he was in Hong Kong or back in England?

231

Henry was studying his pipe, now laid to rest in the ashtray, while he searched in his pockets again, extracting a white handkerchief.

"I had thought Dorothy might like it there. A new beginning, fresh start." George cleared his throat. "I'm sure you understand…" He failed to finish the sentence, thought of the time he had spent talking to his neighbour about Hong Kong: the climate with its brief winter, the proximity to the sea and the breezes it would bring, the vast choice in accommodation. He had even been told of a good school Susan could attend.

"I see. I had no idea." Henry said and scratched his head. "Let me get you another drink." Without waiting for a response, he was gone, ignoring the waiter who had been hovering, waiting to refill their glasses. Or eavesdropping, listening in to George's disbelief, watching his disappointed face.

So now, were his dreams of a new life in Hong Kong being blown away over a drink in a dingy bar, in tin mining territory? He had been looking forward to the discussion with Dorothy; it was so long since she had smiled at him, shown her approval of his plans. At least she would have been given a choice. What would her reaction be to this news? Of course she would want to return to England, but not to Portsmouth, and not with him in an inferior position. He looked over towards the bar where Henry was leaning, chatting to the waiter as he squirted soda water into the glasses. Something about the way Henry had responded to his suggestion, made him go over the exchanges they had just made. It was not difficult to tell when a man had been caught out, was embarrassed by his own reluctance to be honest. Tipping his glass to his mouth, he let the remainder of the melted ice seep onto his tongue.

Then there was Emma. The best chance he had of her fading from his memory was to stay out there. Though she would never entirely vanish. But she would, he had hoped, become a distant recollection of good times, like the summers that never ended in childhood.

Henry was returning empty handed, a waiter following him, carrying the two whisky and sodas on a tray.

Putting his hand out, Henry said, "Look George, sorry to be the bearer of bad news. The Director insisted it be me. Good of him really. Less troublesome this way."

There was little else George could do other than take Henry's hand and shake it. They sat sipping their drinks, frowning up at the wisps of smoke winding upwards towards the ceiling.

"If I have to go back to England, I would rather be in London." George swallowed hard. "For Dorothy's sake."

"I'll see what I can do."

"And you," George asked. "Do you have any plans?" He watched Henry remove his hat from a chair, straighten the band, and look towards the door, as if he were expecting someone.

"Look, old chap. Can't be hanging around too long. Must get back to Matilda. We're playing bridge today and..." He looked at his watch. "Well, you know what women are like." He faltered, the tiny veins in his cheeks started to glow crimson.

"So," George insisted. "What are your plans?"

"I've been offered a transfer to Hong Kong. Matilda's quite keen on the idea." He scratched the side of his nose. "Sorry, old chap. I had no idea you were after a transfer yourself. And that's the truth of the matter."

George lifted his glass to his lips and drank deeply, aware that a couple of the English fellows were staring at him. Hurriedly they looked away, resumed a conversation.

***

The interior of the new trinket box matched the green baize of the table and the lid, propped halfway open with two of Dorothy's books, had intricate mother-of-pearl inlay. Feng had chosen well, according to George's instructions. Even he could see the quality of craftsmanship. Adjusting the position of the box, he tried to conjure up Dorothy's reaction as he presented it to her. Then, he would pour her a large whisky, sit her down in her favourite seat on the veranda... he pondered. Maybe he should tell her his news over dinner, after he had run a bath for her, maybe lit a candle or two.

It was strange being at home instead of at work. As if he were wearing mismatched shoes, or had misplaced his glasses. He fetched the folded newspaper from where he had discarded it on the chair, and reread the first page, turned it to the back page. But he had already completed the crossword hours before. Still, he could not help feeling a sense of pride in the record time it had taken him to finish. Quite at a loss, he paced the rooms of the empty house, and still he had unfinished business at work; forms he had not completed, telephone calls waiting to be returned. And the letters, all those letters from Emma. Why had he not burned them, or torn them into shreds? Would Miss Hall read them all, pass on his secrets to the other secretaries? Not that he would ever see them again.

Walking swiftly down the veranda steps he glanced over towards his neighbours' house as he walked across the lawn. No music came from their direction. The husband would be at work, the wife playing bridge, or tennis, or shopping. But wherever she was, George was glad she was not at home. Avoidance was the best stance to take. Far better than informing them there was no need to discuss Hong Kong any more. As he swung on the swing seat Dorothy favoured, he wondered how far they all were on their journey home. He calculated for the hundredth time, allowing for stops, possible army checks, maybe a slow-down on flooded, pot-holed roads that they should be home within the hour. Probably less, and then he would hear the key turn in the lock.

Half an hour later, the door bell rang. He slopped whisky from his glass, the sound startled him so. Had she forgotten her key? No, they would think he was at work. Taking a comb out of his pocket, he quickly ran it through his hair. Sarah stood at the door.

"I heard," she said. "England again."

"Look this isn't a good idea. Dorothy and Susan will be back any minute." Annoyance at how fast the news had travelled made him brusque in his tone, he realised too late. The words were already out.

"Five minutes. Please."

How could he turf her out? Though the logical side to him wanted to do just that, it would be cruel of him to close the door in her face. As he stepped aside to let her in, he noticed the unhealed scar at the hairline of her temple. A flash of recall; the butt of a rifle smacking her across her face, the scream that followed, and he remembered the day he had been so rough with her, the day of his assault. He led the way into the sitting room.

Without inviting her to sit down, he stood under the mirror on the wall. She moved close to him, the smell of her perfume: lilies again. Sliding sideways, he almost offered her a drink, then changed his mind, stepped away so he was near the veranda doors. To his relief, she did not follow him.

"Dick has suggested I go to England for a while. See more of my son."

George raised his eyebrows.

"Said he didn't want a fuss." She picked up the mahogany box and examined the surface, played her fingers over the mother-of-pearl. "He can't stand fuss. Wants everything just so." She put the box down and traced a circle on the lid with her forefinger. "I'll be leaving next month. Flying. It takes about a week."

"Well, I'm sure he knows best," George said. He gave a small sigh. What a stupid remark. "I mean... I didn't mean."

She raised a hand. "It's all right."

"But you'll like to see more of your son, won't you?"

"Of course. I'd prefer him to live with us. Not stuck in some institution in Sussex. But Dick won't hear of it. I'll be staying with his cousin in Brighton."

The mention of Brighton brought Grace, and her neat twin sets, her pursed lips, and the fumbling Tom, to his mind. Quickly, he made a decision not to tell Sarah of his connection to that particular backwater.

"A peaceful little town, so I've heard."

"Portsmouth's not that far." The words were delivered in a faint voice. She cleared her throat and repeated them.

"I believe not." Best not to mention the change of plan he hoped Henry would see to.

"Do I have to beg you? Can't you see what I'm driving at?" Sarah's arms were outstretched towards George, her face imploring him.

Ten minutes must have passed since she had arrived. He would have to come straight to the point.

"Look, Sarah," he said. "I'm terribly fond of you. But it won't do. We can't see each other any more." There, he had said it. And now he felt sorry, uneasy at the distress he was causing. "We're both married, after all," he added. Watching her swallow rapidly, he hoped that she would leave and not begin to cry.

Taking control of herself, she stood in front of the mirror, her back to him and pulled at her hair, extracting strands from the waves, patting them into place. From the corner of his eye, George watched her reapply her lipstick. He saw her eyes slide to meet his in the reflection. Avoiding them he side-stepped to the door, took a couple of deep breaths. The clock in the hall ticked loudly, a bird settled on a chair outside, bobbing its head up and down. Still, Sarah made no sign of leaving.

"So that's it," she said without turning.

"For the best." He opened the sitting room door, his hand resting on the door handle, a sensation in his lower abdomen turning into an ache. The roar of a car engine made him jerk his neck back and tighten his grip. But the motor carried on, the rumble fading into the distance.

"Please," he said, "they'll be back any minute." Watching her, he felt surges of adrenalin run though him as she made her way to the veranda door. First, he glanced behind him, as if expecting Dorothy to materialise in the hall. Then he noticed Sarah unclasping her bag, before turning to face him and stepping across the rug, her hips swaying, her momentum steady. And it seemed to him that her movements continued to be deliberately slow as she opened a notebook, shook a pen, testing the ink flow. He rotated his fingers on his temples, as she wrote. Clicking his fingers, he turned into the hall, waited by the front door. At last he heard her footsteps. Her face was flushed.

"You will write to me?" She nodded towards the piece of paper as he stuffed it into his pocket. "Let me know how you're getting on."

"Of course I will." He opened the front door, stood on the threshold. The danger was receding; there was no car on the street ahead and Sarah was moving towards him. Sweat dampened his forehead. He could tell she was about to cry, saw the downturned mouth, the blinking eyes as she tried to resist. No time to comfort. He took two steps in one long stride, turned his head towards his gate, her egress. At last he heard her behind him, watched her pass him, retreating down the path. Not once did she turn to look back at him. He admired her for that.

Chapter 23

Her mother's voice drifted out to Susan. Peels of laughter followed, ringing, echoing through the house. Reassured, Susan picked up her skirt again and resumed pinning the hem. Mrs McPherson made her mother happy, her face expanding into mirth; it was she, Susan, who caused such misery and it was her fault, her doing that had made her parents argue, fight, made her mother cry and her father keep his face closed, tight shut. But she missed her father, wanted to wrap her arms round him, feel his stubble graze against her cheek, smell the sleep in him as he ruffled her hair in the mornings. And now, she did not care about the woman who was with him on that day, or about Emma of the letter she had found. Most of all she wanted to go back to the day she saw his car parked on the road and undo all the damage she had caused. She wished she had not strayed from Feng, could not forget the look of helplessness, absolute terror, on her father's face in the jungle. Susan pricked her thumb with a pin. It gave her comfort, letting her blood seep. She counted to sixty. Then fixing a finger to the tiny incision, she put a stop to the flow. There, it was up to her, no one else's decision. Another laugh interrupted her concentration. It belonged to Mrs McPherson, a hoarse giggle, thick, full of carefree fun. What was it that made them both laugh so much? What was Mrs McPherson's secret?

The sound of her mother's shoes clicking across the bare wood came nearer. She turned and greeted her, hid her punctured thumb.

Her mother sat in the long chair, her bare legs stretched out, ankles crossed. Susan smelt the fresh aroma of newly applied perfume, noticed her mother had changed into a dress she had not seen before.

"Susan," she said, "how would you like to go back to Ipoh?"

This was hardly a surprise; Susan knew the date her boat sailed back to England, when she was due back at school. If she left her parents alone, left them to sort themselves out, it all might be better when she saw them again. Or maybe they would prefer it if she stayed away forever, stayed with the narrow beds, cold sheets, the scratchy blankets. "When will we go back?" she asked.

"Feng will be arriving here this afternoon. We leave tomorrow." Legs uncrossed now, her mother brushed an invisible speck off her dress.

"Can't wait to see Daddy again," Susan said. "You do miss him, don't you? I mean everything's all right? Only sometimes..." She stopped. Maybe it was best not to let her mother know her fears.

Her mother stared out across the plantation, gave a slight nod as she cooled herself with a feather fan.

"Well, you've had a bit of a holiday," her mother said. "You seemed to be enjoying yourself at rounders on Friday." She bent towards Susan, kissed her on the cheek, gave her arm a squeeze. "And you like Mr and Mrs McPherson, don't you?"

Part of Susan wanted to stay there forever, if only her father were with them as well.

Her mother's eyes fixed on the blood smeared pin. A look of puzzlement flitted across her face.

"Pricked myself sewing," Susan said. She would stop, she *would*. As soon as they got back to Ipoh and everything was normal again.

"So unnecessary, this habit you've got into." Her mother stared at Susan, her eyes narrowed, searching, as if looking for clues. "You've had enough to deal with. Seeing your father..." she turned away,

240

"like that." She slapped both hands on her lap and stood. "But things will be different now. Very different. Better for you. And me. A better life for us."

"What do you mean?"

Susan watched a rosy glow spread from her mother's neck to her cheeks, accentuating the scarlet background of her smart, new, spotted dress. And she knew that her mother was regretting what she had said. The twiddling of her wedding ring reinforced this knowledge.

"You'll see. Let me speak to your father first," her mother said.

"Different how?" Susan persisted.

But her mother was stepping over the threshold of the veranda. Over her shoulder she grinned at Susan. "Hannah has just made some lemonade. Let's go in. Then we must pack."

"Mummy, please... talk to Daddy about what?"

"Come and have some lemonade."

The back of Susan's neck prickled. She felt her chest tighten. What changes did her mother have in store for her now? A better life, she had said. All Susan wanted was to return to the old one. What could be better than that? She started to breathe fast, the niggling doubt returned, probing her, biting at her consciousness, just like the incessant mosquitoes. Her mother's tone was so familiar, the hesitation, the faltering sentences, all accompanied with a change of gear, a quick exit. Did her mother not realise how much she gave away with her foiled attempts to maintain a code of secrecy? All the murmurings with Mrs McPherson late into the night, the sudden drop in conversation at her presence. Did her mother think she was so stupid not to realise what changes she planned for them now? Poking at her skin again with the pin, she watched the blood ooze bit by bit, then let the pin drop to the floor. She felt better now.

She turned to look out from the veranda at the stubbly grass, at a scrawny cat as it slept, at peace, sprawled out under a palm frond. Today, a sheet of clouds hung over the plantation, unmoving, as if held inert by invisible strings. Distant voices of the tappers meandered across to her in the windless heat and she saw Mr McPherson's tall figure appear in the distance. She picked up her dress, tucked her book under her arm and went indoors.

The lemonade deserved savouring. A small sip at a time was the amount Susan allowed herself; she wanted the taste to stay with her as long as possible. Even the ache of ice, the barely touchable cold was a tortuous pleasure. And she was aware of Mrs McPherson watching her every move, greenish eye-shadow flashing intermittently with every blink, a touch of humour in her face.

"So, Susan," Mrs McPherson said. "Are you going to look after your mother when you get back?"

Susan spotted the reproachful look her mother gave Mrs McPherson.

"When you get back to Ipoh, of course," Mrs McPherson said quickly. "And I hope you'll come and visit us again." The sling-back slipped off her heel as she raised her foot off the ground and crossed one leg over the other.

Susan found herself comparing Mrs McPherson to her mother. Admiring her emerald green dress, the wide belt, the dainty three quarter-length sleeves, and her neat blond curls, she began wishing, not for the first time, that this was her real mother.

Smiling at Mrs McPherson, pointedly, Susan excluded her mother from her vision. She gulped back her lemonade, folded her hands in her lap. "That's for Daddy to do." She stared into her empty glass.

Her mother's laugh was exaggerated, forced, not like Mrs McPherson's loose, easy laugh. Then her expression changed quickly and Susan saw the lines gather on her forehead, noticed tears forming in her eyes. Rushing over to her, Susan gave her a hug, felt tears come to *her* eyes. How could she have wanted to swap her mother for Mrs McPherson?

"You'll feel better when we get back to Ipoh." And a kiss was planted on Susan's nose.

"Will I?" Susan sniffed, embarrassed now, by the closeness she had come to tears.

"Come on, Susan," Mrs McPherson said cheerily. "There's something I want to show you."

"I'll show her Patrick's butterfly collection," said Mrs McPherson. Another quick look, meaningful, loaded with admonitions, passed between her and her mother.

"Go on, Susan," her mother said. She smiled.

Mrs McPherson would know of her mother's intentions, and would, if pressed, tell Susan all. Following her hostess out of the sitting room, she padded along the corridor into Mr McPherson's study. Mounted butterflies covered the walls, the colours vibrant on glistening wings. Susan turned to Mrs McPherson, was about to ask for details, when she heard her mother behind them.

"I've come to see them too," her mother said and linked Susan's arm, like they were old buddies, all secrets shared.

***

The clouds of the day before had been wiped from the sky, replaced by a block of blue, solid and deep, with no heat haze yet to blur the horizon. A beam of early morning sunlight caught in the mirror's reflection, making her mother's eyes appear translucent, the brown turned to gold. A final pat to her hair, a hint of rose to her lips, then her mother turned to Susan.

"Ready?"

"What about this? You're not leaving him behind, are you?" Susan picked up the tiny Buddha hidden by a vase of cannas, petals dropped, scattered on the dressing table. It fitted perfectly into her pocket. She had chosen it with such care, had so looked forward to giving it to her mother. But, then she had hidden in that toilet with the putrid smells, snatching at her throat and nose. If she had not done that, the knowledge of her father's doings would have remained hidden from her; she would not have seen the shame laid bare on his face that afternoon.

She picked up her suitcase, followed her mother out of the bedroom.

Mr and Mrs McPherson were waiting on the porch.

"Got everything?"

"You must come again."

"It'll be so quiet now you're going. Just the two of us."

"We'll write when we get back," her mother said and nudged Susan in the ribs.

"Thank you for having us," Susan said. "It's been super."

"Next time I'll teach you another card game." Mr McPherson shifted his feet. "Better be getting back to work." He offered his hand, first to her mother then her. His grip was powerful, the skin rough, like pumice-stone.

Susan sat in the back of the car again. Her mother drove fast, bouncing over potholes. And in front of Susan sat Feng. Her hair, black, and shiny, the ends shorn abruptly, no curl or ringlet to swing with the movement of the car. Words had been few between her and Feng, kept to the essential, enough not to create suspicion of the simmering resentment that Susan felt sure Feng reserved for her. But her parents had not dismissed Feng, as they had come so close to doing, though Susan knew she was not supposed to know this.

The early morning coolness soon faded as the flat heat of the afternoon set in. It seemed everyone they passed was resting in the shade, waiting, stretched out, sitting on their haunches, marking time, lazily watching the car as it passed. Susan drifted, lulled by the noise of the engine, by the intermittent drone of the cicadas. She dreamt of Mrs McPherson in her pretty, green dress. She was waving goodbye on the step of her bungalow, trying to tell Susan something, her words tangled, impossible to understand. As she dozed, the little Buddha banging against her was swung around by the rough road. They drove for several hours, only stopping twice for refreshment. Each time, as soon as they got going, Susan slept again, secure in her dreaming.

Woken for the third time by the jolt of the car suddenly stopping, Susan's dream was again interrupted: this time she thought she was on the boat back to England, that the warm wind that blew onto her face from the open window was a sultry breeze sweeping across the ocean.

They had stopped outside the office where her father worked.

"He might still be here," her mother said. "Mr Golding's car is still there, so it looks like we've caught him just in time." She smiled at Susan. "I'm doing this for you."

Susan stared back at her mother. "What are you doing for me?"

"You said you missed Daddy."

"Don't you?"

A hand moved to fiddle with her wedding ring. But the movement was brief, scarcely visible. "Won't be a minute," her mother said. "I'll fetch your father and then we'll all go home together." She left the car door open after she had climbed out, turned and waved to Susan just as she got to the office building.

Leaning her arm across the back seat, Feng gazed at the little Buddha, fallen out of Susan's pocket. She slid her eyes up to Susan's face. "You looking well. Away from town good for you. Mr Johnson wait for you. Me too. I miss you too." And she turned back, resumed staring out of the side window.

"D'you think she'll be long?"

"No, not long."

But, not for another minute could Susan tolerate the inside of the car. The metallic box crowded her, was airless, despite the open doors.

"What *are* they doing?" she said to Feng. Impatiently, she circled the car, squinting up to the building, willing her parents to hurry, trying to work out which window belonged to her father's office.

"Better you wait in car," said Feng. "Sun too hot for you. No shade here."

Then her mother appeared. Alone. Graciously, like the Queen, she waved and smiled as she neared the car. "Sorry," she said. "Bit longer than I thought. Let's get you home."

"Where's Daddy?"

"Already there." Eyes downcast, she paused, reached in her bag for a cigarette. Inhaling deeply, she stared at Feng through the window, touched Susan's elbow, guided her to the open car door.

As the car drew up the drive, Susan saw her father standing at the top of the steps. Dashing from the car, she leapt up to meet him. She clung onto him, felt the solidity of his body, smelt his hair, the familiar after-shave and sweatiness of his neck. How could she have hated him before? What if something had happened to him while they were away? Aware that her mother was standing, waiting behind her, she stood to one side, watched her father circle her mother with his arms. But the embrace was not reciprocated. Her mother withdrew, said she was going upstairs to change.

Susan followed her father through the house out onto the veranda. It felt like years since she had been there. Strange that nothing had changed, even the column of ants looked identical to the ones she had watched before.

"Well then," her father said. "Good time? Was Mummy's friend nice?" He indicated a chair with open hand, moved it an inch or so towards her. "Good to have you both home. Not the same without you." A fleeting look of sadness moved across his face. "I'm going to have a sherry. I expect your mother would like a drink too. Orange juice for you?" He hesitated, and a smile made his skin crinkle like fine tissue paper. "Or ginger beer?"

Susan wanted to ask him about the day in the jungle, and about that woman he was with and about this other woman, Emma. There was so much she wanted to know and understand. But, no need to spoil this moment, better to hang on to it, stretch it out for as long as she could. She asked for a ginger beer and watched him striding across the sitting room. "Back in a tic," he called out. "Just going to see what your mother would like."

Already the sun was starting to set; the blue was changing to a darker hue and a pink, the colour of sherbet, spread out across the sky. The low tones of her father's voice drifted down from the balcony above as Susan rocked in her mother's swing seat, pretending to read her book and waiting.

Ten minutes later, her parents came out onto the veranda.

"Well, here we all are," her mother said. A full glass of sherry was clasped in both her hands. "I note it's as hot as ever here, no rest for the wicked." But she did not laugh as she would have done in Hannah's house.

"Has my little girl been good?" Her father asked, a grin plastered on his face.

"I'm not little anymore, Daddy."

"You'll always be my little girl."

"No, George you're wrong there," said her mother. "You made her grow up too fast for her own good. Your actions, your involvement with that... You're so wrong. As usual you can't see what's going on in front of your eyes." Her breathing was fast.

"Dorothy, why do you have to disagree with everything I say? You've only been back two minutes. Why do you always want confrontation?"

"Stop it, stop it," said Susan. "Please."

A large moth was flitting round the light, its wings scratching the surface of the shade. Suddenly it dropped to the table struggling, its wings singed, drooping, useless.

Her mother put her hand on Susan's. "It's been a long day. An early night for you, I think."

"Sorry, Susan," her father said. "Tell me what you did down there in the wilds of Selangor. Did you meet other girls of your age? I don't believe Hannah has any children." He raised his eyebrows as he looked at her mother as if seeking her agreement, a validation of his words.

"No, no children," her mother said quietly.

Susan extracted a long strand of hair from her plait. Winding it tight round her finger, she wondered whether it would have been better for her parents if she had never been born. Maybe then, they too would be as contented as Mr and Mrs McPherson. She thought of Mrs McPherson giggling, the way her husband would blush as he smiled to himself. Perhaps that is just what her parents really needed. For her to disappear completely. Pretend she was not there at all.

Her father was tapping his glass with a finger. An account of Mr McPherson's collection of butterflies, of the translucent blues, of the wings like miniature tiger skins, seemed to placate him for the time being; her mother explained it all in great detail.

"But I do think it's cruel to stick pins in them and hang them on the wall." Susan stared down at the moth, now barely moving, having given up the fight.

After dinner, she lay in her bed, eyes wide open. The explosive sounds of her parents' voices reached her from the room below. She pulled the sheet up, over her head, but this did not block out the crescendos of their quarrel. Part of her wanted to block it out, but the inquisitive side won. Barefooted, she stepped quietly to her door, gently opening it, so its hinges did not whine. Slowly, carefully, she crept down the stairs. Each step that might creak was recognised and avoided. At the middle step she crouched and listened. But the shouting had stopped, their voices were muffled. Had they closed all the doors, lowered their voices to stop her hearing their plans, to prevent her from knowing what they held in store for her next? She heard the rattle of a door knob, the creak of an opening door, her mother's footsteps hurrying into the hall. Deftly, Susan retreated to her room, expecting her mother to come up the stairs, to reprimand her for eavesdropping. A door downstairs slammed shut, the argument continued. Holding her breath she listened hard, but the voices were muted, indistinguishable from the murmurings of the night air. Eyes heavy, she fell into a dreamless sleep.

Chapter 24

Because Dorothy was leaving Malaya, because she had made her decision about George, there was a calmness in her, a tranquillity that was new to her. And she could not help feeling proud of herself, the way she had not allowed George to sway her, to manipulate her with his promises, as he had done before. It was a coincidence indeed that he too was being returned to England. Shame that she could not dump him here; leave him to manage on his own.

She stepped down into the garden and looked across to the pergola and the jacaranda tree. Hibiscus, their pinks almost fluorescent, jasmine, their powerful scents, all bright and cheerful in the lazy sun, climbing, tangled with the humming shrubs. Would she miss them, tire easily of the mildness of the English rose? The lawn was flattened, the blades of grass shorn. Babiya appeared suddenly, noiselessly. She called out, thanked him for his services, wished his family well. He stared at her, a shy smile spreading across his face; she felt a blush rising from her neck, then he nodded. In his broken English, he wished her a safe journey home. The short interaction over, he turned away from her, towards the garden shed.

Closure, an end to her time in Malaya, and there were so few people to say goodbye to, few acquaintances that would miss her. She thought of Susan, the explanation that she had prepared for her, list-like, a summary of events, the future laid out, drawn like a map. And, on cue, Susan was standing on the veranda, the end of her finger in her mouth, the chewing becoming more apparent as Dorothy neared.

Dorothy chose not to remark about the torn nail, the drop of blood which had formed at the finger end, or the acetone smell of hairspray that drifted from Susan's new hairstyle. "I see you've learnt Hannah's hairdressing skills." She touched Susan's hair; it was coarse, stiff, like starched strands of yarn. "Very up to the minute. Pin curls suit you. It must have taken a long time to do." Indicating to Susan to sit down beside her, she rocked, hummed to herself, took Susan's hand, patted it gently, waiting for the right moment. Susan stopped fidgeting, rested her hands in her lap.

"We must talk about the future now," Dorothy said. She turned to look at Susan. "There are going to be some changes for us all." She paused. "I discussed it all with your father last night, and now he's out, I thought it would be a good time for me to explain."

Susan remained motionless, staring out at the garden.

"Your father and I have been having problems, as you know," Dorothy continued. "You know about everything he's done. You saw that woman with your own eyes."

Susan rolled her eyes towards Dorothy, then back to the garden. Still, she made no remark, no comment or sign of agreement. Dorothy continued. "You will, of course Susan, live with me. We'll be staying with Auntie Grace and Uncle Tom at first. And you'll go to a day school in Brighton. You'll like that, won't you? Never really took to boarding school, did you? And I have missed you so…"

"…You said I will live with you?"

"Yes, with me. You'll live with me."

"What about Daddy? Will he live with us too?"

"No, my dear. We're getting divorced. This is what I've been trying to tell you."

Susan was still staring out at the garden and Dorothy followed her gaze, but she could not tell what held her attention. "It'll be nice. Just you and me. We'll have fun," Dorothy said. Watching her carefully, she saw Susan move her head. She was staring at her blunt finger nails, at the pink rawness of the skin. Glancing quickly at Dorothy, she clasped her hands, hiding the damage from her.

"Where's Daddy going to live?"

"He's going back to London. But you'll see him in the holidays." The explanation was in the wrong order, she should have told Susan about her father. And why did Susan remain so composed, so placid in her reaction? Had George pre-empted Dorothy, told Susan his side, his version of the explanations? Would that explain the hushed exchanges she had overheard in the morning?

"So are we all going to England on Friday?"

Dorothy hesitated, wiped her brow.

"We'll all be together on the boat on Friday?" Susan asked again.

"He might go back later. He's fixing the date today."

"Why can't he come back with us?"

"We decided, Susan, that it might be better for us to travel separately."

"Why? Why can't we be like a proper family, like we were before? You always fight with Daddy. I heard you last night. Arguing again. You were shouting at him. I heard you. I want to live with you both. Not just you."

"It's for the best Susan. Your father and I can't continue as we are. You were fine at Hannah's, weren't you? Just the two of us? It'll be just like that."

"But I don't want it. You never think of me. What I want." Susan was fiddling with her new pin curls, unravelling them, tugging them straight. "It's not the best for me. I don't want to live apart from Daddy. I knew this was going to happen. I knew it, I knew it." Breathing rapidly, she turned and ran into the house, up the stairs. Her bedroom door slammed.

Dorothy started up the stairs too, thought better of it halfway up, and returned to the quiet of the veranda. Going over the conversation, repeating Susan's responses to herself, she looked towards Babiya, now leaving the shed, his sinewy arms like sculptured clay, his amble to the back gate, steady.

Had she again, mishandled her own daughter? Would yesterday have been a better time to explain, as Hannah had suggested? Now Susan blamed her. She walked to the end of the veranda, and back, pacing resolutely, until her dress was sticking to her skin. Her flesh itched and sweltered in the midday sun. There was no sound from within the house, she began to worry about Susan, decided to investigate.

Tapping gently on Susan's door she called out, "Susan. Can I come in?" She turned the handle, pushed the door. It jammed, would not give to her efforts. "Susan," she said again, her voice louder. Terrible pictures of Susan with bloodied pins in her fingers formed in her mind. She hammered on the door, but there was silence from within. Then she heard the scrape of wood against wood, of lifting, heaving, until the door opened.

"Why are you making such a noise?" Susan asked calmly.

The light from the window behind partially obscured Susan's face and Dorothy saw the sunlight picking a rosy hue round Susan's silhouette, then noticed the shorn head, the tufts standing up from her scalp. Susan stood aside and Dorothy, picked her way through the fallen ringlets, rigid and hard, scattered on the floor.

"Why?" asked Dorothy. "Your hair. What have you done?"

"Didn't like it."

"So, why did you push the table against the door? Why didn't you let me in? I thought something had happened to you. More than this." A wave of hair, soft, untouched by mists of spray, lay softly on the bed. Dorothy picked it up, ran her fingers through it, ignored her impulse to show her dislike, her distaste for the close-cropped hair.

"I wanted to be alone. Then I decided to cut my hair. I was only going to trim it, but I couldn't stop once I'd started. Then I heard you at the door. And I had to finish cutting it before I let you in."

"It's so short."

"It's better like this. I've always hated my hair." Taking the scissors, Susan retrieved the lock from the bedcover, cut it into four, let the pieces drift back to the floor, tiny wisps floating through the air.

Grabbing the scissors, Dorothy held onto them firmly. "I wish you weren't so angry with me," she said. "I have tried very hard."

"I don't want you and Daddy to split up. We're fine the way we are. If I hadn't gone off from Feng that day, you wouldn't have known about that woman and everything would be normal. Why can't you pretend it didn't happen? Just be like it was before. If I go back to boarding school, it'll be the same. Like it was before I came over from England. Can't we stay the same?"

"No, we can't do that." Dorothy got up and walked to the window. The sun was high, the sky pale with heat. "We'll be back in England soon. We might have a white Christmas." She turned and smiled at Susan. "It could be worse, you know. It could always be worse than it is. You must remember that."

"You always say that."

Suddenly, Dorothy felt she wanted to leave the bedroom, let Susan stay there, alone with her abandoned tresses. "You must try not to think of yourself all the time. It may be hard, but you've still got both of us." Quickly, she gave Susan a hug. "I'll make a drink. Daddy will be back soon." Leaving the door wide open, she left the bedroom.

Downstairs, Dorothy poured out a glass of lemonade for Susan, a whisky for herself. She sipped it slowly as she rocked on the swing seat on the veranda. Susan must learn, she thought to herself, to take things as they come, to accept the fate that was handed to her. It was worse for Dorothy when she was Susan's age; hunger, when the shop's till was empty: a cold dampness, penetrating the bones when there were no shillings for the meter. No questions asked, no demands for explanations. Rocking slowly in her chair, sipping her drink, feeling the warm flow, taking over, soothing, Dorothy thought back to the dance the week before, the tea planter, his ruddy face close to hers, waltzing, relating his search for a wife, a companion, someone to help him take the strain. Of the danger she would be in, he said nothing, assuming she would accept it along with him.

She stretched her legs, stirred the ice in her whisky, brushing a fly off the rim of her glass. A bird was clucking in the jacaranda tree, answering its mate in the neighbour's garden. Glancing up, she watched it fly above the lawn, sit on the pergola and preen itself, its white crest flashing against the blue sky.

Susan was in the kitchen now. Her voice trailed out to the garden as she chatted with Feng. Dorothy felt she seemed more able to manage Susan, had a way of calming her that Dorothy lacked. And she was glad she had persuaded George to retain Feng; a small battle won, though now it would make no difference. The contents of the conversation were indecipherable from the veranda, Dorothy moved closer, stepped into the sitting room, heard a key turn in the front door. Susan galloped back up the stairs and Dorothy went to greet

George, stopping after a couple of steps. Habits so difficult to lose, like shaking off a heavy overcoat. Refraining, she returned to the veranda, finished her whisky too quickly, and wondered how long would it take for her to get used to living without him.

But George did not come straight through to her. Had he been thinking the same? Eventually, he joined her, gave her a quick kiss on the cheek. "I hope you don't mind, but Henry and Matilda are coming over for a drink later. I invited them a bit ago. Before any of this. I had thought it would be a good idea. A nice thing to do. You were always quite fond of them." He started busying himself with the paper, folding it, re-folding it into four, seemingly unaware of the week-old date. "That's all right, isn't it? It's too late to cancel it now." Looking up at her, he added. "Best not to tell them... what you... what we decided last night. No need for them to know."

"Susan cut all her hair off when I told her we are getting divorced."

The paper was rolled, deposited on the chair. But he did not look at her, instead he was gazing at a broken tile in the flooring. His eyes returned to her face, staring, as if he had not seen her before.

"Cut her hair you said. What for? I always thought Susan's hair very pretty... like yours." A smile, a fleeting one, passed across his face.

"You must stop them coming. I don't want to see anyone now. Not after everything... after all that's happened. Pretending everything is as normal. No, George, I can't do it. Not any more. There's time for you to go round there. Tell them I'm not well. Explain to them I've got a terrible headache... anything, anything. Think of an excuse. I can't see them ..."

He interrupted her. "I think they're here now. A quick drink that's all it will be. Half an hour."

The ring of the door bell had eluded her. No time to escape, to hide in her room with a fever, a headache to beat all others she had endured. George came over to her, touched her shoulder. Too late, Henry and Matilda were shown in by Feng. All smiles and out-stretched hands. George poured out drinks, taking his time, holding each measure up to the light.

"Here's to England," Henry said.

"And Hong Kong," added George. "When do you leave?" He sat down and nursed his drink, looked at Dorothy, as though expecting her to join in with the repertoire.

"Not for another two months," Matilda said. "What a rush *you've* got. But I expect you're glad to be going back, aren't you, Dorothy? Not been much fun for you here, really... I mean you've found the climate quite difficult. Am I right?" She smiled at Dorothy. Was it genuine, or one of pity, faked understanding?

"Yes, I prefer a cooler clime," said Dorothy. Her hands refused to stay still in her lap. Noticing her neglected beads, she picked them up, felt the coolness of the amber against her fingers.

"Had quite a time of it one way and another," Matilda continued. "That terrible business with the Communists. Awful for you..." She stopped suddenly, responding to Henry's warning look. "Of course, you'll soon forget all that. An easier time ahead." She picked up the box George had bought Dorothy. "Pretty," she said. "Very pretty." Diaphanous, the mother-of-pearl glimmered.

"Dorothy was saying she'd like you to have some potted plants we've become fond of. Hate them to wither for lack of care." The look George gave Dorothy was one of co-conspiracy, one that would have warmed her once.

"Shall we see them?" Matilda played her fingers round the rim of her glass, replaced the whisky carefully on the table. Opening her mouth, as if about to speak to Dorothy, she turned the words into a cough then followed George out to the veranda. Over her shoulder she said to Henry, "Not really interested in plants, are you, darling?" Daintily, holding her skirt with both hands, she stepped onto the veranda. "Come and have a look though. Such a sweet garden..."

Dorothy watched them, finished her drink, smiled across the room at Henry. "Aren't you going to have a look too?"

"In a minute." After what seemed like an age of watching his wife examine an ornamental plant holder, Henry said to Dorothy, "We're both terribly sorry about everything. I really had no idea that George was thinking of Hong Kong. It was an awful coincidence that I have..."

"George? Hong Kong? He wasn't thinking of Hong Kong..." Her voice trailed. Henry looked surprised, puzzled. He swallowed, realisation stalling him, keeping him quiet.

"Wouldn't you like to go outside? I must see to Susan." She indicated towards the room above. "She's taken it all very badly."

"Of course," he said, without making an effort to move. "So George didn't tell you of his plans... about his request for a transfer?" He stared at her. "Just out of interest. None of my business of course. But what has he told you?"

She darted a look outside. George and Matilda were bending over a plant, pink and yellow flowers in full bloom. From Matilda there was an exclamation of pleasure at a fragrance, a murmur of agreement from George. "Look," Dorothy heard him say. "A babbler." He was pointing to a bird perched on the veranda rail. "Not many of them in Blighty."

"We're getting divorced." Dorothy stood. "So all this is un-necessary, all this stuff and nonsense about Hong Kong. I expect that's why he didn't tell me." As she glanced at Henry, she recalled the longing she had felt for his touch. Now, she felt ridiculous, ashamed of her daydreaming. But had he known, noticed her lengthy looks? Is that why he was here instead of helping Matilda with her choice of plants?

"I see," said Henry. He studied her. "I'm so sorry. I've put my foot in it." He started to make for the veranda. "I'm so sorry," he said again.

Dorothy was standing by the door that led into the hall. She did not reply.

"Let's have a look at these plants. I'm no expert of course. No expert at all." Then he was gone, busying himself in conversation with George.

Upstairs, she found Susan sitting on her trunk, dragged out from the wardrobe, clothes, bags askew on the floor. Head in hands, Susan was shaking.

"I hate it now. It's too short. I haven't got any hair anymore." And she started to sob and pull her short hair from the roots.

"It'll grow again. Soon, it'll be long enough for a pony tail." To-gether they sat, arms entwined, comforting each other. She tried to hush Susan, to stem the tears, the sadness that consumed her. Eventually she quietened; they swayed to and fro together on the trunk, their rhythm united, as one.

Voices rose from the hall, a call goodbye from Matilda, an echo from Henry; dutifully Dorothy leant over the banister, shouted, "Bon Voyage. We must keep in touch. Yes, we'll write. Meet up some-time." She watched as George stood on the step waving, before he closed the door.

Chapter 25

The downpour had turned into a drizzle; the dashes of water on George's sitting room window making his view down to the street below appear blurred. Still, he found the nagging cold of England, the eternal rain and greyness, a keen reminder of the sultry blue skies he had inadvertently left behind in Malaya. And that morning was no better. Ridiculously, he had hoped for a sunny day, for open windows, a soft breeze. Rubbing at the glass, he wiped away the condensation and peered down at the tops of umbrellas. But Emma's umbrella would be a bright colour; the sombre black not for her. Pressing his nose to the window, he searched out the face of a woman stepping down from a cab further up the road. He could just make out the sound of the engine turning over as she leant through the open window to collect her change. Then disappointment, a dryness in his mouth, perspiration dampening his brow, despite the chill air, as the woman walked in the opposite direction, her figure unmistakably someone else. Perhaps she did not receive the letter; maybe her husband found it first, opened it, knowing it was from him. George imagined the row that would have followed, the cycle of accusations and denials; the final decision by her not to see him again. After all, she had managed for over a year without him. Why would she want to start it up again?

But there was plenty of time for him to begin the churn of anxiety again, the state of mind that would continue to keep him awake; still ten minutes to go until the appointed time. He withdrew from the window, from the sharp wind seeping through the sash, and paced the room, straightening the painting on the wall, moving both chairs a touch nearer to the fire, centring the vase of dahlias on the table. And still she did not arrive.

It would be what he deserved, if she decided to stay away. For his affair with Sarah sickened him now. The regret for his unfaithfulness to Emma was acute. If she decided to meet him, would she instinctively know? Or was it merely his guilt that was feeding his insecurity? He picked up his paper, turned to the back page. The crossword was blank, the clues meaningless.

The sound of the doorbell touched a nerve, live and jangling. Emma stood in the doorway, her red umbrella dripping on the lino outside his flat.

"Come in," he said. "Come in. Let me take your coat." In an instant, he saw how unchanged she was; his coveted memory had not misled him.

And as he turned to lead the way he thought how shabby his home was, how inappropriate a place for a day like that. She sat in the chair he usually occupied, and he wondered whether she had been drawn to it by his usual presence there, invisible though it had become. Pulling and loosening the fingers of her gloves, she uncovered each hand. "You've made this room very comfortable," she said and clasped her hands over her knee. The flowers received her full concentration. An opportunity for him to gaze at her profile. Her hair was pinned up in a chignon, his favourite style; he wanted to unravel it, to feel the fragility of the nape of her neck, to remove the crystal earrings, explore her tiny lobes with his tongue. Then a nervousness made his hand shake as he poured out two sherries; he could see her scanning the room, taking in the Rembrandt print over the mantelpiece, the Chinese rug under her feet, the nest of tables, bought the week before, in preparation for this occasion. He extracted the smallest table; placed her glass carefully on the surface. Her eyes smiled at him, the green, luminous and bright.

But he did not dare interpret the sign positively. Not yet. "I'll be moving soon, this is only temporary, till I find something more suitable," he said. So much he wanted to say to her. "How're things in Winchester? Must have taken you a time to get here."

"I'm glad I came," she said, "I had to see you." She looked up at him. "How are you?"

Better now that you're here, he wanted to say. Instead he said. "Takes a bit of getting used to. But I like it here. It's home. You're looking well." A hesitation, an interlude. "Your new life obviously suits you."

She was staring at the gas fire. The heat had returned colour to her cheeks. A glance towards him. "I nearly didn't come. As you say I have my new life," she said and her eyes returned to the hissing fire. "But I'm here now." She picked up a glove from the table, smoothed out the wrinkles. "You're thinner." A smile. "But it suits you."

Rehearsed conversations had been about them, their reconciliation, their longings, his absence. Now he wanted to ask her if she thought she had made the right decision. How long had she toyed with the idea? How close was she to staying at home, instead of travelling here?

He drew his chair nearer to hers, smelt her perfume, so familiar. Reaching for his sherry glass, he took a couple of sips. But it was hard to stop the liquid from spilling, impossible to prevent his agitation. His eyes fixed on the skirt of her dress, the shape of her legs beneath.

"Sometimes, when I was in Malaya, I wanted to pick up a telephone, hear your voice. Letters weren't enough."

There was a smudge of lipstick on her glass. She removed it with the tip of her finger circling the pink as she crossed her legs.

He leant forward. "I thought of you every day out there," he said. "Your memory kept me going."

A nod of agreement. Was it an understanding of how he had felt? Likewise, had it been the same for her?

"Did you like it out there?" She adjusted herself, drew her legs further away from the fire, or was it from him she wanted to distance herself?

"Yes. It was certainly different." He thought of the only letter to her he had never sent. One day he would tell her about the attack in the jungle. Providing he had the chance. "It was interesting. Hot, very hot. You can't imagine the heat. Got used to it eventually. Some Brits never acclimatise. Not properly. Some go mad with it." A thought niggled at him, a recurring nag. What if Emma was here to tell him they could not meet again? "I met some nice chaps at the Club..." he stopped and touched her cheek, lightly, giving her a chance to move away, to turn from him. "I don't want to talk about them."

She turned towards him so his hand could not avoid her lips. Moving his face nearer to hers, he saw her widened pupils, felt her hand on his head, pulling him closer, her fragrance enticing, drawing him to her. Catching her hand, he put his lips to the inside of her wrist, transferred them to her mouth. She loosened his tie, her fingers exploring, touching his neck and throat. The clip of her hair slide was released, coppered hair freed, framing her features. He led her into his bedroom, caressed her face; they held on to each other, their lock interrupted only the pulling of her dress over her head, the unhooking of suspenders. Then it was her skin against his, her softness almost unbearable, and kissing, feeling her mouth on his, touching her breasts, her thighs, tasting the salt on her skin. Their limbs found their places, and they clung to each other. The only words spoken were each other's names, whispered repeated, reassuring of their presence.

The ray of sunlight that had first appeared in his bedroom, through the dusty pane, vanished in the two hours they passed in his bed. And the crisply-ironed sheets were damp, the smell of laundered cleanliness replaced with her scent, the mingling of their bodies. Heavy rain had started up again, and distant noises from the street below, a shout from the outside stair, reminded him of the presence of others, of the normality of life beyond this room. Running her hair through his fingers, he splayed it out fan-like on the pillow case, and watched her closed eyes, her long lashes curled at the end. He didn't ask what time she had to leave. An inkling of an idea formed; if they did not talk about their parting, maybe time would not move on. But he got up and made coffee, fearful, that somehow she would be gone when he returned to the room.

Sitting on the edge of the bed, sipping his coffee, he said, "We should be together. I can't imagine life without you again. Not any more. I want you to be with me all the time. To live with me, for you to leave your husband." Hopeless though he knew it was, he had to suggest it. A picture formed in his mind of a gabled house, a garden, a swing erected by him for their children, Emma in a summer dress. "I have better prospects now that your father has left. Easier to get promoted now. Get back to a position similar to the one I had before. Before…"

"…There's nothing I would like more. But it'll be difficult."

"I know." He lay on his side, his face close to hers.

A door was slammed in the flat below, voices shouting.

"If he were to find out… you understand how it would be… for me, at least. I don't know how I'd cope if he found out. If he divorced me. My father is so ill at the moment. He could have another stroke if something like this upset him." She lifted George's hair back from his forehead.

The same as a year ago, her father was standing between them, his disapproval a barrier, perhaps more so than her husband. Flopping on his back, he stared at the twisted light flex, at the glass shade with the veins of fake marble. What was she telling him? Was this indeed the last time they would meet? "So do you still want to see me?"

She rolled on top of him, slid her hand down his torso. "How could I not see you? Tell me how I can do that?" She kissed him down the length of his body, then turned onto her back bringing him with her.

Emma kept her eyes open this time; she wanted to watch George's face, see the change in his expression, the sweat collect on his brow. He held her hands up high above her, his eyes searching hers, his breath, hot, brushing her skin. The exhaustion she had felt before, vanished; she was only aware of George's closeness, his body part of hers until finally, her eyes closed involuntarily and she gripped his hands digging in with her nails.

George rested his head on her shoulder while she stroked his back, felt his heart slow down and his breathing steady. She wanted to stay there forever with him, close her other life behind her, shut the door, start again.

The cold of the winter afternoon, unnoticed before, was making her shiver. A strange weakness set in, as if she could not move. They both pulled the covers over themselves. She turned on her side, lay her head in the crook of his arm. She thought back to the first time they had met, how she had nearly passed out as he touched her arm, the absurd happiness when he asked her to meet him again. And the realisation that her near faint had been from desire for a man she barely knew. With her fiancé away in Germany, she thought she could get away with it; just one time, only one meeting, that was all she thought it would be, that is all.

"Tell me about your house," he said. "When I get your letters, I want to be able to picture you writing them, and you reading mine."

"Won't that make it worse for you?"

"I want to know everything about you and about the way you are, when we're apart." He removed his arm from under her, clasped his hands under his head.

"The army has provided us with a large house." She raised herself onto her elbow, studied his face, drew a line with a finger along his cheekbone. "You don't need to know more."

His eyes closed as if he were trying to imagine it. "Where do you write your letters?"

"I sit at the dining room table. It looks out onto the garden."

A deep sigh and he opened his eyes. "So now I'm getting divorced and you've just married. It's ironical, back to front…"

"As if there is always something to keep us apart." How many times had she relived, reinvented the roll of recent events? There had been an opportunity to delay the marriage date, but how could she have possibly known George would return so soon, alone? And then there was George's suggestion before that; run away together, abandon everything, just be together. She remembered how close she had come to believing it was possible. "I didn't think I would see you again. I thought when I saw you last…"

"The Café Royal. It was raining then too. I remember. I told you I'd come back. I promised you." He got up and roughly pulled the curtains together. "Just as well one of us kept our word."

Why was he angry with her? Now, after what they had just shared? She watched him as he started to put his clothes back on. No backward glance at her. Flicking the end of his tie into a knot, he walked across the room, checked it in the mirror. Although she could clearly see his eyes in the reflection, he refused to meet hers.

"Why are you being like this?" she asked.

"I can't stand thinking of you with Christopher. That's his name isn't it? Christopher?" Still he did not turn round.

What was she supposed to say? Whatever words she chose would hurt him.

"I can't understand why you married him. Was it to please your father, make him proud of you? Or were you not being altogether honest when you told me you didn't love him?"

The reference to her father made her flinch. What was he talking about? How could he possibly know what it had been like for her while he was away? She should have told him more in her letters, let him know he was not the only one who'd paid for their actions, for her father's fury. And now she wanted to get dressed, her nakedness was making her feel vulnerable. "I thought I loved him." Sitting up, she kept the sheet loosely around her waist, started to slip on her underwear. He turned round and watched, sat on the bed next to her. Picking up a stocking where it had fallen to the floor, he handed it to her. "Is that what you really think? That I married him to please my father?" she asked him.

Relief spread through her as he put his arm round her, kissed her hair. "Sorry. I didn't mean that. It's hard for me to think of you as married now. I can't get used to the idea." He stood.

Watching him carefully, she saw him take a breath; stare at the pillow where she had just laid her head.

"When can we meet again? How often?" He tipped her chin towards him.

"As often as I can get away." It was time for her to leave. She could not delay it a minute longer, had not realised how long she had been in George's flat. If she got back too late, there would be no time to compose herself, to prepare for Christopher's return. "It's not often he's away?"

George looked at her quizzically.

"He's been in Germany for a week. Back later on this evening. It was coincidence that you asked me here, the last day he's away."

"And if he hadn't been away..."

"...Yes, I would have been here." Better that he did not know how close she had come to not arriving. How she had let a London train go and turned to the exit, nearly stepped into a taxi to take her back home. And now she had to face Christopher, concoct plans and stories, hide this memory, conceal the excitement for future meetings. This, she knew, would be the hardest for her to achieve.

It was after four o'clock when they left his flat and ran down the three floors, out into the bitter cold of twilight. The street lights were on, the fluorescence ghostly, made hazy by the blowing rain. Standing with her in the downpour, he saw an empty taxi on the other side of the road. It swung round, pulled up at the kerb.

"I'll ring you up next week," she said. "One afternoon." She removed a glove; his face felt her fingers slither down his jaw line, quickly, hardly meeting the surface. Then the sensation was gone, stolen, and she stepped into the taxi. "Don't forget. No letters." She pulled down the window, lent through it. Hair blowing across her face. "Wait until I phone."

Drenched, he stood alone in the street; watching the exhaust fumes of her taxi evaporate, merge with cars lights, vanish into the fog of rain.

Chapter 26

Ripping the old wallpaper off the wall was easy, an enjoyable task, even therapeutic; in any case an unblemished pleasure. Eventually the last shred, a long brown piece, stubborn, as though desperate to cling to the wall was torn from the plaster, revealing the plasterwork bare and potholed ready for her choice of decoration. Dorothy leant back against the wall, observed the pile of curled shavings, the plaster dust that had accumulated on the floorboards. Why wait for Tom to prepare the wallpaper? Why not make a start herself? It looked simple enough. And it was time to show off her new found independence.

Unfolding the pasting table looked easy enough; the legs pulled out obediently and, though the board was cumbersome and a bit big for her to manoeuvre on her own, she eventually succeeded in erecting the apparatus. From the kitchen she fetched the packet of paste and a bowl of water, tipped the powder in and stirred, then brushed the wallpaper with glue scooped from the mixing bowl. Lumps were sliding, popping up in the glue; she beat it, whisked it round like a cake mix, crushing the lumps with the back of a wooden spoon. She began to brush the wallpaper again. The pasting table sagged dangerously in the middle, and the paper started to slide towards the floor.

She took a couple of deep breaths. *Breathe deeply*, Moira had said. Hands on abdomen, she practised the newly learnt technique, swallowed the curse for George that rose in her throat. She thought again of Moira, her new friend; her only friend in Brighton. How she managed somehow to make Susan laugh, to giggle helplessly as she used to before.

Her attention returned to the wallpaper; it was curling at the edges, the paste was beginning to dry. The sheen of glue was disappearing and setting despite all her efforts to keep it moist as directed on the instructions. Lifting the sheet carefully, she started to climb the ladder, holding the sheet away from her, but still the bottom end stuck independently to the middle of the wall. No directions were given on the packet for this turn of events. Wiping perspiration from her forehead with a sticky hand she stepped down from the ladder to survey her work. But the wallpaper was wrinkled and creased, and looked like a furrowed field. She would have to start again. Just as she was halfway up the ladder, she heard the front door open.

It was awkward to turn and look at Grace, Tom, and Susan whilst balancing on the ladder, but she managed it and tried to smile serenely. "Thought I'd make a start."

Not one of them replied for a minute, then they all spoke at once.

"What are you doing, Mummy?" Susan said, surveying calmly, hands on hips.

"Tom said he'd help. Decorating is no job for a woman…"

"You could have fallen from the ladder…"

"Broken a leg. As if you haven't got enough…"

"I'll do it tomorrow, I said before." Tom grinned, surveyed the room, glanced at the pot of paste, at the wallpaper hanging as if in mid-flight or undecided whether to stick or collapse to the floor.

"Got a lot of groceries for you," said Grace. "Thought your larder might need filling."

"And Susan helped us so much," said Tom. The wide beam on his face remained, as though stuck to his features.

271

"You're being very kind," said Dorothy. As she led them into the kitchen.

Susan leant against the kitchen door post. "I want to go out in a minute, Mummy. I've been invited to Jane's," she said.

"I had wanted you to help me." Dorothy sighed. "There's so much to do." She saw a plaster stretched across the back of Susan's hand. Was that here this morning? Now she was not sure.

"Uncle Tom and Auntie Grace are here now. They can help."

Staring down at her daughter's face, Dorothy saw the impatient frown, the bitten lips, the dark smudges under the eyes. Her hair was scraped back into a ponytail, the strands stretched and pulled, as if Susan had thought this action would encourage the growth of the shorn hair. "Wouldn't you rather stay here with us, your family?"

"He should send you money to decorate," Grace said as she filled the kettle. "It's outrageous that you should be expected to do your own decorating, while he sits pretty in his big house." She pulled out an envelope from a shopping bag and handed it to Dorothy. "I bought this for you. You need someone to watch over you. Now George has abandoned you."

"I said I'd do the wallpapering," Tom repeated. "No need for you to do anymore."

"It's I who left George. I did explain." Dorothy opened the envelope. Inside was a Patience Strong poem bordered with pink roses and framed in gilt. Dorothy scanned the first line: *Life is never futile when there is something you can do.* Was this some kind of joke? Looking at Grace's earnest face, Dorothy knew the present had been given in good faith. "And it's for the best." She nodded towards the kitchen where Susan was now making toast for herself.

"He might as well have abandoned *you*," Grace continued.

The automatic angry response to her sister remained on her lips. For Grace meant well, had taken Dorothy's side, instead of blaming her as had been the expected reaction. She bit her lip and smiled at Grace, wiped the mantelpiece with a cloth, put the framed poem in the centre, pride of place.

"I'd rather have someone in the family help me, than have a strange man coming into my flat," she said, the lie slipping easily off her tongue, well practised as she was at covering the truth, protecting herself or Susan from an abrupt reality. But exactly why she was defending George, she was not quite certain. Inwardly, she seethed when she remembered the phone call to his office. A few weeks, he had said, to let him get settled, then he would send some more money; *for any extras that might be needed* was how he put it. But three weeks had passed since that particular promise.

Making pretence, a big to-do of fixing her hair in the dusty mirror, tucking a stray strand behind her ear, she pulled her shoulders back. "Anyway," she continued. "I am enjoying my new life. And it's pleasant earning my own wage. To spend money as I see fit." Another half-truth, but if she told herself enough times that everything was fine, would that not eventually be the case? Besides she was missing George less and less, though sometimes she thought she heard the rustle of his newspaper, the little grunts he made as he pondered over a crossword.

"Mothers should be at home with their children..." Grace started to say.

"But I don't need looking after. I'm at school all day," Susan interrupted, munching toast. "And I'm going to Jane's now. I did tell you." No kiss on the cheek, no look of affection, instead a frown and an unbecoming scowl. The door was slammed; her feet sped down the stairs, the echoes reverberating round the stairwell.

Dorothy felt beaten, unjustly so. Why did Susan's behaviour change when Grace and Tom were around? Was it intentional? A way of showing her up to be a bad mother? Tom was staring out of the window, humming softly to himself, hands in pockets jingling his change, his rotund figure fatherly, a comfort to a growing girl. Maybe, Susan secretly wanted to go and live with them, be part of a proper family.

As if on cue, Grace cut in on Dorothy's thoughts. "And," she said, "you know we'd be more than happy to care for Susan, if it all gets too much for you." A smile creased the loose flesh round her eyes and she stooped to pick up a discarded cup and saucer. Her head was turned away from Tom, Dorothy noticed, a deliberate move, preventing her from acknowledging him, his sigh, the grumble of his cough.

"I'll decorate this flat in a twinkling of an eye," he said. "Not to worry yourself about that." His face was growing redder; he put his hand up to his cheek, but dropped it to his side quickly, as if the heat was burning him. "Excuse me," he said, and left the room.

It was not long before Grace started in the kitchen, opening cupboard doors, rearranging the jars and tins, emptying packets, filling caddies and arranging biscuits on a plate. To Dorothy, it was a reminder of Feng, the constant attention, the removal of ordinary chores from her daily routine. A box of books sent over from Malaya lay untouched, unopened, slammed up against the kitchen wall; tales of murder, of mayhem solved by men with spy glasses, held little interest for her now.

She sneaked a custard cream from the plate and wandered back into the dining room to observe the chaos she had left for Tom to sort out. Outside, two sparrows squawked and fluttered, settling onto the windowsill, observing the disarray with their little, darting eyes. The strip of wallpaper had fallen, and now lay in an abandoned state on the floor, one end still sticking hopefully to the bottom of the wall. But she was glad she had chosen the pattern with white stars spread across a turquoise sky. They reminded her of the cool evening nights here, the nearness of her flat to the tug of waves across the English Channel; the sky clear and bright instead of the murky nights of Malaya, heavy and saturated with a cloying dampness she would never forget.

Finally, Tom and Grace left the flat, taking bags of rubbish down with them, along with their promises of another visit soon and an invitation to lunch on Sunday after church.

Dorothy changed out of her slacks and blouse, threw them into the laundry basket, put on a pretty wool dress, blue with a white trim. She sat by the window in her bedroom, sewed buttons on a dress she had been making for Susan, then hemmed it, her fingers moving swiftly, deftly across the fabric, An early moon was rising, its crescent sharp against the cloudless sky. With elbows resting on the window sill, Dorothy leaned out, staring down at her new street, at the Victorian mansions stretching away towards the sea. She breathed in slowly tasting the salt on the wind, listening to the call of mothers bringing their children in from play.

She thought of Susan, in her new school uniform, still chewing on her finger nails, scabs, scars where she hurt herself, so bad-tempered too. The company of other families sought in preference to Dorothy, the avoidance of all remarks or comments about Malaya, refusing to enter into discussions about it; as if the country did not exist, as if Susan had been nowhere before Brighton. She thought of George's response. *Send her back to boarding school,* he had said. *She was happy there. She told me so.* Too stunned to slam the receiver down, Dorothy had sat heavily on the chair. *I'll pay,* he had added to her silence. *I don't want you worrying on that account.* Strange that money was available for the priorities which suited him. Or perhaps he thought by sending Susan away his guilt would be expunged. For what else could he offer her?

As she stared across at the glittering lights of the pier, just visible through the mist-filled half light, she suddenly longed for Susan to be with her, for them to be watching the view out to sea together, their arms linked, heads touching, laughing at the seagulls as they fought over a crust of bread.

The doorbell rang. Moira was on time. To her surprise, Dorothy found herself bobbing her hair at the nape of her neck and replenishing her lipstick before she went to open the front door. Her friend stood in the doorway, swinging a brown handbag from one hand. It was oversized, slightly ungainly, but suited Moira's large frame.

"I brought you a present for your new home," she said as she followed Dorothy up the stairs. They sat opposite each other at the kitchen table.

The brown paper was fastened securely round the heavy box. Dorothy was aware of Moira chaffing her lower lip. Impatient at Dorothy's inability to successfully attack the sealed parcel was making Moira lean over the table, a whiff of Lux soap emanating from her scrubbed face.

"You shouldn't have," Dorothy said. "You've done enough for me." A nail snapped as she picked at the unyielding cord.

"Shall I help you?" Moira asked.

Dorothy was acutely aware of Moira rubbing her hands together. The coloured string was unravelled from the first knot. Three more to go. She pushed the parcel across the table.

"I'm all fingers and thumbs today." She studied Moira's face as she picked at the knots. Just about devoid of make-up, only a sliver of lipstick to colour her lips a washed-out red. Greying hair pinned back behind her ears, the grips clearly visible, mismatched in colour; some grey, one brown or black. One grip, manufactured for blondes securing an overgrown fringe out of the way.

The box was free of wrappings. Moira indicated. A nod, a shy smile. "You open it," she said. "It's your present."

A rush of excitement turned Dorothy's cheeks into furnaces. She opened the box, lifted the books out one by one.

"*Madame Bovary,*" she read from a front cover. She picked up the next one. "*The Fables by Aesop.*"

"For your daughter." Moira lit a cigarette with a match, sat back, blew smoke out of an O-shaped mouth.

"*Wuthering Heights: Pride and Prejudice: Jane Eyre,*" Dorothy read out loud. "You really shouldn't have." She laid the four books out on the table, their hard covers shiny, new, untouched, ivory white. She turned to the first page of *Pride and Prejudice.* The paper smelt fresh; as if the ink had barely dried, the pulped wood only just gone through its metamorphosis. "I'll start this one tonight. When I'm on my own, while Susan is tucked up in bed." And there was a part of her that could barely wait, that relished the idea of escaping into another world on her own.

"I'll make us some coffee. But I won't stay too long. Leave you to the vistas and romances of old England," said Moira suddenly, as if she had been delving into Dorothy's inner mind.

Despite Dorothy's objections, ignoring her pleas to act the proper host, Moira laid a tea tray, placed a tartan tea-cosy on the teapot, beckoned to Dorothy to lead her out of the kitchen, to show off her dining room, the walls stripped bare.

"Very up to the minute," was Moira's comment as she touched one of the white stars. "I've always lived with my father, as you know... never had the opportunity of choosing my own decorations. But not for much longer. The Corporation is going to demolish our street. Re-house us all in modern flats with indoor toilets, so I'm told." Her purple flowered dress swung as she turned and faced Dorothy. "But my father refuses to budge. Says they'll have to drag him out dead. His father, and probably his father's father, lived in Edwin Place. Clearance, they say. For better housing. Damp, we're told, is bad for us. And it's true enough. My father wheezes like a rusty hinge every time he climbs the stairs to his room. The new house is proper brick, so they say. Nice and dry." She paused, pulled her cardigan across her large bust. "But, you don't want to hear about all that. You've taken to your new home like a duck to water. Hard to believe you've only been here a few days."

Returning to the kitchen, they sat and sipped their tea without speaking for a while. Dorothy thought of Hannah, how her religion forced her to stay with Patrick. Then there was Moira's father unhappy with a move, preferring to remain in a crumbling terrace with an overgrown path to the privy. Now, Dorothy had her own home, could pick out her choice of furnishings, colour co-ordinated to suit her moods and was able to move her own bed so that she could watch the retreating sun.

A crashing of footsteps up the stairs brought Dorothy back from her musings. Susan's head appeared round the door frame, as she peered into the kitchen. When she saw Moira, she came up to Dorothy and kissed her on the cheek. She greeted Moira, her voice sweet, angelic. Willingly, Susan started to peel potatoes, to help Moira with a shepherd's pie.

"But you have to get back to your father," Dorothy said, as she started to rise from her chair.

"Don't be daft. Besides, you've been decorating all day. Put your feet up. Read. Susan and I will cook dinner."

And so she did, settling herself into the horsehair stuffed sofa in the sitting room, avoiding the springs which threatened to poke her and only shifting herself from the comfort of her seat, when the smell of fried onions and mince meat enticed her back into the kitchen, to be in the company of the two cooks.

***

Even though it was not yet April, with the wind gusty and threatening to blow off her hat, the day was sunny and it brought Dorothy on a route along the seafront to work. Most people she passed had their coats buttoned, their scarves wrapped round tight, keeping their heads bowed, close to their chests. But Dorothy wanted to be open to the ocean blasts. She walked close to the railings, leaning her face out towards the frothy sea. It was inky blue and the tide was coming in fast, the waves whipped up to a frenzy, trawling up the beach and dragging the contents back in their wake.

And it was working, this onslaught, the battle with the wind. Her mind was easing, the night before she had not slept, had barely contained a fear that she was returning to the madness, the solitary confinement of her time in Ipoh. Fighting with the blankets, still unused to the heavy layers, she had felt the return of a headache, the once familiar throb beating at her temples. She felt a little better now. After all she had her job to look forward to. But it was hard sometimes, not to wonder what George was up to, to hope that he was lonely, regretting the actions that had caused her to, finally, leave. She wanted him to suffer, could not rid herself of her bitterness. And his ungenerosity of spirit gave her plenty of fodder on which to feed.

She turned up past Poole Valley and took a route along East Street and through the Royal Pavilion gardens. Daffodils and crocuses filled the beds, they were a pretty foreground to the flowering shrubs, the shades gentle on the eye, unlike the bold colours of the tropics, the bossy petals always demanding her attention. She arrived at the library and headed straight for the Ladies to comb out her hair and straighten her collar. To dust an extra touch of blue eye shadow on her lids and to powder her nose.

Moira was already in the reference library, talking in a low voice to a man with an unfashionable bushy beard, with grey sideburns curling down his cheeks. She led him over to one of the shelves, and started to climb a set of steps to reach the top and extract a thick volume. So Dorothy took her place behind the counter, observed the rows of bent heads, listened to the quiet rustle of paper and the scribbling of pens, the tick of the minute hand as it travelled round the clock. Her father's daughter, here she was, presiding over other people's needs. Only instead of slicing pork pies and weighing out cheeses, she was waiting on the learned, those with an enquiring mind.

At one o'clock, Moira turned towards her and tapped her watch. Most people had left, only a woman remained, her hat still secured to her head with a pearl-tip pin. She was ensconced in a week-old copy of *The Times*, her lips moving as she followed the lines in an obituary. Finally, she closed the paper, folded it, thanked them both and left.

"Let's have a cup of tea on the Pier," Moira said.

Linking arms, their steps in time, they hurried down to the sea front.

"I've finally persuaded my father to seriously consider moving," said Moira as she cut their sandwiches into four, then poured the tea. "With a bit more persuasion on my part, we'll be moving into the new house in a fortnight's time." Two sugar lumps made a plopping sound as Moira dropped them into the cups of steaming brown liquid; the bubbles rose to the surface. "It's really thanks to you. I told him how nice your flat is, how you'd moved from Malaya, just you and Susan, how you'd taken it all in your stride. Doesn't like to be shown up by a woman, my father doesn't."

"I'm glad." Turning to face the sea, Dorothy watched a boy fishing off the pier, winding in his line. She saw he had a large crab caught on his hook. Dangling, twisting, the crab waved its legs, its pincers snapping uselessly at its hunter, who dropped it in a bucket, a look of triumph on his face. Moira was watching him too, one hand clasping her huge handbag, the other holding the delicately painted handle of a teacup as she sipped her afternoon tea. Her thoughts switched to Susan; she remembered her laughing with Moira. Chopping onions, tears running down her face, the giggles unsuppressed and free. There was some kind of understanding between them, perhaps it was a shared secret, a defined longing that gave each of them empathy for each other. Of Susan's need to damage herself, Moira, she suspected had no idea. She would tell her, Dorothy decided; seek her help, another opinion.

She touched her coral necklace with the tips of her fingers and looked out to sea, at the churning surf crashing on the shore.

Chapter 27

George opened the back door to his house, stepped out of his kitchen onto the yard and looked with satisfaction at his lawn, tidy, in preparation for the day. A finch was tugging at a bug in between the blades of grass, the air smelt fresh, washed by the night rain. A sliver of moon was still perched high in the sky. No haze, all clouds dissolved. A good sign, thought George; enough of doubt, uncertainties. He was owed a respite, a more relaxed way of life. Clasping his hands behind his back, he lifted his face, breathed in the smell of grass clippings; nostalgia, memories he could not quite place. A popular tune came into his head, and he began to whistle - for the first time in many months.

Back in his house, he picked up his paper, took it through to the sitting room. The front page showed a picture of a huge passenger ship bound for Australia, trunks, boxes and suitcases piled on the quay. He was reminded of his journey to Malaya, the emptiness he felt, the unwillingness to go on. But he must not become maudlin. All that was in the past. Emma would be there in an hour; her voice at last calling out to him, her footsteps light across the hall floor.

But he would have to be careful, have to hide his relief, his elation. For Emma would still be in mourning, missing her father, brooding over questions she would never be able to put to him. Sympathy for Emma, he certainly felt, along with the reluctant empathy for Moorcroft, for the suffering he knew he had endured at the last.

Of course, he felt guilty in his sense of exultation about Moorcroft's death. Thoroughly un-Christian, not that he particularly cared about that. Though it was strange, irritatingly uncanny how hard it was to rid himself of the inbred doctrine of his childhood, no matter what he told himself he believed. And so, was he doomed for thinking ill of the dead? By so doing had he encouraged some kind of curse on him from old Moorcroft's ghost? It was as if there had been a bullying spirit calling the shots from the mortuary where Moorcroft had lain; frigid, bloodless, but able still to arrange his own burial to take place on the day Emma was due to see George. Fortnightly meetings were hard enough to bear. But four weeks? He did not know how he had endured that length of time without hearing her voice. To add to his difficulties and the impossibility of the situation, the nightmares had returned, worse, than before.

He walked to the window that looked out onto the street, watched his neighbour leave her house, fussing on the doorstep, calling out goodbye to her cat.

If he told Emma about the day in the jungle, would that help dispel the face that reappeared every night, the flattened features, blank eyes, bayonet drawn back? But how would he explain his presence in the village? Another concocted story to remove the existence of Sarah. And part of him knew that it was his remorse that invented the bad dreams. But he could not tell her – not that day. For he would have to be gentle with her when she arrived.

Folding his paper, he placed it on the arm of the chair. The crossword could wait for his full attention later. He admired the roses cut from his garden first thing in the morning. He had chosen them carefully; most of the red ones were still in bud, the white fully open, their stamens heavy with nectar. It was with pride that he made sure a vase of flowers, a different variety each time, was ready and waiting for Emma's visits. Not for the first time, he wondered whether Emma's husband showed the same thoughtfulness. Always her favourite bath salts, the tulip-shaped jar filled, next to the matching talcum powder, sitting on the rim of the bath. Scented flowers on the dressing table, her robe washed and ironed by his char lady. But it was not that he cared too much about her husband's choice of flowers. If only she would give more details about him, how they were together. It seemed impertinent to continually ask her, more sensible for him to have abandoned the subject long ago. Though not knowing made his imagination churn during the two weeks they were apart. For details of her sexual relationship with her husband, she refused to discuss, would not elaborate, other than to comment only that she felt unable to deny him that aspect of their marriage. And so her admittance fed what he conjured up in his mind; the pictures torturing him of Emma allowing her husband to make love to her, of him touching her where he did, of her shuddering in his arms.

George stood abruptly, headed for the decanter, poured himself a full glass, knocked it back in one go. But for one thing he was certain, her father was dead, everything would be different. No danger of killing Moorcroft off with irresponsible actions on her part, no parental approval to be sought. Only the husband to be dealt with. A marriage that should never have taken place, she had told him so, in as many words.

The room darkened slightly and he looked up to see raindrops spattering on the window pane. Next door's clock chimed the hour. Apart from that, there was silence. Should he put some music on his radiogram, as he usually did? It was hard to know what to play. Difficult to calculate which composer would not induce a sense of melancholia in Emma and so magnify her sadness. Clouds, weighed down with rain, moved across the sky, hiding the sun, putting his room into shadow, more reminiscent of an early evening. He switched the standard lamp on, and the light on the drinks cabinet.

A niggling doubt worried away at the back of his mind, itching to present itself in the forefront, jostling for full recognition. The other possibility was terrifying, too ghastly to contemplate. How would he be able to tolerate it, if she still had made no decision, or worse still, that her social status meant more to her than a life shared with him? That the fortnightly visits would continue, leaving him in limbo for every thirteen days with the dread that she would not return, his mind becoming dulled, his body listless, aching for her closeness. No, she could not continue this. She had said so before, told him it was as bad for her, the in-between, the holding on.

He realised that he had been pacing the room; a crack of thunder startled him. The lights flickered for a moment. He finished his sherry. She was fifteen minutes late. Always the same; the doubts would start to gnaw, clawing at him; the closer the time to her arrival, the nearer the possibility that she had not been able to get away. Maybe the train had been delayed, or the tube was still idling in a tunnel, dawdling, its passengers staring out at the blackened walls.

The sound of her key in the door relaxed his jaw muscles, the tendons in his neck. In the time it took for her to open the door and step onto the mat, he imagined that she was coming in from a shopping trip, a morning at the hairdresser's, and that her return was a daily occurrence, that she had departed only earlier that morning.

Her long, tresses no longer adorned her neck and shoulders, they were scraped back with a black band, secured in a fashion that held them off her face. Stepping towards him, she kissed him quickly on the lips. He told her he liked her hair, that it suited her and wondered whether the severe hairstyle was a kind of sackcloth reaction to her father's death. Indicating to her usual chair, he offered her a sherry. She nodded and he noticed how tired she looked; her eyes had lost their lustre.

"It must be very hard for you," he said. "I'm really sorry."

"I'm just like you now. No parents, an orphan." She looked towards the flowers. "Roses today." Her voice was level, without expression. "There were mostly lilies on his coffin." After she had taken a sip, she twiddled the stem of the sherry glass between finger and thumb. "I know how much you disliked him, there's no need for you to pretend."

"I'm not pretending how your sadness makes me feel." He put his hand on hers as it rested on her lap. It was cold, still damp from where the rain had penetrated through her gloves. A nervous smile crossed her face. The day of the funeral was relayed to him in detail; the mourners, the sermon, her choice of music.

"I have to talk about it. You understand that?"

"Of course," he replied.

A pause, while she took breath. He waited, felt some warmth returning to the hand which rested under his.

"It's so strange being here again. As if nothing has changed."

"Nothing has." Was it his imagination, or was she more distant, aloof, apart from him? Not yet five weeks since her father's death he reminded himself.

She pulled her hair band off, shook her head, loosening the strands with her fingers. She was staring at the roses again, resting her head against the back of the chair. "Always the flowers," she said, almost inaudibly.

She continued to talk about the funeral, the gathering of dignitaries, the sympathy they showed for her loss. He listened quietly as they sipped their sherry, sitting round the unlit fire. He wanted to ask her what she had decided. Realised, how unlikely it was she had thought of anything other than Moorcroft, her father. Then he felt disappointed, rejected by her grief. Their talk dwindled to silence; the neighbour's clock chimed another hour. She said she wanted to go upstairs. Surprised at her sudden eagerness, he started to lead the way.

Sitting in the armchair next to the bed, he waited for her to finish in the bathroom. Comforted by the sound of water gurgling down his pipes. It would be easy to take his clothes off, lie ready, naked under the cover. But he felt somehow that this action would be inappropriate. Better that they undressed together.

The smell of freesias was heady, filling the room with their aroma. Emma was taking a long time. He stared at the green vase that contained them, placed next to the bed they would soon share. Emma was thinking again of her father's death. He remembered Dorothy's disgust after his father's funeral, at his need for sexual release; the incident long forgotten, trawled out, dragged to his consciousness only now. Wandering over to the window, drawn by the sky, clear again, he looked out at the apples, fallen onto his lawn like dropped tennis balls, muddied, abandoned by the players. Other people's gardens, spread out, fading greens into the distance; an insight into their summer's day. A girl of Susan's height was leaning a ladder up against a tree, her mother looking on. Emma was taking a long time. There was no sound from the bathroom.

Tentatively, he knocked on the bathroom door. "Everything all right? Don't wish to intrude…" It was not locked, he pushed it open.

She was sitting on the edge of the bath, one hand was cupped, the other was playing with some bath salts in her open hand.

"Sorry," she said. "Have I been a long time?"

"Were you about to take a bath?" Though she remained fully dressed, and no water filled the tub. He sat down beside her, on the rim of the iron bath. Blood emptied from his face. A coldness ran through him.

"You always make sure there are enough. Always the same fragrance. Lavender." She tipped the bath salts back into the jar, looked down at her empty hands.

"What's wrong? Something's wrong."

She was tugging her hair. "I thought it might make it easier. If we were close again. Thought it might… Sorry."

"Make what easier. What?"

"It's hard to tell you. I was putting it off."

"Hard to tell me?" He licked his lips, his mouth was dry, so parched.

"I have to stop."

"Stop. Stop what? I don't understand."

"I can't anymore."

"No," he said. "No."

"You're the same. I can tell."

"No." Standing, facing her now. "The same? Same as what?" Leaning towards her he took hold of her arms. "What are you talking about?" He tightened his grip, shook her. "What are you saying?"

"Don't. Please."

Relaxing his hold, he put his hands to his face.

"Maybe we should go downstairs."

"Explain what you meant," he said.

"I'm sorry." She was starting to shiver. "I want to go downstairs."

For a minute, he remained where he was, listening to her footsteps, slow, as they dropped down the stairs. Then he followed her, saw her standing, her back to the window.

"I thought if we made love, it would be better. Thought it might help."

Her words bounced away from him. She did not know her own mind. How could she, after all she had been through? "Look, you've had a terrible shock. You were very close to your father. You need time to adjust. Before you make plans for the future." A sensible approach. How could she know what she felt at a time like this?

"You're not listening."

"You're not telling me much. Help what? You thought it might have helped what?"

"I nearly didn't come today. I'd written you a letter." She was wringing her hands. "I'm going to stay with Christopher."

"You need time. I can understand that."

"I'm not going to come here anymore. I can't."

"What about our plans? All our plans for the future? Both of us living here? That's why I moved to this house." He was shaking so much, he could barely remove a cigarette from its packet. "Look, we'll have some time apart. Give you time to grieve in peace. Come back when you're ready. If that's what you want." The flame from his lighter soared high as he held it to the tobacco. And he watched her closely. For a sign of agreement, acknowledgement that he was right.

"George," she said, then stopped. "All right. Some time apart."

He inhaled deeply, anaesthetised. "But you will come back. Come back to me. Won't you?"

Silence. Then, "No."

His legs could not hold him upright any longer. Sinking into the chair, he felt his heart race; nausea swamped him.

"I'm sorry." And she was gone, the door closing softly behind her.

His muscles were paralysed, rigid, he was aware of voices, outside: children's, laughter.

289

He came to, shot up from his chair, moved swiftly to the door. "Why?" he called out as he ran down the path. At his gate, he shouted, "Why? You didn't tell me why." But there was no sign of her, though he hurried down his street, followed the curve of the road. She was nowhere to be seen. How could she have walked so fast? He came to a halt, leaned against a garden wall; saw the woman from the house opposite returning, her shopping bag, bulging, a tin of golden syrup balancing at the top.

"Good morning, Mr Johnson. Lovely day." she said, though she did not stop to wait for an answer.

***

Fields flashed by, the hedges forming a long dark streak, sometimes jerking, jagged with the movement of the train. Steam billowed from the engine, obliterating Emma's view. She turned to face the man sitting in front of her, his paper held up high, feet planted sideways, perhaps to give her extra room. And next to him, his wife, her arm bumping into his, unaware of the irritation she was causing, ignoring his sharp movements away from her, as she unwrapped a sandwich folded in greaseproof paper.

The train was slowing down, the fields replaced by terraced houses, washing drying in the squat yards. The brakes screeched and squealed, the woman sitting opposite put her hands to her ears, grimaced, smiled sympathetically at Emma.

And Emma was glad when she saw the last of her travelling companions leave the carriage. Alone, she looked out onto Basingstoke station, at the porters busy taking cases, leading the way to the exit. And a man shoving a broom along the platform, pushing a line of dust and dirt. Pausing, he leant on the handle, looked up at the station clock. A family stood in front of her window, the man carrying a picnic hamper, head turned sideways, watching the line beyond Emma's train; the woman was crouching, wiping her daughter's cheek, adjusting her Peter Pan collar.

At last the train moved away; this time an elderly woman sat opposite Emma, her back bowed in arthritic pain. Another woman rushed in, as the train began to chunter. Panting and sighing, she unbelted her coat, flung it on the rack above.

The train was slower this time; more time to absorb the meadows, the sheep munching or lying, dozing in the shade. Emma rested her hands on her stomach. Soon it would be swelling; she closed her eyes but did not sleep.

Chapter 28

Susan woke early, just as the sun peeped in through a crack in her curtains. She stayed where she was for a few minutes, listening to the breakfast chatter from the flat below. Someone switched a transistor on, the tinny melody drifted upwards. She pulled back the covers, stepped out of bed and sang along as she put the kettle on and splashed her face with cold water. Opening the window to let the warmth in, she looked down at the garden far below with its washing line, clothes pegged and swinging in the soft breeze. Susan stayed at the window, watched a black cat amble along a wall, took in the smell of fried bacon from one of the flats below. She dipped back into her room, popped some bread under the grill, still humming the tune that she knew would be with her all day.

Then she dressed. Attention to detail. Never mind the summer's day, she would wear her white boots: they looked so funky. Besides, all the other students at her night class wore them. Better to merge in, not to look too different. She brushed her hair until it shone, until it started to fly, full of electricity. Today was a special day. The decision was made and she would not allow Dr Matheson to change her mind. Then there was the afternoon. But she would dwell on that later.

Lipstick on, the final touch, she sat at her table and looked at the golden painted Buddha, recently discovered by her mother at the back of a cupboard. Next, she pulled a box towards her. It was one of her mother's; a relic from Malaysia, rescued from the dustbin with her mother's other memories of that year. This box was larger than the rest, just the right size for Susan's purpose. The painted pink hibiscus flowers were faded and chipped, the leaves smudged with wear, but the inside was untainted, the red velvet smooth and soft, as if it were new. Susan tucked her hair behind her ears and opened the box. Unwrapping the velvet cloth, she laid it on the table and, without touching, studied the pen knife, the box of swabs, the bottle of TCP. *Today will be a cut-free day.* She said these words out loud, just as Dr Matheson had instructed her, then she folded the implements into the cloth and replaced them in the box. One final cup of tea with her toast. Then, time to go.

An hour later, she arrived at the West End. She decided to walk the half mile rather than catch the tube. After ten minutes, the glittering shop fronts gave way to houses with brass plates and knockers on their doors. A green Rolls Royce glided down the street. A woman with a poodle on a lead bustled past her, a wake of perfume left dwindling in the London air. The song from the transistor radio was getting louder in Susan's head. Softly, as she made her up the steps of Dr Matheson's office, she sang it to herself: *Ba ba ba ba Barbara Ann - Ba ba ba ba Barbara Ann.*

She rang the bell.

"Please take a seat," the receptionist said after she'd ushered her in.

Susan lowered herself into one of the green upholstered chairs. There was no one else in the waiting room. The receptionist was filing her nails. The song sped round Susan's head, as she stared at the tiny striped fish in the tank opposite as they swam round and round their home.

Dr Matheson's door opened and he beckoned Susan in. She trotted into his office and sat in the black leather armchair that was squishy and soft and squeaked when she moved around in it. He sat on a stool in front of his desk. The lights were low. His hands were clasped as if in prayer, pen and pad balanced on his lap.

"How are you today, Susan?" he asked.

"I've made a decision."

He sat back. "Would you like to tell me?"

"I'm cured. I'm better. It's four weeks two days, three hours since I last... you know."

"Cut yourself?"

"Yes."

He wrote something on his pad, then tugged at his goatee beard and looked at her.

"Last time you were here." He glanced at his paper. "Two weeks ago. You were still very upset about your visit to Brighton."

She did not reply immediately; she knew he liked long gaps in their conversation. Mulling time, he called it. Getting things straight in her head. She tugged at the hem of her skirt, shorter than she usually wore. Should she have put on her black maxi-skirt? But it would not have looked right with her white boots.

"Yes," she eventually said. "I was."

"So how do you feel now? About seeing..." he glanced at his paper again. "Sarah, on the sea front?"

She thought of the woman; it was the teenage boy with her that had drawn her attention. She had stared, though she knew it was rude. But she was curious to know how he managed with that limp, wondered what caused it. Then her eyes had slipped to the woman walking slowly beside him. Unmistakably Sarah, though the woman had not recognised Susan. She had nearly told her mother and Moira but had decided not to. Instead she stayed awake all night, planning other coincidental meetings, scheming how she would confront her.

"I got my box out after I'd been here. After you'd made me talk about that day in the jungle, after I'd thought about that woman, Sarah with my father. After I'd remembered all the lies I'd been told about the other woman, Emma. I even put the pen knife to my wrist." She pulled up her sleeve where the scars from three years ago stayed stubborn, a reminder, a mark for future guidance – if needed. Dropping her hand to her lap, she stared at Dr Matheson's shiny shoes, at the laces all done up neatly, a bow of the same size on each foot. "That's why I think I'm better. Because I didn't."

"How do you feel now?" he asked again and looked at her with his steady gaze.

"I don't want to talk about my childhood anymore. That's why I've decided."

"But what have you decided?"

"I'm cured now," she repeated. "I don't need to come here anymore."

He was writing something down again. "These conditions can take time to cure, you know. Four weeks isn't long."

"It's long enough for me. And it's twelve years since we came back to England."

He sighed. "Good, good. That's very good. But one step at a time."

The phone rang in the waiting room. Then it stopped. The song ran round Susan's head. She stared at Van Gogh's *The Yellow Chair*, positioned above Dr Matheson's desk, every hue and shape as familiar as the tools in her lacquered box.

"You were very ill when you first came to see me." Dr Matheson was saying. "You've made splendid progress."

She nodded.

"Maybe we should tail the sessions off. Rather than an abrupt withdrawal."

Another interlude. Time to plan. So much to do. Her mind drifted to Brighton, to the sea front, to her mother's flat, to Moira.

"Is there anything else you'd like to share with me?" His eyes flicked beyond her face, to the clock on the wall.

She still said nothing; the room was thick with silence. Then she decided to tell:

"I think my mother is a lesbian. I saw them kissing in the kitchen. They didn't know I was there. Lesbian sex is all the rage now. Two of my friends at college are trying it out." She dropped her eyes from the Yellow Chair, fixed them on Dr Matheson's face. Not even a little twitch or a flutter of an eye lid.

"And how does that make you feel?"

"I suppose I've known for a long time." She thought of the other signs, like the looks they exchanged, the care they showed each other. "I didn't like the idea before. It made me feel sick – Mummy kissing Moira, but when I saw them – well, I suppose it seemed..." She searched for a word. "Normal." Then she sighed. "Mummy's much nicer to me than she was before."

"Perhaps that's because you're feeling happier with yourself. Maybe the world is a better place than you thought it was." He smiled, then wrote something on his pad. "And what plans do you have now, Susan?"

"I'm going to visit my father this afternoon."

He placed his pen down carefully on the pad. "How do feel about that?"

"I've been invited. I have to go. He likes to see how I am."

296

"And do you enjoy these visits?"

The Yellow Chair drew her attention again: it seemed to be tilting over even more than usual. "They're OK. We have lunch, then I go home."

Dr Matheson put his hand to his mouth, coughed. "You don't think you're perhaps putting a little too much pressure on yourself? Going to see him so soon after this session."

"Well, I was supposed to come here on Thursday evening, not today."

"Indeed. And thank you for being so flexible. As I expect my secretary told you, my wife had the baby rather earlier than expected."

"How is your wife? Is it a boy or a girl?"

"A girl. Thank you for your interest."

"What are you going to call it?"

"Susan. This session is for you. It isn't appropriate that I discuss my personal life with you." He paused, clasped his hands together. "Are you ready to see your father again? Has your anger faded?"

She wondered about Dr Matheson's personal life, tried to imagine him embracing a wife. "As I said, I'm fine now." She slid her bottom round in the big black chair. The song in her head started up.

"Good, good. Well you know what you must do. Everyday."

"Yes, I do."

"Well, the session has ended. Would you like to make another appointment? Just in case you have the need of it? You can always cancel."

Now the time was up, she was not sure. She rubbed her wrist, felt the bump of her scar. What if she had the urge again? What if she needed to sit in his room and stare at the *Yellow Chair*?

"No," she said. "I've decided."

"Good luck then." He held his hand out.

She shook it, said goodbye.

Outside, she wanted to skip down his street. Instead, she paced herself. Better to show restraint, best to act as if nothing extraordinary had happened, as if she stuck to important decisions all the time. The song was still in her head: she started to hum as she strolled in the direction of the tube. The streets were deserted, her footsteps rang out. She wondered if she was disturbing other sessions with grave and important therapists cocooned behind their heavy drapes. Perhaps the patients could hear her singing: maybe the tune would traverse the bricks and mortar to land inside their heads. Then her thoughts switched to her father. What would they talk about today? *Have you seen your mother recently?* He always asked, and she always said "yes". *So how is she?* What would he say if she told him what she had seen in their primrose kitchen with the sea gulls screeching outside? But she knew she would not tell. She owed her mother that. And if she felt like tormenting him, if he said something out of place – an indirect reference to her "condition," a wish that she would "settle down," then she would tell him about seeing Sarah with the limping boy, how he held her hand to steady his walking. But then they would have a disagreement, and she would have to find refuge in her cutting knife. Slowly, she descended the steps to the tube station, holding her skirt at the hem to stop the gusts lifting it up.

For sure, he would ask her how college was, and what she planned to do. He would pour her a sherry and look longingly at the crossword which he never finished when she was there. But today was a special day. For she had some news. And she would not tell him about seeing Sarah. She would not allow herself to get upset.

It only took an hour for her to reach his tube stop. The sun was high, the heat bounced off the pavements, her feet were hot inside her new white boots. And as she turned the bend in his road, she saw his neighbour talking to her tabby cat, telling it she had some nice fish for it in her shopping bag.

Her father opened the door, smiled, kissed her on the cheek.

"Lovely day," he said. "How are you?"

She told him she was fine and followed him through into the sitting room. It looked different, though at first, Susan could not see how, until she realised the blue sofa with wooden arms was new. But there was something else. Then she saw a vase of white roses in an earthenware vase.

"Sit down, sit down," he said and poured out a sherry. He glanced out of the window. "We'll have lunch in the garden. Would you like that?"

"That would be nice." She wanted to ask him if he thought about her in between her visits. Perhaps now she was better she should see more of him. Tugging at the hem of her skirt, she wished again that she had not worn such a short one today. Perhaps he was embarrassed. Is that why he kept looking away? "I have something to tell you," she said as she took the glass from him.

He sat in the chair opposite and smiled at her and she felt all warm inside: how could she have thought this visit would be so terrible?

"And I have some news for you." A cigarette packet was ready, open on the table beside him. Shaking one out, he offered it to her. She shook her head. "But you can go first."

The song started up in her head again. "What?" she asked. "What's happened?"

"After you. I insist." Smoke was blown out of his nostrils and she saw him sneak a look into his garden. "It's rather good news actually. I hope you'll agree. But please. What is it that you have to tell me?"

She considered refusing to play her part, to sit there tugging at the hem of her skirt, humming the song that spun round her head until he told her first. She took a sip of her sherry. "I've finished with Dr Matheson. I'm better. I don't need to see him anymore." She paused, looked up at the mirror above the gas fire, at the reflection of the other wall: blue and white striped wallpaper. Was that also new? Now she was not sure. "So thank you for helping me. Thank you for paying for Dr Matheson."

He was studying her. "You say you're better. So you've stopped…"

"…Yes."

"I hoped he might help. Trained in America, I believe."

"He said I had a troubled childhood." An urge to sit next to her father came over her, but she stayed put on the sofa that was beginning to make the back of her legs itch.

"We tried," he said. "Your mother and I… we tried very hard." He scratched an eye. "As long as you're all right. That's all that matters." She saw him look out of the window again, as he fidgeted with his tie. "Such a lovely day. Are you hungry, Susan? Come on outside. It's so stuffy in here." Picking up her drink, he headed for the kitchen. "I'll just take the lunch outside," he called out to her. She heard him open the back door. She waited.

Her finger touched her left wrist. A fragrance from the roses wafted across the room.

300

"Come on. It's all laid out and ready," he called.

Letting go of her wrist, she stood. Best to follow him out; see what he had to say. Once inside the kitchen, she saw a floral apron slung over the back of a chair, all daisies and buttercups strewn across the fabric. She stepped into the garden; saw her father standing over a table - green checked cloth, cold meats, hard boiled eggs, beetroot salad, pickled onions in a jar.

"Rather a splendid spread, wouldn't you agree?" he said. "Can't take all the credit, though."

"Bit much for two."

"Have a seat."

He remained standing, staring at the feast.

"You remember the woman I became rather fond of, here in England? Emma?"

Finger touching her scar, just to make sure. "Emma. Yes, I remember."

"I nearly told you last time you were here. Six months ago, wasn't it? Wasn't sure how you'd take it. Didn't dare. Perhaps I should have done."

She gripped her wrist again. "Told me what?"

"We're seeing each other again. Her marriage was..." he faltered. "Well anyway so she and her son..."

"Son?"

"Yes, Michael. He's eleven now." Then he paused, sliced a piece of ham in two. "You don't mind, do you, Susan? I mean, you're an adult now. You have to understand how these things happen." An egg was divided into four. "She makes me happy, you see." He rearranged some salad leaves. "Maybe you'd like to meet her?"

She looked at the flower beds, pink, red and orange, a clump of white roses, the newly clipped lawn, and she remembered Sarah on the sea front, open camel coat flapping in the wind, then she thought of her father sobbing in the bathroom next to her room in Ipoh. Her mind flicked to her mother in her yellow kitchen, a cheek resting on Moira's shoulder, a smile on her tired face.

"Not yet," she said. "Maybe sometime soon."

"That's fine. Let's eat. She prepared it for you, specially. Before she went out shopping for a new coat."

A face was conjured up, a woman at the sink. Rinsing lettuce, slicing tomatoes, boiling eggs on the ring. One day, she would meet her and whoever this son was.

"What colour's her hair?" she asked.

"Red, and her eyes are green."

The picture of the woman was adjusted; she wore a blue dress too, like the dress she had spotted beneath Sarah's flapping camel coat. And did this Michael have red hair as well, or perhaps he had the same colouring as his father. But she did not want to ask: she did not really want to know. Not today, at least.

"Eat up," he said. "Then tell me what you've been doing."

As she munched on the picnic lunch, she answered her father's questions while she sweltered in the sun.

Until there was no more to be said: she told him she must go. And she saw him blinking rapidly when she kissed him on his cheek.

The sun was low when she came up from the tube. Past the chip shop with its smells of frying batter and vinegar, across the road, down an alleyway, and she was nearly home. Up eight flights of stairs she ran.

Inside her room, she opened the window, looked out: the washing had been taken down and a black cat was squatting on the wall. *Ticket to Ride* blared out from the flat below.

Sitting in front of the little Buddha, she pulled the hibiscus painted box towards her, laid out carefully on the velvet cloth, the pen knife, the box of swabs, the bottle of TCP.

She stared at all her implements for a little while. One by one she returned each of them to the waiting box. "Today will be a cut-free day," she said.

THE END

I would like to thank Jonathan Buckley and Todd Kingsley-Jones for the support they gave me while I was writing this novel. I would also like to thank David Williams for his tireless support, encouragement and belief in my writing.

Amanda Sington-Williams

Sparkling Books

Tony Bayliss, *Past Continuous*

Anna Cuffaro, *Gatwick Bear and the Secret Plans*

Daniele Cuffaro, *American Myths in post-9/11 Music*

Nikki Dudley, *Ellipsis*

Alan Hamilton, *Two Unknown*

David Kauders, *The Greatest Crash*

L. A. Abbott, *Seven Wives and Seven Prisons*

Harriet Adams, *Dawn*

Grace Aguilar, *The Vale of Cedars*

Gustave Le Bon, *Psychology of Crowds*

Carlo Goldoni, *Il vero amico / The True Friend*

M. G. Lewis, *The Bravo of Venice*

Alexander Pushkin, *Marie: A Story of Russian Love*

Ilya Tolstoy, *Reminiscences of Tolstoy*

For more information visit:

www.sparklingbooks.com

Sparkling Books